Death Offerings

by

Alicia Dean

A Monroe Donovan Novel

Death Offerings

Contact Information: info@thewildrosepress.com

Cover Art by *Lisa Dawn MacDonald*

The Wild Rose Press, Inc.
PO Box 708
Adams Basin, NY 14410-0708
Visit us at www.thewildrosepress.com

Publishing History
First Edition, 2022
Trade Paperback ISBN 978-1-5092-3986-3
Digital ISBN 978-1-5092-3987-0

Previously Self-published
Published in the United States of America

My mouth felt stiff when I made myself speak. "You did this… you killed her so I'd keep writing the articles?"

"We have a connection. I know you feel it too."

"I don't even know you. If you're really the one doing this, please just stop."

A low chuckle rumbled over the line. "Stop? I did stop, but my life wasn't complete. Something has been missing. Now, you've given me a new purpose. I'd gotten bored with the girls… the same old routine, blah, blah blah. You made it fun again."

"You killed her because of me? For me?"

"When I read your articles, something sparked." He paused, and when he continued, I detected emotion in his voice. "I can't explain it, but…" He sighed. "Forget it. I don't want to get all gushy. You get me. I know you do. Did your detective friend tell you about the penny?"

"Penny?"

"Your pennies from heaven story inspired me. I left a penny in the girl's hand, along with one of her teeth."

Bile, thick and overpowering, clogged my throat. I swallowed hard and whispered, "One of her teeth?"

"Yeah. With a little coaxing, I got her talking. Telling me about her life. She lost her first tooth in '03 when she was six. I found a penny dated 2003 and put it in her hand with the tooth. I bet the cops don't want that released. There you go. A human interest touch for your article." He sounded proud, like he'd just solved world hunger.

My body went cold. My mind whirled with warring thoughts… find out something useful… hang up… keep him talking….

Dedication

To LaDonna and Debbie, my amazing friends of many,
many years.
Thank you for your support and encouragement.

Chapter 1

I think about dead people a lot.

It makes sense in my line of work—I'm a crime writer for the *Northland Chronicle,* and my former job was writing obituaries—but that's not the reason.

I don't think about dead people *because* of my career, and I didn't choose my career because I think about dead people. They both just sort of happened, independent of one another.

Maybe it's partly because my entire life has been shrouded in death. Not only is my father a mortician, but my mother named me Monroe, after Marilyn, the dead sex goddess. Growing up, I hung out at the funeral home a lot with my father. I went to my first funeral when I was five—my aunt Karen—and touched the body when my mother encouraged me to do so. When I was in school, the kids called me Elvira, the Queen of Death. I presently live next to a cemetery.

But mostly, my connection with the dead is about what happened to Katie. Katie, who was one of my childhood friends. Katie, who was only twelve when she was snatched from my backyard and murdered. Katie, whose murderer was never caught.

I don't just think about the dead, I see them. Not in the same way as the boy in the movie. I see their pictures on the web. Each and every detail etched into my memory, ready for retrieval and study.

Specifically, I think of dead girls—young, murdered girls.

It's not as creepy as it sounds. I think about them because they deserve to be remembered and to be mourned. But also so I can learn all about the hows and whys of their murders. I hope by doing so, it will help me learn the who of Katie's.

For the past six months, I'd been writing feature articles on unsolved murders. Mostly, the stories were about young girls in and around the Kansas City area. The series was finished. I'd covered all the unsolved murders of young girls in Missouri and Kansas. It didn't stop me from researching the details of others. I couldn't seem to help myself.

Although I should have been working on material for tomorrow's article on the rise of street gangs in south Kansas City, I was reading about the six-year-old murder of Jessica Browning. Her case had been solved.

Shutting out the sounds of the newspaper office that floated around me, I read the details on my computer screen. Jessica was fifteen when she was murdered, but in the photo displayed with the article, she looked to be about twelve or thirteen. She wore a white, puffy-sleeved, baby-doll blouse. Her brown hair was shoulder-length and badly cut, with bangs that were longer on the right side than the left. Still, she smiled, all white teeth and freckles.

Jessica lived in a small town in Pennsylvania, but was kidnapped from a school field trip in New York City. The class had gone to the Empire State building and somehow, somewhere among the many floors, the confusion, and large number of high school kids, a maniac had gotten his hands on her. Her raped and mutilated body was found a week later, among a pile of rubbish in an alley.

The man they'd finally arrested was an ex-convict out on parole for rape. He'd been found guilty of second degree murder and was now serving a twenty year sentence. He hadn't 'planned' the murder, so no life sentence or execution for him. In our justice system, murderers were rewarded for *spontaneous* acts of evil.

"Monroe?"

The voice came from my left, and I shook out of my trance. My boss, Adam, stood next to my desk. Strands of blonde hair fell over his tanned forehead, and his full, sensual lips were drawn into a frown.

"You okay?"

I tucked my hair behind my ear and squinted up at him, trying to blink the computer blindness from my eyes. "Yeah, sure. What's up?"

Adam didn't respond right away. He stared at me like a Leprechaun stares at a pot of gold. Not only was Adam my boss, he was also my ex-boyfriend. He'd cheated on, then dumped me, but his affections were rekindled last year. I'd inadvertently saved him and his fiancée—the woman he'd cheated with—from a psychotic killer.

Shortly after, Adam broke up with the fiancée, gave me the promotion he'd been promising me, and declared his undying love. Much to his surprise and disappointment, I was officially over him by that time. His baby greens no longer had the power to weaken my knees. Not since I'd fallen for Detective Lane Brody.

"A body was found at Riverside Park," Adam said. "Possible murder victim."

"You're giving it to me?" I asked, even as I came to

3

my feet and grabbed my purse. Phillip Conan was the other crime writer, and it was technically his turn.

Adam grimaced. "I thought you might want this one. Young girl. Phil will get the next two."

A young girl. My insides froze as Katie came to mind. Had the killer resurfaced?

No reason to think so. Not yet, anyway. This case could be totally unrelated. The last victim with a similar MO had been over three years ago. Maya Pittman. Seventeen years old. One of her teachers—with whom she'd been having an affair—was questioned and released. No one had been charged with the crime.

Whoever had committed the murders was still unknown. Maybe he'd died, maybe moved on to another area, maybe had a change of heart. Regardless, he'd never been caught, so…

Anticipation and dread warred inside me. I'd find out soon enough.

"Thanks." I flashed Adam a smile before brushing past him and heading toward the door.

"Hey," he called out.

I paused and looked back.

Sadness was etched on his too-pretty-for-a-man face. His lips quirked in a humorless smile. "Say hi to Lane for me."

****

Detective Lane Brody squatted next to the girl's body, squinting at the afternoon sunlight that glinted off the diamond piercing in the side of her nose. Her jeans were undone, resting low on her slender hips, showing a strip of pink thong underwear. Ligature marks around her neck indicated strangling, although whatever had been used to squeeze the life from her was nowhere to be found.

She lay half on-half off the slide. Her head and upper torso rested on the hard ground—reddish brown hair splayed around her—while the lower part of her body remained on the slide, as if she'd been sliding on her back, head first. It was unlikely she'd actually been playing on the playground. For one, she was too old—probably sixteen or seventeen. For another, from what he could see of her exposed torso, postmortem lividity had colored her lower body a dark reddish purple. Had she died in this position, lividity would have been fixed in her face and neck.

She'd apparently been murdered elsewhere and brought to the park for some kind of twisted display. The killer had posed her body with her arms crossed over her breasts, vacant eyes staring up into the blue sky.

Lane's partner, Detective Tony Webber stood on the other side of the victim. "Matches the others," he muttered.

"Looks like it."

"What the hell, Huck? It's been nearly three years. Why all of a sudden?"

Since Lane was from the south—Montgomery, Alabama—the guys at the station called him Huck, as in Huck Finn, even though *The Adventures of Tom Sawyer* was actually set in Missouri. Lane had given up on correcting them.

Lane shrugged and rose to his feet. "Beats me. If it is the same guy, he sometimes went years between killings. Who knows what the sick bastard is thinking."

The girl had likely been killed last night. Two brothers, six-year-old Tyler and eight-year-old Brendan, had found her when their mother brought them to the playground this morning. Tony and Lane had questioned the woman and sent her home. Neither she nor her boys had any information that would help. They hadn't seen anyone around. No one, that is, except for the still unidentified young murder victim.

Frustration settled in Lane's gut, followed by rage and helplessness. The victim had been discarded... like she didn't matter. That was almost as bad as the murder itself.

"She looks to be... what... sixteen or so?" Tony's voice sounded strained. "She's just about Paxton's age." His face had gone pale, his features tight and drawn. Paxton was Tony's fifteen-year old daughter. He was divorced and his kids, Paxton and her younger brother, Cadence, were spending the summer with Tony while their mother went on her honeymoon.

Lane didn't have kids, so he couldn't imagine what it would be like to lose one... especially losing one like this. Judging from the look on Tony's face, he could imagine it all too well.

The park had gone eerily quiet. Normally, on a nice spring day like this—sun shining, birds singing, flowers blooming—the place would be overrun with people and the sounds of laughter and children shouting. That's the way it had been when he and Tony arrived, but not anymore. His team had cordoned off a large section surrounding the playground, and the people who remained hovered on the other side of the crime scene tape, gawking curiously.

Lane made another circle around the slide. He'd already been over the entire area, but would keep going over it until he found something important—or until he was damned sure there was nothing to find.

"The others were left in wooded areas," Lane mused aloud. "It appears our guy wanted this girl found quickly."

Tony glanced around the park, peeling rubber gloves off his hands. "He had to know the odds were good that little kids would find her. Is he trying to send a message or just being a full on douche bag?"

Lane started to answer, but a figure in the crowd beyond the police tape caught his attention. Her dark hair lifted in the breeze, and she brought a hand up to push it out of her face.

Monroe.

Just the sight of her made it difficult to breathe. He grinned, knowing he must look like a besotted fool, but unable to help himself. She gave him a finger wave, and her full lips pulled into a brief smile.

A popping sound caught his attention, and he turned to find Tony snapping his fingers in his face. "Focus, dude. Dead girl, remember?"

Lane scowled. "I remember."

Tony snorted a laugh. A touch of his typical carefree cockiness came back into his expression. "Go say hi to your woman. We're still waiting on Keaton anyway."

"She's not my woman. Not really."

Lane had started divorce proceedings, but Monroe wouldn't take their relationship to the next level until he was actually divorced. Nor would he press the matter. She'd been hurt badly by cheaters and refused to become one. Lane knew exactly how she felt.

"For God's sake. Go talk to her. Then maybe you can pull your head out of her ass long enough to work the scene."

Lane hesitated, but because he couldn't stay away

from her, even if he'd wanted to, he acquiesced, heading to where Monroe stood. The closer he drew, the more airy and light his chest felt. He could smell her scent just before he reached her—that special fragrance that was hers alone, the scent of summer rain and fresh cut grass—fresh and intoxicating.

"Hi there," she said.

Her brown eyes glowed almost golden in the sunlight, but they held a hint of worry. He wanted to reach out and touch her... run his hand along her soft cheek, reassure her that everything would be okay. But too many people were around for him to give in to the temptation. Besides, everything would *not* be okay. A young girl had lost her life to some sick son of a bitch, and no matter how happy just looking at Monroe made him, right now he had a crime scene to work.

"Hi," he replied softly, trying to keep from drawing the attention of the others in the crowd. But it was useless. Half a dozen reporters migrated to the area where he stood, microphones thrust out like fencing swords.

"Detective, can we get a statement?"

"Who's the victim? You have an ID yet?"

"Is this a homicide?"

"Who found the body? Can we speak with them?"

Lane pushed out a heavy breath and winked at Monroe. "We'll talk later."

She nodded, her smile gone, her expression solemn. Her change of mood matched his. It was difficult to remain cheerful at the scene of a murder.

Holding his hands up in a halting gesture, he addressed the ravenous media. "We don't have anything for you yet. If you'll hang tight, we'll have a statement shortly."

With one more quick look at Monroe, he walked back to where Tony and the crime scene techs waited. The CST's had already scoured the area and taken pictures of the body, but none of them could touch her, or anything on her person, until the Medical Examiner was done.

No sooner had the thought materialized, than the man himself—Byron Keaton, the ME—arrived, ducking under the crime scene tape. He strode toward them, his thick, curly hair flopping around his head like a red mop.

Lane and Tony had been here for hours, waiting. Now, not only would they get some answers, they could finally finish processing the scene.

Byron squatted down, slipped gloves over his hands, and lifted Jane Doe's bruised chin to study her neck. Without raising his head, he said, "Cut off her air by squeezing her larynx. Didn't crush it, though. Looks like he squeezed and let go, over and over, making her death a long time coming."

Lane's jaw tightened. Sadistic bastard.

Keaton searched through the girl's pockets. "No ID," he said. "You guys know who she is?"

"Not yet."

One of the patrol officers had gone back to the station to run a check on reports of missing teens. So far, no hits.

"Huh," Keaton said, his voice tinged with speculation. The victim's right hand was clenched, while her left lay open. He pulled back the fingers on her right hand and retrieved two objects, holding them up for inspection. "A tooth and a penny. Odd." He used his gloved fingers to part the girl's lips and nodded. "It's her tooth. Front incisor. Removed postmortem. No blood on the gums."

A chill moved through Lane's veins as he stared at the coin. "A penny? That's a new twist."

Tony squinted at him. "Dude, you look like you're about to hurl. What's the big deal about a penny?"

"You don't read Monroe's articles, do you?"

"Nah." Tony grinned. "But then, I don't want in her pants."

Lane forced a corner of his mouth into a half-smile, but the chill had turned into an icy wind that swept through his soul. "She wrote about some theory… a pennies from heaven thing. Supposedly, some people believe that loved ones who've passed on send messages from beyond for those they leave behind. Pennies."

"Pennies?"

"Yeah. Pennies with significant dates. Supposed to be some kind of sign that the dead are reaching out to the living. Monroe's friend who was murdered… Katie? Her mom found a penny dated the year Katie was born in her bedroom right after her body was found. Then, just a few months ago, she found one on her grave dated 1969."

"Is 1969 supposed to mean something?" Tony asked. "You don't believe in that hocus pocus crap, do you?"

Lane shrugged. "I don't believe the pennies mean anything, but it's possible the killer left it because he read Monroe's articles."

Keaton peered at the penny through the plastic bag. "This one is dated 2003."

Lane forced calm into his voice. "Once we get an ID, we can question her family. See if that year has any significance."

Tony frowned. "So, you really think this has something to do with Monroe?"

"Could be."

"Maybe." Tony stroked his goatee, his frown still in place. "Then again, maybe not."

Yeah, right. The girl was murdered while gripping a penny. All teen girls carried a single penny around in their hand. And maybe the killer yanked her tooth out and stuck it in the same hand, totally by coincidence.

Lane's mind clicked over all the scenarios, all the possibilities, but with each one, he came up with the same conclusion. He believed the penny had nothing to do with Monroe as much as he believed the tooth fairy would swing by to replace the extracted incisor with a few more coins.

****

I pulled into Linus's driveway to drop him off after taking him on his errands. Although he only lived across the street from me, I didn't want my elderly neighbor to lug his grocery bags even that short distance. He was independent and feisty—but the pain of age had begun to tighten his expression more often as the days wore on. I'd known him for five of his nearly ninety years, and his approach toward the century mark was starting to take a toll.

Before getting out of the car, he lifted a hip and tugged his wallet from the back pocket of his overalls. Fingers that slightly trembled fished out two one dollar bills.

"Here you go, Marilyn." He found it amusing to call me Marilyn, found it amusing that I was given the name of a promiscuous bombshell who died ten years before I was born. "For your gas and your trouble. Thanks for taking me around."

I suppressed a grin. I'd driven him on errands for half the day. With gas at nearly four dollars a gallon, the two bucks would barely get me out of his driveway.

"Really, Linus. You don't have to." I held up a hand in protest. "The Jesse James stuff you've given me is worth more to me than all the gas in the world."

He pursed his lips as if considering, then slowly replaced the bills. "If you insist. You're a good girl, you know. When I'm gone, the whole collection is yours."

I raised my brows. Linus was a descendant of Jesse James, and he had an amazing collection of memorabilia. From time to time, he'd given me a piece as a thank you for helping him out. It had never occurred to me that he'd bequeath me his entire collection.

The thought made me simultaneously sad and thrilled. But mostly overwhelmed that he thought that much of me. I'd always been fascinated with Jesse James—all the more so because he was from Kearney, a town less than twenty miles from where I lived in Parkville, Missouri. I'd been drawn to his mystique and legend since childhood. Even though I wanted the collection more than I'd ever wanted anything—well, almost anything—I said, "Shouldn't you leave it to your family?"

"None of my kids care a whit about it. They'll get money, and that's all that really matters far as they're concerned. 'Sides, you spend more time with me than they do."

He fumbled with the door handle and climbed slowly from the car, reaching into the back to retrieve two loaded-down grocery sacks.

"You need some help with those?" I asked as I

stretched across the console.

"Heck no. Day I can't carry a few sacks of groceries ten feet is the day they can cart me off to an old folks home."

He winked, but the merriment in his expression faded as he stared over the hood of my car at something across the street. I followed his gaze. My pulse rate kicked up a notch when I saw Lane's Crown Vic in my driveway.

Linus closed the door, but leaned into the open window. Strands of his white hair blew around his head like dandelion seeds. "Ain't none of my business, but I'm gonna say it anyhow. You're a good girl, like I said. And Detective Brody seems like a nice fella. But he's married. Don't care if he's happy in it or not, married is married."

Heat warmed my cheeks, and I felt like a chastised child. The fissure of guilt I'd been toting around reared its head. Still, I attempted a defense. "I realize that. We're just friends. Besides, he's getting a divorce."

Linus harrumphed as he straightened. "Getting ain't got, remember that."

Before I could respond, he turned and slowly made his way to his door.

I frowned, trying to push back the unease—the awareness that Linus was right—and watched until he was safely inside. I then backed out of his drive and pulled into mine, parking next to Lane.

A smile lifted the corners of my mouth as he climbed out of the car and moved toward me. An answering smile touched his lips.

The navy blue suit hung carelessly on his body, and his shiny light blue tie was off-center. Dark hair, lightly streaked with gray, was messy, as if from the breeze. But, I knew it always had that mussed, just ran his fingers through it, just climbed out of bed look. I drew a deep breath, reining my thoughts back in—and out of bed with Lane Brody.

"Hi again. Good to see you." His whisky tones, tinged with a hint of a southern drawl, washed over me as he moved closer. His voice lowered, and he reached a hand out. "Good to finally get to touch you."

I stepped back before he made contact, casting a quick look across the street. Linus's opinion shouldn't matter so much, but it did. I adored the old man and wanted him to keep thinking I was a 'good girl.'

"Let's go inside," I suggested.

Lane frowned, then followed me into my small, but comfy home. My friend, Josie, had been staying with me for the past few months while she worked on her sobriety. But last week, she'd moved into her own place, and mine was now delightfully quiet.

As soon as Lane shut the door, I went into his embrace. His touch warmed me, filled me with a sense of peace. I relaxed and released a long, contented sigh. Pulling back, he pressed a kiss to my forehead, his lips gently gliding down, over my temple, then my cheek. He tilted my chin and lowered his mouth to mine. Heat rushed through my veins as he coaxed my mouth open, and his tongue explored, sending tingles along my flesh. His hand skimmed my back, resting on my bottom, pulling me tighter against him. I whimpered, lifting my arms to entwine around his neck.

Something in my brain admonished me to stop before we went any further… before we went *too* far. I ignored the irritating intrusion. Being with Lane felt so damn good… so right…

But, in reality, it wasn't right. Linus's words came back to me, hitting me like a bucket of icy water. *Married is married…*

I pulled back, stepping out of Lane's embrace. He let out a groan and closed his eyes. His hands fell away from my body. "You're killing me, you know that?"

"I know." My voice was hoarse, and I cleared my throat. "Killing me too."

"So, how does this work? We can finally make love when the papers are filed? The divorce is final? When?"

I arched a brow, and he lifted his hands, shrugging innocently. "I'm just trying to get the facts straight, find out what the target date is, you know, so I don't spontaneously combust or something."

Letting out a chuckle, I said, "I was thinking we should at least wait until the divorce is granted. How's that?"

He smiled. Little crinkles formed at the corners of his ice-blue eyes. He brought his hand up, brushing a strand of hair from my face. "I'd wait an eternity for you. Matter of fact, I'd be content with you even if we never had sex."

I snorted. "Right."

"What? You don't believe it because I'm a man?"

Tiptoeing, I rested my hands on his shoulders and placed a quick kiss on his lips. "No," I whispered. "I don't believe it because *I* wouldn't be content if we never had sex."

The corner of his mouth lifted in his sexy, half-grin. "I'm meeting with my mother-in-law and our attorneys this evening. We'll hammer out a few details, then get the papers signed and filed. Smooth sailing from here on out."

Lane's wife was in a mental institution, in a near catatonic state, where she'd been for the past three years. She was undergoing evaluation to see if she would improve enough to stand trial for the murder of her lover… the man she'd cheated with while married to Lane. As her guardian, her mother would stand in for her in the divorce proceedings. The woman apparently adored Lane and didn't blame him for divorcing her daughter, but nothing about the situation sounded like smooth sailing to me.

A chill of foreboding rippled through my insides. "Don't say that. You'll jinx it."

"You're a superstitious little thing, aren't you?" A teasing light twinkled in his eyes. "It's not like you can speak bad things into existence. Bad things happen every day, with or without jinxes."

The mention of bad things quickly sobered the mood in the room. Like me, I figured he was thinking about the dead girl in the park.

"Did you ID the victim?" I asked.

He released a heavy breath and dropped onto the edge of the couch. Resting his elbows on his knees, he scrubbed his hands over his face and nodded. "Her parents were waiting for us at the station. They'd been looking for her. She left a friend's house a few nights ago, and they hadn't seen her since."

"They didn't file a missing person report?"

"Apparently, she took off frequently like that without letting anyone know where she was. They usually found her sooner." Another long sigh escaped him. "And alive."

I lowered onto the seat beside him and placed my

hand over his. "Was it like Katie? Like the others?"

A muscle in his jaw jumped, and he was silent for a while, as if considering how much to tell me. Finally, he answered, his words slow, cautious. "There were some similarities to the other murders."

Feeling a little callous, but needing to make notes for my article, I took a legal pad and pen from the end table. "What was her name?"

"Charity Munson. She would have been sixteen in July. Two young boys found her body on the slide, arms crossed over her chest."

I had been scribbling furiously, but I paused, lifting my pen. "Arms crossed over her chest? Were the other girls found that way?"

He hesitated, then shook his head. "I can't say much. I wouldn't have shared that with you if the media didn't know. The mother and boys have already been interviewed."

While at times, I was left a little frustrated at the lack of information my relationship with Lane afforded me, I also admired his principles. He was too good a cop to jeopardize his cases simply because he had the hots for me.

"Was the girl nude?"

Lane shook his head. "Her pants were pulled partway down. Looks like maybe the killer either had them off and put them partially back on, or he just tugged them down a ways. Not sure which. Or why."

They'd find out in the autopsy whether or not she'd been raped. Of all the murder victims over the years, the ones that were similar to Katie's, each of the girls had been raped. Except for Katie. The knowledge had provided a small measure of comfort over the years—for me and Katie's parents.

When I wrote my article, I'd leave out the part about Charity Munson's pants being pulled down. If I were a parent, I wouldn't want to know about that. More sickening details would emerge as time went on. I could spare them at least this one at the moment, although I couldn't expect the same from my peers.

I nudged Lane for a few more answers—some he sidestepped pretty effectively. He looked at his watch and stood. "I need to get going. I'm expected at the meeting in fifteen minutes."

"Sure. Good luck. Hope it goes well."

"You and me both." He studied me, and my concern must have shown in my expression. He stroked a finger down my cheek. "It will. Don't worry."

I nodded, then walked him to the door. We shared a chaste kiss before he left.

Moments after he drove away, my cell rang. The caller ID showed a number I didn't recognize and the words "Magic Construction." Frowning, I answered the phone.

A male voice—gruff and unfamiliar—said, "Did you like my gift?"

"Gift? What gift?" There was something unnatural sounding about his voice. Like he was purposely disguising it.

"The gift I left you in the park."

The strength drained from my legs and nausea tightened my gut. I dropped onto the edge of the recliner. "Who are you? What kind of sick joke is this?"

"No joke. It's very real. You don't sound happy."

"Happy? Are you out of your mind?"

I knew it was unlikely this jerk was really the killer.

He was probably just some asshole screwing with me. But the fact that anyone could be this sick made me ill.

A raspy, unsettling laugh rumbled across the line. "I did it for you. Your articles were ending. I liked reading them. Liked that you were writing about me. Now, it doesn't have to stop."

I swallowed a lump in my throat and tried to still the heavy thud of my heart. Instinct told me this guy was for real.

Fuck me.

I was talking to the killer.

Chapter 2

As soon as Lane drove away, thoughts of Catherine crowded out thoughts of Monroe. He was on his way to divorce the woman he'd once believed was his world. He'd never forget the first time he saw her. Long auburn hair, eyes so blue they glimmered like jewels. Tall, graceful, body made for worshipping. He couldn't believe someone like her was interested in him—a sloppy, mid-salary, average-looking cop.

But she had been. And he was caught up in her spell from day one. When they first met, she'd shown him only the side she wanted him to see. Loving, charming, in need of his protection. Exactly the kind of woman he wanted—at the time. Eventually, he discovered it had all been an act. Rather than loving, he learned she was a sex addict—although ironically not with him, not after the first few years of marriage, anyway. Her 'charm' was, in reality, manipulation—a skill she honed to an art. 'In need of his protection' proved to mean that she was high-maintenance, helpless, greedy. Nothing he did or gave her could ever be enough.

From the beginning, he'd thought her far too beautiful for someone like him. Turned out, she agreed. No one man could love her enough, could adore her enough, could keep her satisfied. Guys at the station had eyed him with envy, called him lucky bastard and ribbed him about how he 'better keep an eye on that one.'

The teasing had ended the night he and his partner got a call to a shooting. They'd entered the cheap, run-down motel room where the half-naked woman—wearing nothing but a sheer, gaping robe—stood over the bleeding man.

Lane's mind registered facts in pieces, until they clicked together in one big horrific puzzle. Catherine—stunningly gorgeous, in spite of the crazed look in her eyes, tears streaming down her cheeks, matted hair, blood splattered on her porcelain skin.

Insanely, Lane's first thought had been, *how could a woman as beautiful, as special as Catherine, end up in a crappy dump like this?*

Immediately, the other thoughts piled on top of that one. The man was naked. Lane's wife was nearly naked. She held a pistol. Judging from all the blood pooled around the victim and the vacant, cloudy gaze, the man was dead.

Catherine turned to Lane with wide, traumatized eyes. Her throaty voice ravaged with tears, she whispered, "He was going to leave me. In spite of all we've been to each other, he was going to leave me."

After the first few days of hysteria, Catherine had gone silent. In the nearly three years since that night, the only other word Lane had heard her speak was the man's name. *Joseph.* Each time he went to visit her, she'd turn expectantly to him and say, in a death-like monotone, "Joseph?" Hoping that, instead of her husband, her dead lover had arrived.

On the day of the shooting, a hole had opened up in Lane's chest. Over the years, that hole had slowly filled with a block of ice so solid, Lane didn't think he'd ever feel anything again, other than cold.

Then, he'd met Monroe. Her sensual, yet understated beauty, her calm, caring spirit, her fire, had melted that ice and now, all he wanted was to be near her warmth for the rest of his life. Tonight was the first step toward making that happen.

The attorney's office was in semi-darkness when he walked in. Since they were meeting after hours, the reception desk was empty.

One of the interior doors opened, and his attorney, Hank Boggins, appeared. Hank stuck out a hand, and Lane gripped his long, bony fingers in a handshake. The man was so tall he almost had to duck to keep from hitting his head on the top of the door frame.

"We're in the conference room down the hallway," Hank said. "But I wanted a word with you before we go in."

"Is something wrong?"

Hank's graying brows drew together in a frown. "I'm not sure. Your wife's doctor is here."

"What's he doing here?"

"They didn't say. Wanted to wait for you."

A knot of worry formed in Lane's gut. Had something happened to Catherine? Suicide? He'd long suspected if she'd had a way to take her own life, she'd have done so without hesitation. Maybe she'd finally found a way.

He nodded, but didn't speak. Couldn't speak through the fear rising to his throat. Although he no longer loved her—although she'd cheated, betrayed, ripped his world apart—he didn't want her dead. What he wanted was to divorce her, for her to get her mind back, and pay for the crime she'd committed. He wanted justice. Not particularly for the asshole she'd killed…

just... justice.

Unsteadily, he followed Hank into the conference room. His mother-in-law, Miriam, sat at the table between her attorney and Dr. Posell. Hank held a hand out toward a chair on the opposite side of the table, and Lane sat.

Miriam gave him an uncertain smile, and relief whooshed out of his lungs. Catherine's mother wouldn't be smiling if her daughter were dead.

He relaxed back in his chair and nodded to Miriam, then turned to Dr. Posell. "I didn't know you were going to be here."

The doctor cast a quick look at Miriam before bringing his gaze back to Lane. "It was a last minute decision. There's been a development."

Lane frowned. "What kind of development?"

Miriam leaned forward, her smile growing. Blue eyes that were a replica of her daughter's sparkled. "Catherine. She's..." Miriam sucked in a breath and pressed bent knuckles to her lips. After a few seconds, she continued, "She's better, Lane."

"Better?"

She nodded. "She's getting better. I went to see her yesterday, and she recognized me." Tears filled her eyes, and she scooted forward in the chair so she could reach across the table and clasp Lane's arm. "She spoke to me. She actually spoke." Her words ended on a reverent whisper.

Shock kept Lane silent for a moment, then he turned to the doctor. "What does this mean? Why would she suddenly improve after all this time?"

Dr. Posell pushed his glasses up his nose. "We've seen this before, although not often. Patients suddenly have breakthroughs, and there's not always a logical explanation. The good news is, with this kind of improvement, we can probably expect to see more progress… rapid progress." He held up a hand, adding a disclaimer. "Not in all cases, mind you, but most of the time."

Lane tapped his fingers on the table, trying to decide how much he really cared about the news. He was divorcing her. She'd either remain in a mental institution, or she'd get better and face a trial. Either way, he was no longer part of her life.

His gaze went to Miriam, to the joy he saw in her still-pretty face. She'd always been kind to him. They'd stayed close even after the incident with Catherine. Miriam had always been on his side—angry and appalled at what her daughter had done, how she'd hurt him. But, no matter what, Catherine was her little girl. For Miriam's sake, he was glad she'd improved.

"I'm happy for you," he told Miriam. He turned to Hank. "So, does this mean that Catherine can act as the party in the divorce, or since she's still somewhat incapacitated, will we proceed as planned?"

Hank opened his mouth to speak, but Miriam cut him off. "That's the thing, Lane. About the divorce." She glanced at the doctor, then stood and came around the table. Sitting next to Lane, she took his hands in hers. "We think… Dr. Posell and I think it would be best if we hold off for a little while."

Lane looked from the doctor to Miriam. "Hold off? On the divorce?" At Miriam's nod, he said, "Why?"

The psychiatrist squared his shoulders and cleared his throat. "Catherine's mental state is improving at a swift rate. She's becoming more aware of her surroundings... her circumstances. Before long, she's going to recall everything that happened. She'll be traumatized. She'll have a lot to work through. We feel that adding a divorce at this time would be detrimental. She needs to cope with one issue at a time."

Lane tugged his hands from Miriam's and stood. "You can't seriously think I should stay married to her just because her mental state is improving?"

"Lane," Miriam said, her tone taking on a pleading note. "She asked for you. She wants to see you."

Lane's gut tightened. His wife hadn't wanted to be with him since the shooting... for that matter, since a long while *before* the shooting. Why did she suddenly want to see him now? He'd been to visit her nearly every day since she'd been hospitalized, and she hadn't even acknowledged him. Now that he wanted rid of her, now that he'd found someone he could truly love... she suddenly wanted to see him?

He shook his head. "No. We go through with the divorce. I won't be pulled into Catherine's games."

Miriam looked at the doctor. "Tell him the rest."

Dr. Posell hunched over, resting his linked fingers on the table. "As the memories have been coming back, Catherine has begun to show suicidal tendencies. She's in a very precarious place. If she feels she's being abandoned, it could push her over the edge. Force her to do something drastic."

Anger and resentment burned in Lane's stomach. What about what *he* wanted? What he needed? At one time, he'd wanted Catherine to love him, to be a faithful wife. Since she'd chosen to become a cheating murderess instead, why should he still be bound to her? Why was it his responsibility?

He crossed his arms and jerked his chin toward the psychiatrist. "Aren't you the mental professional? Isn't it your job to make sure that doesn't happen?"

The doctor's face colored. "Well… of course I… I mean, there's more to it than—"

"Can I speak with my son-in-law alone?" Miriam interrupted.

Shit. She was playing the son-in-law card.

The three men excused themselves. Once they were gone and the door closed Miriam said, "You made a promise to her. You said you'd stay with her as long as she needed you."

Before Catherine had slipped into her near catatonic state, she'd been hysterical and clingy and terrified. Although his heart felt like a herd of elephants had used it for a trampoline, he'd assured her he'd stick by her, that he'd be there for her as long as she needed him. Miriam had been trying to get him to divorce her ever since the shooting. Now she was using his words against him?

"I did. I stuck by her during this entire ordeal. She never uttered a word to me, never recognized me. She never needed me."

"Well, she needs you now."

He clenched his jaw, trying to remain calm. "Maybe it's too late now."

"Lane, please. I know what she did to you was terrible, but she's still my child."

"Are you sure you even want her to improve?" At Miriam's confused expression, he continued. "If she gets well, she's facing murder charges. She could end up in a place far worse than this." He knew it was cruel, but it was true. She might as well face up to it.

Miriam's face paled. "I know that," she whispered. "She might end up in prison, but I could go see her. I'd be able to communicate with her. Women's prisons aren't that bad. The hospital is a prison too."

He gentled his voice. "Have you thought about the fact that she could get the death penalty?"

She began shaking her head before the words fully left his mouth. "No. Her attorney said they wouldn't put the death penalty on the table. It was a crime of passion."

"He can't—" Lane stopped. Shook his head. He started to tell her that the attorney couldn't make that guarantee, but Miriam was obviously going to believe only what she wanted to believe. He also didn't mention that Catherine had taken the gun to the motel with her. A fact the prosecutor could use to show pre-meditation.

"Besides," Miriam said. "I'm terrified if she finds out everything at once, she'll take her own life. That would destroy me. Please just hold off until she's stronger."

"It could take months. A year. Maybe longer."

"That's true. And I know you've found someone else. But I'm trying to save my daughter, Lane. All I'm asking for is a little more time. If Monroe loves you, she'll wait."

That was the thing. Monroe had never said she loved him, and he'd never admitted his love for her. They were moving slowly, but definitely wanted to move forward. It wouldn't be fair to ask her to wait for him. She'd been let down too many times in her life. He only wanted to make her happy—never wanted to be one of the people who hurt her.

He looked at Miriam, at her beseeching expression, and knew that was exactly what he was about to be.

****

I gripped the phone and squeezed my eyes shut. Although I realized there was something I should say that would make him give a clue to his identity, something I could share with the police, my mind wouldn't work properly. Nothing clever came to me.

My mouth felt stiff when I made myself speak. "You did this… you killed her so I'd keep writing the articles?"

"We have a connection. I know you feel it too."

"I don't even know you. If you're really the one doing this, please just stop."

A low chuckle rumbled over the line. "Stop? I did stop, but my life wasn't complete. Something has been missing. Now, you've given me a new purpose. I'd gotten bored with the girls… the same old routine, blah, blah blah. You made it fun again."

"You killed her because of me? *For* me?"

"When I read your articles, something sparked." He paused, and when he continued, I detected emotion in his voice. "I can't explain it, but…" He sighed. "Forget it. I don't want to get all gushy. You get me. I know you do. Did your detective friend tell you about the penny?"

"Penny?"

"Your pennies from heaven story inspired me. I left a penny in the girl's hand, along with one of her teeth."

Bile, thick and overpowering, clogged my throat. I swallowed hard and whispered, "One of her teeth?"

"Yeah. With a little coaxing, I got her talking. Telling me about her life. She lost her first tooth in '03 when she was six. I found a penny dated 2003 and put it in her hand with the tooth. I bet the cops don't want that released. There you go. A human interest touch for your article." He sounded proud, like he'd just solved world hunger.

My body went cold. My mind whirled with warring thoughts… *find out something useful… hang up… keep him talking….* But the will to contain the screaming inside my head was all I could manage.

Steeling my resolve, I drew in a deep breath and tried to force calm into my voice. "That's… that's clever." I nearly choked on the words. "I'm flattered that you paid so much attention to what I've written. Since we have a connection, don't you think we should know something about on another? You know my name. Tell me yours."

He emitted a burst of laughter that sounded like it was filtered through a broken speaker. "I'm not an idiot, Monroe. Please don't think you can patronize me."

Lifting a trembling hand, I scrunched the hair on top of my head. "You're right. I didn't mean to. I just… you fascinate me." It took everything I had to get the words out of my throat. Stroking the ego of a psycho was nauseating. "As you can see from my articles, you've fascinated me for years. I want to know you better."

"You will." His tone softened. "In time. For now, I have to go. In case you're trying to start a trace. I'll be in touch, though. Can't wait to reconnect."

"No… wait!"

But he was gone. The arm holding the phone suddenly felt too heavy. I dropped the cell onto the sofa cushion beside me.

Dear God.

Lane.

I had to call Lane. I picked up the phone once more, then remembered he was in a meeting. I dialed Tony instead.

He answered after a few rings. "Monroe? Is everything okay?"

"Not-not really." My teeth began to chatter, and I clenched my mouth shut to stop them.

"What is it?"

"I think I just got a phone call from the killer."

I heard a sharp intake of breath. "Jesus Christ. I'm heading over right now." Noise in the background came through the line—shuffling movements, then a sound like he was gathering his keys. "Did you call Lane?"

"He's in the meeting with his attorney and mother-in-law. I figured his phone would be off. I didn't want to bother him."

"Yeah. Okay. Are you all right?"

"I'm…" Was I all right? Hell, no. I was freaking out. "Fine," I said, trying to sound as though I meant it. "I'll see you soon." *But hurry,* I wanted to scream.

After I hung up the phone, the son of a bitch's words came back to torment me. He'd done it for me. A shudder ripped through me. I'd been the cause—the inspiration—for that poor girl's murder. My hands trembled, then the vibrations moved through my entire body until my teeth were chattering again—this time, so hard, I thought my jaw would break. That girl died because of me. I sat shaking for I don't know how long, before a knock pounded on the door.

I froze. The killer?

No, of course not. It had to be Tony. I looked down at my hands, surprised to see them dampened with my tears. I pushed myself from the couch and stumbled to the door. When I saw Tony standing on my porch, shaved head, tall and muscular, able to intimidate even the bravest of thugs, I threw myself in his arms.

"Are you okay?" he mumbled against my hair, giving me a reassuring hug.

I nodded, then shook my head and burst out sobbing.

"Shh. It'll be okay. Tell me what happened." He spoke softly, led me to the couch and lowered me onto it—settled beside me.

"He-he called." My voice sounded hollow through the roaring in my ears. "He said he'd left me a gift. The g-girl in the park." I squeezed my eyes shut, trying to recall his exact words. "He said he killed her for me. So I'd keep writing the articles." I looked at Tony. "It's my fault that girl is dead." I started shivering all over again.

Tony wrapped his arms around me. He wasn't Lane, but the human touch still comforted.

"It's not your fault. This guy's a sick fuck, and you had nothing to do with it. How can you be sure it was even him? There are a lot of crazies out there. They like to take credit for things that other twisted mother fuckers do."

"It was him. I'm sure." I frowned. "Or, at least. I felt like it was him, you know? In my gut. He sounded so…" Then I remembered. There was one way to be certain. "Did the girl have something in her hand? Something the cops are holding back from the public?"

Tony blinked and pulled his gaze away from mine. "You know I can't talk about the case with you, Monroe. No more than I can release to the public. I trust you, but—"

"Was it a penny?" I cut him off. "And a tooth?"

He turned back to me, his eyes wide. "Son of a bitch."

"He said he put them in her hand." The trembles started again, and I was freezing, in spite of Tony's

31

comforting hold.

He stood and looked around the room, then snatched an afghan off the back of my arm chair. "Here." He wrapped it around me, but the shaking only slightly eased.

"He left them as some kind of sick tribute to my pennies in heaven story."

"Fuck," Tony whispered.

My phone rang, startling me so badly that I jumped. My heart slowed to a normal rate when the caller ID showed it was Lane.

"Lane?" I answered shakily.

"Hey there. Mind if I come by? I need to talk to you about something." His voice sounded down… troubled, like he'd been the one to get a call from the killer.

"I need to talk to you, too. Tony's here. Something's happened."

"What is it? Are you hurt?"

Moisture leaked down my cheeks, and I wiped the tears away. "No. I'm not hurt. I'm fine. We… the killer… I got a call from the killer."

"What? You're sure it was him? What did he say?"

"I'll explain when you get here. Please hurry."

I hung up the phone and wrapped the afghan around me. Lane would be here soon, but that wouldn't change the fact that a killer had set his sights on me… had left me a twisted gift that cost a young girl her life.

****

Lane saw Monroe shivering, even from the doorway. She stood, tightening a blanket around her shoulders. He stalked over and pulled her into his embrace, rubbed his hands up and down her arms. She felt so small, so vulnerable, the quaking so severe, he could feel it to his core. He wanted to mangle the bastard who'd done this to her.

He pulled away slightly and ran his gaze over her pale, drawn face. "Tell me exactly what happened. What he said, and why you believe it was him."

The lines around her eyes tightening, Monroe drew in a shaky breath and began to speak. When she got to the part about the pennies, Lane's throat closed. *It was him.* The asshole had Monroe's phone number. And a sick fascination with her.

"Give me your phone."

Monroe retrieved it from the sofa. "I didn't even think about that," she said as she passed it to him. "He called from Magic Construction. You can find him from that, right?"

"Shit," Lane muttered, looking up to meet his partner's eyes. The girl's parents had wondered what happened to Charity's cell phone. Now they knew. The cocksucker used it to terrorize Monroe.

"What is it?" Monroe asked.

Lane sighed heavily. "The victim's father owns Magic Construction. The killer called you from the girl's cell."

"Oh, my God." Monroe caught her bottom lip between her teeth and sucked in a shuddering breath. "He kept her phone. Used it and—"

"And I'm sure he's thrown it away by now," Tony bit out. "He knew we wouldn't be able to find him if he used the victim's phone."

"He wants me to keep writing articles," Monroe said. "He said that's why he started killing again. He wants me to use the information about the penny and the tooth in my article." Taking in another gulp of air, she pressed a clenched hand to her mouth. "He left the penny dated 2003 because that was the year she lost her first tooth."

Lane grimaced. They hadn't gotten far enough to figure out the symbolism, but apparently, the murderer was happy to impart the information to Monroe.

Monroe turned wide, horrified eyes to him. "Did he take her tooth while she was still alive?"

"No." That much he could say with certainty. At least he could offer that small comfort. "The ME said he pulled it postmortem."

Monroe nodded. The tension in her expression abated slightly, but she still looked as though she'd been in the middle of a war zone.

"Don't print it," Tony said. "That's something we don't want leaked to the public. Can you do that for us? Keep that out of the article?"

"Of course." Monroe favored Tony with a slight lift of her full lips.

Lane's heart ached for her sadness, but at the same time, he suffered a twinge of jealousy that Tony was the recipient of that brief smile.

"You know, maybe I shouldn't write the article at all," Monroe said. "If he killed her so I'd keep writing about him, maybe if he doesn't get what he wants, he won't hurt anyone else."

Lane nodded slowly. "Maybe But it's a gamble. It might just piss him off."

"Right," Tony said. "But she has a point. If he's doing it to revel in the glory of her articles, and he finds out that's not going to happen, maybe he will stop. Or maybe he'll do something to draw himself out in the open, and we'll nab him."

"I'll talk to Adam," Monroe said. "The paper will definitely want to run the story, but Phil can write it. That way, I'm not going along with the sick bastard."

"Good idea." Tony stood. "I'd better go. The kids are at home."

Monroe stepped away from Lane and said to Tony, "Thanks for coming over."

"Sure." Tony cocked his head toward Lane. "I'll be a stand in for this asshole any time." He winked at her, drawing a real smile this time.

For a second, Lane wanted to punch his friend's face in. Tony was a notorious womanizer, and Lane knew it was his nature to flirt. He just didn't want him flirting with Monroe. The cave man in him didn't want another man near his woman. Of course, once he told her the latest development, she would no longer be his. The thought caused a fierce pain to grip his gut.

"I'll walk out with you." Lane told Tony, following him out onto the porch.

They stood in silence for several seconds. Lane stared out over the neighborhood. Just past the end of Monroe's drive was a cemetery. Headstones rose above the blanket of darkness covering the ground.

"It's definitely our guy." Tony was the first to speak. "Just don't know if we can do anything about it. Maybe we can figure out a way to use his phone calls to Monroe to trip him up."

"Phone *calls*? You think he'll call again."

"Don't you?"

Frustration and worry for Monroe weighted Lane's chest, making it difficult to get the words out. "Yeah. He will."

Tony nodded and fell silent again.

"Did you know that over the years, pennies have been made from various materials?" Lane said. "Since copper is so expensive, in 1982 they started making them from 97.5 percent zinc and 2.5 percent copper."

"Is that right?" Tony said, although not with any genuine interest. Everyone who knew Lane was accustomed to his quirk, knowing he mainly spouted insignificant trivia when he was troubled. Tony stepped off the porch, then looked back at Lane. "So, how did it go with the attorneys? When will you be a free man?"

Lane took in a deep breath and let it out between pursed lips. "Not sure." He explained what Miriam had asked of him.

"You're not going to do it are you?"

"I feel like I'm caught between a dog and a fire hydrant." Lane shrugged. "I think I have to. For now."

"For now, my ass." Tony's voice rose, and even in the darkness, Lane could see his face redden. "You'll lose that woman, and that'll make you the dumbest mother fucker around." He shook his head and shoved his hands in his pockets. "You and I both married royal bitches. I hooked up with a shitload of chicks and barely remember any of their names. You've got something good with Monroe. Women like her don't come along every day."

"You think I don't know that?"

Tony shrugged. "You might know it, but you damned well better remember it." He jerked his chin toward the door. "She needs you. You should get back inside. And, for now, how about you don't drop your little torpedo?"

****

The next morning, I could barely drag myself out of

bed. Lane had stayed late—until I insisted I was okay and convinced him to leave. As much as I enjoyed being with him, I didn't need a babysitter.

After he was gone, I called Adam. I had to tell him about hearing from the killer in order to convince him to allow me to give the story to Phil. He reluctantly agreed and promised not to let anyone know the maniac had called me. Phil had already turned in his story for the next morning, so Adam asked me to write about the murder, and Phil and I would just trade bylines.

I stayed up half the night writing the article. What would normally take only a few hours took an eternity. I couldn't concentrate. I hated the thought of giving the bastard his spot in the limelight—even if Phil would be taking credit—but I knew the other papers would run it. Besides, although I'd talked Adam into letting Phil have the story, there was no way he would agree to the *Chronicle* not running it at all.

When I arrived at the newspaper office just after eight a.m., my friend Asia was waiting by my desk. I was once again struck by how lovely she was. Not only was she beautiful on the outside, she had inner beauty that radiated in the glow of her perfectly smooth, mocha-colored skin. Although she was slightly heavy, her impeccable fashion sense downplayed her weight. Today, she wore a white gauzy thigh-length caftan over a designer burgundy pantsuit.

She handed me a cup of coffee, her dark brown eyes filled with sympathy. "You okay?"

My heart slowed. Had she heard about the killer's phone call? Tony and Lane had asked me not to say anything, and I promised I wouldn't. Adam promised he wouldn't. She couldn't know. Could she?

"I'm fine," I answered tentatively.

She pointed at today's newspaper lying on my desk. "Sounds like it might be the same killer. That's got to be tough after thinking he'd stopped."

Relief swept through me. She was talking about the murder. "Yeah. It's tough. Poor girl."

She reached her hand out and squeezed my forearm. "I'm sorry. That really sucks." Flashing white teeth, she gave a smile. "At least it's Friday. Only a few days til MPM Monday. That should help get your mind off of all this."

MPM was Melting Pot Mojito night. Each Monday, myself, Asia, and a few other girls from the office went to Happy Hour at the Melting Pot. It was one way to get through the drudgery of Mondays. I forced myself to return her smile. "Looking forward to it. Are you and Darion going to the Spring Carnival tomorrow?"

"We can't make it. We have plans with Darion's family. How about you?" She paused, her eyes gleaming with merriment. "And Lane?" Asia would like nothing better than to see me with Lane—partly because he and her husband were friends, but mostly because she'd like to see me with a decent guy, period.

"I'll be there. I'm not sure about Lane." We didn't make a lot of public appearances. Didn't want it to seem as though we were dating. At least not until he was divorced. I realized then that I hadn't even asked him how last night went with the attorneys. In light of what happened, it seemed somewhat trivial.

"Good article, Monroe."

I turned at the masculine voice to find Adam striding toward me. Asia snorted and whirled, heading back to her desk. Although Adam was her boss, she didn't show him much respect. She hadn't forgiven him for cheating on me. If I still cared, I wouldn't have either.

"Thanks." I thought about the pennies from heaven angle and how much better the story would have been if I'd given Phil that detail. Adam would kill me if he knew I'd hidden such a juicy tidbit. But jeopardizing the investigation wasn't an option, even for a phenomenal article. Whoever this bastard was, he had to be stopped.

"Maybe I could take you to lunch today to show my appreciation?" He said it casually, but the hopeful lilt to his voice gave him away.

I picked up the newspaper, avoided eye contact. "Thanks, Adam. But I don't think that would be a good idea. Favoritism, you know."

"Yeah, and I'm sure lover boy wouldn't like it." He stepped closer, too close, but I didn't move away. I stared up at him, feeling his emerald orbs reaching into my soul. "If you ever get tired of holding out for a married man, let me know. I'll be waiting."

I opened my mouth, intending to offer a scathing retort, but nothing came out. Adam had a point. He held my gaze for a few moments, then without another word, retreated to his office.

I released a long sigh. Taking a sip of my coffee, I let the warm, strong brew soothe my jagged nerves. If Lane didn't get this divorce handled soon, I'd have to start wearing a big scarlet 'A' on my chest.

****

He gripped the newspaper, hands trembling so badly, he could barely read the words. But he could read them well enough. Not only did the article not mention the penny, but Monroe hadn't even written it. Some other bozo had. He'd gone through all that trouble, wasted all that creative energy, and she hadn't even done the story. The article that they ran barely mentioned him at all. Hadn't mentioned the connection to the other murders. It referred to him as 'the unknown assailant.'

Damn her.

How could she treat him so casually? How could she ignore his demands?

"Fuck," he growled, ripping the paper to shreds and flinging it across the room. The anti-celebratory confetti floated to the ground—mocking him. Just as *she* mocked him.

She was the only one in the media who knew about the tooth. He'd given her the gift of the girl, then added a bonus to the package. And she hadn't appreciated it. Had thrown it back at him like it meant nothing.

Not only would it have made an extraordinary article, he'd fucking *told* her to print it. Who did she think she was messing with?

If they were going to be soul mates, she had to learn to respect his wishes.

One way or the other. She had to learn.

Chapter 3

Josie and I pulled into the parking lot at the river where the Spring Carnival was being held. We climbed from the car, and Josie dug in her purse, pulling out a pack of cigarettes. She lit one, leaning her rear end against the hood of my car as she smoked.

"You coming?" I asked.

"You go on ahead. I'll be there in a little bit."

I narrowed my eyes, peering closely at her. Since she'd stopped using drugs, she'd added some meat to her delicate frame—not much, but enough that she didn't resemble a refugee from a concentration camp. She wore jean shorts and a green tank top that matched the color of her eyes. Her pale complexion now had a bit of healthy color, but her blonde waif-like appearance hadn't changed all that much. She still looked fragile, just a healthier version of fragile. But now, her eyes darted around nervously and the hand that brought her cigarette to her lips trembled.

"What's wrong?"

She shrugged and took another pull from the cigarette. "I'm just not used to being around this many people."

"Come on, my family will be there."

"Yeah, but your mom hates me."

"Mom hates everyone except her sons." I smiled, shooting a glance at her from the corner of my eye.

"Mitch will be there, and he doesn't hate you." Mitch—Mitchum—was one of my brothers, and the childhood crush Josie had on him was still very much alive.

She flushed, adding even more color to her cheeks. I hadn't seen her looking this good in a long, long time. She'd fought an extensive, hard battle—one she hadn't won yet—but she'd made huge strides. Since high school, I hadn't known her to stay clean for more than a week. Now, she had nearly six months sobriety.

"Mitch is going to be here?"

"I think so."

She considered for a few seconds, then crushed the butt out beneath her flip flops. I picked it up off the ground, tossed it into a trash can, then headed toward the carnival with Josie.

As we drew closer, I heard music coming from the bandstand. A local country band playing a Billy Currington song. The smells of funnel cakes and corn dogs followed us as we passed food booths and carnival games on our walk toward the river. I found my family gathered beneath a blue canopy not far from the river's edge.

My father sat in a lounge chair, reading a newspaper. He'd brought a newspaper to a carnival? And not even the *Chronicle*. I shook my head. He'd mentally absented himself from the family years ago. I should be used to it by now.

My mother sat in a lounge chair, holding my three-month old niece, Sierra. Sierra's mother, Naomi, and my brothers, Coburn and Mitchum, sat around a picnic table. Coburn was tall, blond, charming—yet slightly egotistical. Mitch was handsome in a not quite so obvious way. He had thick chestnut hair, hazel eyes, and

42

a crooked grin that attracted females like ants to a crumb.

My brothers stood to hug me and Josie. I tried to be unobtrusive as I watched to see how long Mitch and Josie's hug lasted. Now that she was on the path to getting her shit together, I hoped she would find a decent guy—someone like my brother—rather than the abusive asshole she'd been seeing for years.

"Hello, Mom, Dad." I bent to give Dad a peck on his cheek, then went over to Mom and did the same. I brushed my finger along Sierra's perfect, soft, round baby face. "She gets more beautiful every time I see her." My heart squeezed with an emotion I'd never experienced before, not until Sierra was born. I was all at once in awe, protective, and humbled by the precious gift… the miracle that was my niece.

My mother sighed. "Yes. We're blessed to have her. Doesn't look like you'll be giving me any grandchildren." Her mouth pulled down in a frown. "Especially as long as you're keeping company with a married man."

I'd grown so accustomed to my mother's long-suffering litany I didn't even acknowledge it. "Can I hold her?" I asked, already reaching for the pink-swaddled sweet smelling bundle.

My mother reluctantly released the baby, a glow on her aging face. "Isn't she perfect? She looks just like her daddy."

I frowned. "She doesn't look all that much like him. Other than the black hair, she's the spitting image of Naomi." It was somewhat true, but I mostly said it to get under my mother's skin. Sierra had Naomi's eyes and Coburn's dark hair, but she mostly just looked like her own little individual self. Since my mother thought

Coburn was second to only Jesus Christ, and since my other two brothers fell into place right below Him on her perfection scale, I took every opportunity to make little digs regarding her sons, just to rile her. She'd named each of them after Marilyn Monroe's various leading men, and it was quite poetic that the three of them were the leading men in her own life.

"Where's Gable?" I asked as I chucked Sierra's chin. She smiled, cooing with delight.

"He's manning a craft booth for the church."

I handed Sierra back to my mother. "I'm going to find him, say hello. Josie, you want to come?"

She slid a glance at Mitch. "I think I'll hang out here for a while."

Mitch smiled. "Would you like a beer?" He stood and moved over to an ice chest, then halted, his face reddening. "I'm sorry, Josie. I—sometimes I forget."

"It's okay. Do you have a Dr. Pepper?"

"Sure. That actually sounds good." He pulled two Dr. Peppers from the cooler and returned to the bench, this time settling next to Josie as he handed her a can. I hid a smile. Mitch *hated* Dr. Pepper. Maybe Josie's crush wasn't one-sided.

I found Gable—sans priest garb—standing at a booth with a long table literally covered with hideous-looking hats, scarves, shawls, and other sundry knitted items. He flashed a smile when he saw me. He wore a white linen button-up shirt and faded jeans. With his dark hair and dancing black eyes, he was almost too handsome to be a priest. No doubt women all over the Kansas City area were trying to figure out how to entice him away from God.

I lifted my hand to shade my eyes from the sun and

took in the bright colors of the items he was attempting to sell. I laughed and shook my head. "You don't really expect to sell these, do you?"

"You'll buy one."

"Yeah, but I'm your sister, and I love you. They're atrocious, you realize that, right?"

He scowled and shook his head in mock reprimand. "The women in my church worked their arthritic fingers to the bone making these. Of course I'll sell them. Watch."

Two young women who looked to be in their early twenties slowed as they reached the booth. One was heavy-set with blonde streaks in her brown hair, the other was a thin, almost attractive brunette.

"Hello ladies," Gable said, favoring them with his signature smile of white teeth in naturally bronzed skin. "Could I interest you in a scarf? A hat, perhaps?"

The heavy one curled her nose up as she gazed at the items. "Really? It's, like, spring, almost summer. Besides, they're ug—" She halted, smiling timidly at Gable. "They're not really my style."

"You're kidding, right?" Gable's brows rose. He plucked a knit cap and matching scarf in a bright fuchsia and sea green pattern from the table. He held them up next to the girl's face. "This sets your eyes and complexion off perfectly." Peering at her, he said, "Are your eyes really that shade or are you wearing colored contacts?"

Her face reddened. "These are my real eyes—I mean—uhm—color."

"Wow." He set the items down on the table and turned to her friend. "With your lovely, slim figure, one of these shawls could make you look like a runway model." Taking a lavender shawl from the table, he settled it around her shoulders, then stepped back and let out a low whistle. "Beautiful."

Blushing furiously, both girls hurriedly dug money out of strappy purses and paid Gable for their purchases. He squeezed each of their hands as he said goodbye. "Don't be a stranger. I'll be here all day. Tell your friends, and hurry. All of this will probably be gone in a few hours."

After they left, turning back a time or two to glance at him over their shoulders, he favored me with a wicked grin. "So, tell me again how I won't sell any of this crap."

I shook my head and laughed. "Isn't it a sin to lie? Sometimes, I think you forget you're a priest."

He slapped a hand over his heart as if wounded. "Lie? I said it *could* make her look like a runway model. I just didn't follow up with the news that it didn't. Then, I said, 'beautiful.' I didn't say *she* was. And, I asked if the other one wore contacts. Where, in all of that, was the lie?"

I chuckled. "I think you got me on a technicality. I hope God sees it that way."

He grinned. "It's all for the greater good, sis. Proceeds go to the homeless shelter. While my methods might not be exactly honorable, my motives are completely pure."

All joking aside, he was right. His motives were always in someone else's best interest. He was the kindest, most loving and selfless person I knew, but it hadn't always been that way. When he'd decided to become a priest at the age of fifteen, it had surprised everyone who'd ever met him. Our family was Catholic, but not the most zealous in our religious devotion. Gable had been a hell raiser, to say the least. Not long after Katie was murdered in our back yard, something in him changed. That night changed my whole family—Josie, too. It was the beginning of her journey into the world of drugs that lasted more than twenty years. At least Gable's change was for the better.

****

He eased the back gate open and grinned when he spotted him. The old man knelt at the edge of a vegetable garden, his plaid-covered arm rocking back and forth as he wielded the trowel. Linus Tompkins was so involved in his task, he didn't look up as he approached.

Good. The old guy would make it easy. Breaking into a house was always a tricky thing. Although he'd had a lot of practice, sometimes the unexpected happened. No reason to worry about that now. His victim was outside, easy pickings.

He drew near, and the old man's motions stilled. Based on the hearing aid visible in one ear, not to mention the man's age, it was doubtful he'd heard him. Most likely, he sensed something was amiss.

Tompkins turned his weathered face upward, squinting at the sun's glare. "Can I help you?"

By way of answer, he bent and yanked the trowel out of the old man's hands. "On your feet, old-timer. We're going inside."

"Now, listen here—"

"No, *you* listen here." Maybe he wasn't going to make this easy after all. "You either come with me quietly, or I fuck you up right now, then I go visit your neighbor, Monroe."

Tompkins' eyes watered, and his shoulders slumped in defeat. Bracing liver-spotted hands on his knees, he rose slowly to his feet.

"Atta boy."

Tompkins shot him a look over his shoulder that said he wanted to do anything but meekly obey. He grinned, following Tompkins inside his house.

A Jack Russell greeted them at the door, growling low in his throat when he saw his master wasn't alone.

"Hush, Rowdy, everything's okay." Tompkins' trembling voice held no authority, but the dog went silent. The old man squared his shoulders and lifted his chin, his voice brave, considering the circumstances. "Do what you want to me, but please don't hurt my dog or Monroe."

He let out a long sigh and shook his head. Tightening his grip on the trowel with one hand, he flipped a coin in the air with the other, catching it in his palm. "Do you have any idea how hard it was to find a penny dated 1929, you old fuck?"

****

I hung around and chatted with Gable for nearly an hour, watching him work his magic on a multitude of females from the age of twelve to eighty. By the time I headed back toward the canopy, more than half of the knitted eyesores had been sold.

Torn between not wanting to face my mother quite yet, and yearning to see Sierra again, I chose to take a short walk along the river, away from the crowd. The gentle flow of the water soothed me, and the spring breeze rifling through my hair felt heavenly. I took in a deep breath, inhaling the scent of honeysuckle and river water into my lungs.

As I neared a storage building set back a ways from the river bank, I smelled cigarette smoke and heard girlish laughter. The reporter in me curious, I headed away from the river and rounded the corner of the green shack.

Tony's daughter, Paxton, was half-sitting, half–leaning on a rail that ran behind the shack. A middle-aged man stood talking to her... much too close for my comfort. He reached out a hand and ran it down her cheek, eliciting a smile from the girl.

Fury swept through me, and I stormed over to the two of them. "Paxton, does your dad know you're back here?"

She turned to me, her face going bright red. "What's it to you?" she muttered sullenly.

I engaged the pervert with my gaze. His eyes were a dull bluish color, his brown hair showing signs of receding. He wore khaki shorts, and a Kansas City Chiefs T-shirt stretched over his paunch.

I tried to tamp down the rage crawling from my belly into my throat. Speaking to Paxton, but still looking at the man, I said, "With your father being a cop, he worries about you." I was satisfied to see the man flinch when I said the 'C' word. "There are all kinds of creeps out in the world who take advantage of young girls."

The man scowled and licked his fleshy lips. He looked familiar, but I couldn't place him. I stuck out my hand. "I'm Monroe Donovan, and you are?"

I thought I saw a flicker of recognition at my name dawn briefly in his eyes, along with some emotion I couldn't identify. He swallowed audibly, then took my hand in a brief handshake. Shifting his gaze from side to side as if looking for an escape route, he said. "Name's Cameron."

"Last or first?"

"Huh?"

"Is Cameron your last name or first?"

"First."

Geez, this guy was going to make me drag it out of him. "And your last name?"

"Come on," Paxton whined. "Chill. We were just talking."

Still looking at the creepster, I said, "And now, *I'm* talking to *him*. What's your last name?"

His mouth drew in, making him look even older than he had before. "Cooper."

Cooper? Cameron Cooper? I knew why the asshole looked familiar. "When did you get out?"

"Huh?" he said again.

"When were you released from prison? After you served your sentence for rape."

****

Lane pulled into Shelley Crane's driveway. He'd elected to further question the mother of the boys who'd found Charity Munson, rather than go to the carnival. Although being with Monroe held more appeal, he couldn't see her again without telling her the news, and like a chicken shit, he was putting it off.

Shelley Crane opened the door, her eyes widening slightly when she saw Lane on her porch. He gave her a smile that was meant to reassure. "I'm sorry to bother you, Ms. Crane, but I have a few more questions. May I come in?"

She was around thirty, but her beaten down expression and extra twenty pounds made her look much older. With a hesitation bordering on reluctance, she stepped back and swept her arm out in invitation.

They entered a small living room that smelled of

cigarettes and stale food.

She didn't invite him to sit, so he stood. "One of your neighbors said you might have… remembered something you didn't tell us before. Something about an ex-boyfriend of yours?"

She flinched, then turned away from him, squinting out the window, as if that would tell her which of her neighbors had ratted her out.

Her voice was flat when she spoke. "Johnny doesn't live here anymore."

"Not now. I know. But he did up until a few days ago, right? Even though he's a registered sex offender?"

Once her neighbors learned an RSO was living in their neighborhood, around their children, they'd called the police and Johnny Price had left the house. But it didn't mean he wasn't somewhere nearby. Didn't mean he hadn't murdered Charity Munson before he took off to whatever hole he burrowed into now.

She shifted from one foot to the other. "It was a long time ago when he did that." Her gaze went to a picture of her sons that hung on the wall. "And it was a girl he did it to. He'd never hurt my boys."

Maybe she should win an award for Mother of the Year for only allowing a violator of little *girls* around her sons.

"Where is he now?"

She shrugged and didn't meet his eyes. "I have no idea."

Lane blew out an exasperated breath. His internal lie detector told him she was full of shit. "I think you do. I think you know exactly where he is. If I find him without your help, I'll charge you with aiding and abetting. If you help me, we'll forget that little white lie you just told."

Her head whipped around. "You can't do that. You can't charge me with something like that."

Lane allowed a grin to crease his mouth. "You'd like to think that, wouldn't you? You'd be surprised at what I can do. What I will do."

Her face blanched, and she turned. Jerky strides took her to a small end table where she yanked open a drawer. Lane was surprised when she pulled out a pack of cigarettes instead of a piece of paper to write the guy's address on. Guess he wasn't quite as intimidating as he thought.

With shaking fingers, she lit a cigarette. She crossed an arm over her stomach and rested her elbow on it, continuing to puff on the cigarette, blowing smoke toward him and glaring like she wanted to cause him bodily harm.

"He didn't do anything." This time, her protest had lost some of its conviction.

"Then you won't mind if I have a chat with him, will you?"

She dropped onto the couch and stared at the ground. Taking another drag of the cigarette, she let the smoke out with a sigh, then looked up at Lane. "He's at the Stay All Night motel off of I-29. Room 326."

Lane tilted his head toward her. "Thanks. If I have any other questions I'll let you know." He walked to the door and put his hand on the knob. Turning back, he said, "If you're thinking about calling him to warn him, I wouldn't advise it. If I don't talk to him soon, I'll be back to talk to you."

She glared at him, violently stubbing her cigarette out in the ashtray.

He lifted his brows. "And I'm sure neither of us

want that, am I right?"

Chapter 4

Paxton gasped, and Cooper took a step back.

"I don't need this bullshit," he said, his voice trembling. "Don't need any trouble." He kept backing, and then turned, stumbling before he took off at a run toward the parking lot.

I frowned as I watched him retreat. Could he be the killer? I tried to match his voice to the one of the caller, but couldn't. The caller disguised his voice, though, so that didn't really mean a lot. I didn't sense the confidence in Cooper that the caller exuded, but that could come from him being able to hide behind the phone line.

"What the hell are you doing, butting into my business?" Paxton demanded, her voice bringing my attention back to her.

I kept my tone level as I stared her in the eye. "Business with a rapist?"

Cameron Cooper had been a suspect in the killings long ago. In Katie's murder. The son of a bitch had done time for rape, but they'd never been able to pin any of the murders on him. Now he was out of prison, and another girl was dead.

Reluctantly, I acknowledged there had been a few killings while he'd still been in prison. Still, there was nothing to confirm that the same person committed the crimes. Cooper definitely bore watching.

Paxton took a puff from her cigarette and slid off the

rail. "I'm outta here."

"You're pissed because I ran off a pervert? What, did you *want* to get raped?"

"I'm pissed because I don't need another parent. The two I have are fucked up enough." She lifted her chin defiantly, but tears shimmered in brown eyes that looked so much like Tony's. "Besides, who'd want to rape me? Look at me."

My heart clenched. This girl's self-esteem was so low she was complaining that no one would want to rape her? She was slightly overweight, and in today's world of anorexic-looking women plastered on magazine covers, it was no wonder she might feel unattractive. In spite of that, and the acne scars that were poorly concealed by too-dark foundation, she was a very pretty girl. Her long, dark hair was the kind of smooth, sleek style I envied. She had perfect white teeth and long, thick eyelashes.

I lifted my brows. "Are you kidding me? You're a lovely girl. Lots of guys would want to go out with you."

A faint blush rose on her cheeks. "Right." She took another drag from the cigarette, but settled back on the rail.

"You have another one of those?" I asked, pointing to the cigarette.

Her eyes widened. "You smoke?"

"Sometimes." I didn't—hadn't in forever—but she didn't need to know that.

"Here." She pulled a pack from her jeans pocket and shook one out for me. She lit it, and I took a drag, resisting the urge to curl my nose. They didn't taste as good as they had in high school.

"So, you're going to rat me out to my dad?" she

asked.

"I have to tell him about that asshole you were talking to."

"Geez, great. He'll ground me the entire time I'm here. Like my summer isn't going to suck enough."

"It's not your fault the guy was talking to you. I'll explain that to your dad, but the man could be dangerous, and I need to let the police know he's out of prison and in the area. You know about the girl getting killed, right?" I waited, but she didn't respond. "A girl about your age was found in the park on Thursday morning. She'd been strangled to death, probably raped. The police think this same guy has been killing for years. The man you were just talking to was a suspect in the case twenty-five years ago."

Her face paled underneath the make-up. "You think it was him?"

I shrugged. "I don't know. But he's a bad guy, a rapist, Paxton." I took another pull from the cigarette. Somehow it didn't taste as bad as it had at first. I stubbed it out quickly. With all the stressful shit going on, it would be so easy to pick up the habit. I tossed the butt in a nearby trash can. "So, what do you guys have planned for the summer?"

"Me? Nothing. My dad and brother will hang out together. My dad will attend all his games, and go on and on about how great a ball player he is, and how he's going to be the next George Brett. I'll sit around and watch TV. Thing is, it won't be much better when I go back home. My mom is off on her honeymoon with the asshole she married, so fun times ahead. Yay me," she ended bitterly.

"You don't like your new stepfather?"

She shrugged, and I got the feeling she didn't like much of anyone, especially not adults.

"He's not mean to you is he?" I asked.

"Nah. He barely even knows I'm around. Kind of like my dad, especially when he's with one of those sluts."

Damn. Talk about attitude. The girl had it oozing from her pores. "So, you don't care for the women your dad dates *or* the man your mom married?"

She snorted. "Sucks that old people like them can hook up, and I can't even get asked to the junior prom." As soon as the words were out of her mouth, her eyes widened, and she jerked her face toward me, almost as though she'd forgotten I was there. "Look, it's really lame that you're trying to bond with me or whatever. Just tell my dad anything you want." She slid off the rail again and flung her cigarette on the ground, then stalked away. I knelt and stubbed out the smoldering butt, then tossed it in the same can where I'd thrown mine.

I caught up to her. "I know how you feel." She glanced over her shoulder and gave me an annoyed look, then kept walking. I refused to slow my pace or let her off the hook. I continued like she'd invited me along instead of hurrying her step to try to lose me. "My mother is always riding my ass. Telling me how I need to stop slouching, asking why I can't find a boyfriend, that I'm not getting any younger, I need to drop some weight, blah, blah, blah."

She stopped and turned to face me, her brows scrunched together suspiciously. "*You* need to lose weight?" She looked me over. "You look... amazing. You're not fat."

I shrugged. "I could stand to lose a few pounds, but

57

according to my mother, I need to do that, and more, if I ever want to land a man."

Her expression softened ever so slightly, then the rebellious look came back. "Right. I don't believe you. You're thinking if we have something in common, you'll get to me, and I'll pour out all my deep dark secrets so you can go running to my dad with them." She started walking again, then called over her shoulder, "Just leave me the hell alone, okay?"

"Not quite yet." I hurried to catch up with her. "We're going to find your dad, and I'm telling him about that Cooper creep. If I let you take off and something happens to you, I'd never forgive myself."

"You tell my dad whatever you want, but you can't make me go with you."

"I'm not going to leave you alone until we find your dad and tell him about Cooper."

"Fuck," she bit out. "Let's just get it over with then."

In a few minutes, we were to the canopy where my family was. Tony stood talking to Mitch, Paxton's little brother next to him, looking from one man to the other, seeming to hang onto every word.

"There he is," I said. "Let's go."

She let out a huff, but sauntered behind me when I approached her dad.

Tony looked up. "Paxton, is everything okay?"

She rolled her eyes and didn't answer. Before I could, I heard my mother's voice behind me. "Have you been smoking?" I turned to see her looking at me with aversion.

"I had one cigarette."

"That's a disgusting, filthy—" She abruptly stopped. "You know, it might not be a bad idea after all.

It will help you keep your weight down."

I heard a sharp intake of breath and turned to find Paxton staring at us, wide-eyed. I lifted my brows in an 'I-told-you-so' way as I met her gaze. Tony scowled at my mom, looking like he wanted to say something.

I reached out and took his arm. "We need to talk. Come on." I said over my shoulder to Paxton, "You need to come with us."

Once we were away from my mother, I told Tony about Cameron Cooper.

"Shit." His face paled as he stared at his daughter. "What were you doing talking to a scum bag like that?"

"It wasn't her fault." I put in. "She had no idea. I just wanted you to know he was out, and he's in the vicinity. You think it's a good lead on the latest murder?"

"I have no idea, but we'll check it out. Did you tell Lane?"

I shook my head. "He's not here, is he? I haven't seen him."

"No. He was finishing up questioning some witnesses."

For a brief moment, I detected pity in his eyes that made me wonder if something was going on I didn't know about.

"I don't know if he'll make it here or not, but we'll check Cooper out. Thanks, Monroe. And as for you," he turned back to his daughter. "You don't go off like that without checking with me. Don't talk to strangers either. Hasn't your mother taught you anything?"

Her chin came up, and her lip quivered, but to her credit, she didn't tear up. "Yeah, she taught me the same thing you did. How to get laid."

Tony's mouth dropped open, and I realized mine

was doing the same. Before either of us could respond, Paxton gave her back to us and stalked away, calling out without turning around, "I'll be waiting in the car whenever you're ready to leave this lame ass carnival."

Tony looked at me and let out a long, loud breath. "Damn. She's a handful. I think she hates me."

"I think she hates herself most of all. Maybe she just needs a little love and attention. From her father."

He frowned down at me. "I love my daughter. I love her very much."

I shrugged. "I believe that. Question is, does she?"

****

Josie and I left the carnival, and I'd just dropped her off at her house when Lane called. "Sorry I couldn't make it," he said.

"No problem. It was kind of lame." I grinned, thinking of how fond Paxton was of the word. "Did Tony tell you about Cameron Cooper?"

"He did. We're checking into it."

"Any luck with the questioning?"

"Nothing much. Shelley Crane was dating a sex offender who moved out of her house just before Charity was killed. I questioned him, but he's got a pretty tight alibi. We're keeping tabs on him, though."

"Geez. That's kind of disturbing. She has two little kids."

"Right." Sarcasm colored his tone. "But it's no problem, because the kids this asshole molested were *girls*. Apparently, her sons were in perfectly good hands."

"Ah, so that was her excuse."

"Yeah. Sometimes you just gotta wonder about people."

I didn't want to seem needy, but I'd been disappointed when he hadn't shown at the carnival. I really wanted to see him. But then, I always wanted to see him.

"So, what are you doing now?" I asked. "Do you have time to get together for coffee?"

"Actually, I'm sitting in front of your house."

My pulse did a little dance of joy until he said the next words.

"There's something I need to talk to you about." From the sound of his voice, it wasn't anything I wanted to hear.

"Okay. I'm almost there. We'll talk."

I pulled into the driveway, and we exited our cars at the same time. He didn't speak or make an attempt to touch me as we stepped onto the porch and I unlocked the front door.

He walked in, still not speaking, and moved to stand in front of my Jesse James collection. I sensed something was troubling him, but I remained silent, giving him time. His demeanor unnerved me, caused the hair on my nape to rise.

"I remember when I first saw this stuff." He turned to me with a wistful smile.

"I know. You thought I was some kind of lunatic criminal."

"I thought you might know more than you were telling me, and as it turned out, you did."

He had been looking for Josie to question her about her asshole boyfriend's whereabouts. I'd withheld the info that Josie was in town, because she was coming off a bad bout with drugs. I didn't want him harassing her.

He moved closer to me and looked down into my

face. "I should have toughened up on the questioning, but I was distracted. All I could think about was how sexy you were."

I released a burst of laughter. "I had on ratty pajamas, no make-up, and my hair was a mess."

He reached up to brush a strand back from my face and let his hand linger on my cheek. "A beautiful mess," he murmured. He leaned forward as if to kiss me, then stepped back, closing his eyes and shaking his head. "Damn."

Internal warning bells clanged in my head and my heart. *Don't say it. Whatever it is, don't say it.*

I moved close to him, reaching up to wrap a hand around his neck.

His blue gaze filled with torment, he stared down at me. "Monroe, I—"

"Shh." I placed a finger against his lips. "Don't talk." I replaced my fingers with my mouth. Pressing tightly to him, I kissed him. At first, he resisted. Then, a small moan left his throat and his arms came around me. His tongue slid inside my mouth, sending tingles of delight over my flesh. Warmth seeped from his hard chest to my breasts, even through our clothing.

Dizzy with desire, I clung to him, clung to what was happening now, between us, ignoring whatever had his eyes stormy with emotion, his sexy mouth tense with dread.

If he doesn't say it, then it won't be…

His shoulder muscles tightened beneath my fingers, and his hands left my waist, coming to rest on my upper arms as he set me gently away from him. He stared at me with half-lidded eyes, his breathing ragged. The earlier agony in his expression was still there.

"What is it?" I asked. Enough pretending. He had something to say, and I wanted to hear it… or at least I needed to. Wasn't sure I wanted to.

"I have some… news I need to tell you, and I don't know how."

Any icy chill grabbed my insides. "Just say it," I demanded, my voice harsh with the anxiety welling in the pit of my gut.

He shoved his hands in his pockets and released a long breath. His sky blue eyes stared into mine, shimmering with moisture that looked suspiciously like tears. But Lane Brody—tough guy cop—wouldn't cry. No way.

"Lane, dammit, just tell me."

He tightened his lips, then said, "The meeting with my mother-in-law and attorneys didn't go well." He raked a hand through his hair and shook his head. "Catherine is coming around. She's starting to get her mind back, it seems."

I frowned. "But that's a good thing, right? Now you can divorce her, and she can stand trial for what she did."

His gaze fell away, and his shoulders dropped. "You'd think, but her doctor was at the meeting. He said Catherine was extremely fragile right now. That a divorce would be a huge setback in her progress." He lifted his head to look at me. "They asked if I'd hold off for the time being."

"Hold off? As in halt the divorce proceedings?"'

He nodded. From the look on his face, I knew what he'd decided.

Still, I rushed on, avoiding the inevitable. "But you don't have to, right? I mean, she treated you horribly. She cheated on you and murdered her lover. You don't owe her anything."

"I made a promise to her after the incident. I told her I'd see her through this thing."

My vocal cords froze for a moment as I took in his words. One of the things that I admired most about Lane was his unfailing loyalty. Now that very trait was biting me in the ass.

Finally, I sputtered, "You're kidding, right? After all she's done, you're sticking by your promise? What about me? Us?"

He laughed, but the sound had no humor, and it ended with a slight hitch to his breath. "That's what tears me up. I wanted so badly to be free, to be with you. Now this." He gave me his sexy half smile, but it was filled with sadness and regret. "You're strong, tough, independent. You don't need me like Catherine does."

I need you, my heart cried out. *I need to finally have someone I can trust, that I can love.* But then, I couldn't really trust him now, could I?

"I can't believe you're doing this." My voice refused to go above a whisper. I hated how pathetic I sounded, but I couldn't seem to help myself.

"I can't leave her right now. If I did, I wouldn't like the kind of man that would make me." His lips twisted. "You wouldn't like that man either."

I swallowed back tears. "Well, I guess this is it then." My voice came out stronger than I expected, considering the ache growing in my heart. "You need to leave."

He studied me in silence. He removed his hands from his pockets, pinching the bridge of his nose between his fingers. "It won't be forever," he promised, his tone husky with emotion. "It will probably only be a few months."

"Really?" I barked a bitter laugh. "You know this? So, it appears you're more qualified than her psychiatrist. Maybe you should be the one treating her."

"Roe…" He reached out a hand toward me. I didn't know his intentions, but I stepped out of his reach. "Please," he whispered. "Please don't give up on us. I love you."

His words sent a wave of desperate rage through me. "No! Don't say that." I took another step back, maybe afraid of what I might do if I stayed in striking distance. "You don't get to say that now, not when you're staying with your wife." My voice rose, trembling with hurt and anger. "You never said it before, and you damn sure can't say it now."

He shrugged. "Not saying it won't make it any less true."

I could see my own pain reflected in his gaze. I knew I was being hard on him, knew he was torn, trying to do the right thing. But I wouldn't let up. I couldn't. He had chosen her over me, and the knowledge of what he had done twisted my graciousness into an ugly knot. Even if he was doing the right thing, his actions didn't sit well with me. I was on the losing side of a battle I didn't start. A casualty of war. I curled my lip in disdain. "Then I guess you have a problem, don't you?"

He stared at me with an injured look, and unable to stand it any longer, I stalked to the door, flinging it open. "Get out, please. Now."

He nodded, slowly heading toward the door. When he reached me, I smelled his achingly familiar scent of woodsy aftershave and soap. I caught my breath, tensing my hand on the knob until he passed. Once he stepped outside, I slammed the door and locked it behind him.

I made my way to the couch and dropped heavily into the soft cushions, resting my head back, my eyes tightly shut as tears squeezed between them.

Turned out, my mother was right. God, it sucked admitting that. Even to myself.

****

That evening, tired of wallowing in self-pity, I called Josie to see if she wanted to catch a movie.

"I'd love to. I'm going a little stir crazy. What do you want to see?"

"I don't know." I shrugged. I didn't care what we saw. I just needed to get out of the house. "Let's be adventurous. I'll pick you up in half an hour, and we'll go into whatever movie is starting then."

"Wow." Josie's voice held amusement. "You are a wild and crazy girl. What's next, floating caution lights?"

I laughed, my spirits lifting slightly. I'd tell Josie about Lane once the movie ended. But for a few hours, I'd pretend like I was going to have my happily ever after, just like the people on the big screen. Well, not all of them had happily ever afters, but the ones who didn't usually died and didn't realize they weren't going to.

I brushed my hair and put on lip gloss, not bothering to change out of my jeans and Rock Louie T-shirt. Tonight, as most nights, my attire would be casual.

As I closed the screen door, a flash of something that didn't seem to belong made me look down. It sat just to the side of the front door. Had it been another foot to the left, I'd have tripped over it. Tissue paper stuck out of the top of the red gift bag.

A present from Lane? An 'I'm sorry I stomped on

your heart' gift, or maybe an 'I was an idiot to even think about going back to Catherine' gift? Not likely. Had either of those thoughts occurred to him, he'd probably just have knocked on my door and told me.

I picked up the bag and pulled out the tissue paper, reaching in to retrieve the objects. One was a document that I recognized from Linus's Jesse James collection. It was a letter Jesse had written to his mother, Zerelda, while he and his brother Frank had been on the run. The paper was so old, so brittle and fragile, that Linus kept it locked in a glass case. No one ever took it out. No one ever touched it.

Chills washed through my blood as I gently replaced the letter inside the bag and looked at the other item in my hand. A penny. Dated 1929. A quick calculation told me that was the year Linus was born.

My stomach lurched in fear, and I dropped my purse and the bag. While my mind hadn't yet accepted what this macabre gift meant, my legs were already pumping, carrying me across the street to Linus's house. I grabbed the door knob and turned, shouting Linus's name as I slapped my hand against the wood. *Locked.* Shit.

I stood on tiptoe, feeling along the top of the frame for his spare key. Through the door, Rowdy's frantic barks sounded. With shaking fingers, I unlocked the door, screaming as I flung it open, "Linus? Linus, are you here?"

Rowdy met me at the door, whining and wagging his tail. The dog turned and trotted to the kitchen. I followed.

Just inside the door, I halted, my breath leaving my body in a terrified rush.

"Oh no. Oh God, no." I dropped down next to Linus,

touching my fingers to his neck to feel for a pulse. Thank God. He was alive. My cell was in the purse that I'd left behind in my panic. Scrambling to my feet, I rushed to Linus's phone and punched in 9-1-1.

I murmured to Linus, even though I knew he couldn't hear me, "It's going to be okay. Just hang in there." My voice caught on a sob. "Help's coming. You're going to be fine."

When the operator answered, I managed to shriek out enough words that she got the gist of my emergency.

"Is he breathing?" she asked, managing to infuse sympathy into her clipped, professional tone.

"Yes," I whimpered, moving back over to Linus and once more kneeling beside him. "He's unconscious, but he's breathing. Please hurry."

"An ambulance is on the way. Do you see where he's injured? Do you see any blood?"

My eyes roamed over his too-still body, landing on a dark puddle beneath his head. "Oh God," I cried. "Yes. There's blood. He's bleeding from his head."

"Was anyone with him? Does it look like he had some kind of accident?"

I gulped in air, trying to stop sobbing, then opened my sweaty palm where I still gripped the penny.

"It was no accident," I choked out. "That mother fucker did this to him."

Chapter 5

I sat by Linus's hospital bed, a prayer playing over and over in my mind. *Please let him wake up soon. Please let him be okay.*

With his face relaxed in sleep, his wrinkles were more pronounced. His false teeth had been removed, causing his mouth to sink inward. He looked pale, frail and vulnerable—smaller than normal.

The door opened, and I turned to find Lane and Tony entering the room, their faces set in grim lines. I met Lane's gaze. His eyes held a look of sympathy and longing. The sympathy I would take. The longing was his problem. I pulled in a deep breath as they joined me at Linus's bedside.

"How is he?" Lane whispered.

"He won't wake up." My voice broke. "The doctors said he should be okay. But, at his age, something like this could—"

"My age, hell!"

The words were slurred, whistling from Linus's toothless mouth, but his voice was firm, strong. Hope lit my chest as his eyes fluttered open. "Linus!" I reached out and took his cool, wrinkled hand gently in my own. "You're awake."

He turned his head to look at me. "Yeah, but I got a mother of a headache."

"I'll call the doctor."

"Don't need no doctor. Need a drink."

I poured water into a cup from the pitcher next to his bed. Holding the straw near his mouth, I waited for him to drink.

Scowling, he took the cup from me in a trembling hand. "He knocked me on the head. Didn't break my arms." He sucked from the straw, then set the cup on the nightstand and lay back against the pillows. "Ain't no invalid," he grumbled.

His voice had gained strength, and the sparkle in his eyes was back. I knew then that he'd be okay. *Thank God.*

He looked over my shoulder at the detectives. "I guess you fellas are here to take my statement. Well, I'm ready to give it to you. That no account son of a bitch. I swear, if I was fifteen years younger…"

I hid a grin. If he were fifteen years younger, he'd still be in his late sixties.

"Yessir," Tony said. "We have reason to believe the man who attacked you could be responsible for a string of murders. Anything you can tell us will help."

"I'll get out of your way." I stood and stepped back, giving Tony and Lane access to Linus.

Linus recounted what happened, and my anger grew with each word. How could the asshole hurt a poor, sweet old man like Linus? Then again, how could he savagely murder young girls?

"Can you give us a description of your attacker?" Lane asked. I could hear the eagerness in his voice. This was the closest they'd come to catching him. The only witness he'd left alive. The question was why? Why hadn't he killed Linus?

Linus huffed out a frustrated breath. "Damn sure

wish I could. He was wearing a fedora hat and sunglasses. And a fake beard and mustache. You could tell they wasn't real. He had this cocky grin, like he thought it was funny that he didn't even try to make it look natural. Like it was all some kind of game. Son of a bitch," he muttered. "I wanted to wipe that grin right off his face. Sorry I ain't more help."

Lane's shoulders drooped. "That's okay. How tall was he? Fat, thin? What did his voice sound like? Did you notice any scars or tattoos? Any particular smells? Body odor? Cologne?"

Eyebrows puckered, Linus said, "He was around six foot. Average build. Kind of on the thin side, not muscly at all. A little bit scrawny, if you ask me." He smiled, the observation seeming to please him. Speaking slowly, he continued, "He had a normal voice. No scars or nothing unusual. He wasn't there long, though, before he conked me on the head. I didn't have time to see much."

"You're doing great," Tony said. "If that's all you can think of for now, we'll let you get some rest. You might remember more after you're feeling better."

"I remember one thing. He threatened Miss Marilyn. Said if I didn't go inside with him, he'd pay her a visit." Linus's lips trembled. "I tell you what, made me spittin' mad. I was wishin' I had my gun. I'da shot him where he stood."

My heart warmed at his fierce protectiveness. I caught Linus's eye, giving him a smile.

"We appreciate your time, sir." Lane pulled a card out of his shirt pocket and laid it on Linus's bedside table. "If you think of anything else, give us a call."

Linus lifted his head, glaring at Lane. "I didn't say I was done, did I?"

I flinched at his tone. His ire no doubt had to do with mine and Lane's relationship. He'd be happy to know that was a thing of the past.

"He gave me a message to give to Marilyn. Said to tell her, maybe she'll listen next time. Said he spared me because killing me wasn't part of their special connection, whatever the hell that means. He said if she didn't listen, though, he'd be willin' to break the rules."

Cold tingles washed over my skin. It wasn't as if I didn't know this was some kind of warning, but hearing those words from Linus's lips made it real. Made it deadly serious. If this was the maniac's way of warning me, I'd damn sure listen. No way was I taking a chance with anyone else's life.

****

The ringing phone woke me much earlier than I would have liked. I'd stayed with Linus most of the night, then downed half a bottle of wine when I got home.

I blinked my eyes open and fumbled for the phone. My tongue stuck to the roof of my mouth, but I managed to squeak out a greeting.

"Monroe, did I wake you?"

All remnants of sleep fled when the tinny voice came over the line. I swallowed painfully, but my mouth was so dry it only made me cough. I reached for the bottle of water on my nightstand, unscrewed the lid, and took a gulp of the tepid liquid. "Who is this?"

"Come on, let's not play that little game each time we talk. You've pushed my patience to the limit as it is."

"What?" I sat up and leaned against the headboard, shoving a mass of hair out of my face. I had to play this right. I damn sure didn't want a psycho killer pissed at me. I'd seen firsthand what that could cause. "I didn't mean to upset you."

"You *did* upset me." His voice rose. "We're supposed to be a team. I went through all that work for you, and you don't appreciate it."

"I'm sorry. I… uh…" Why was it that I could never think of what I needed to say when conversing with a lunatic? Maybe I hadn't had enough practice. Something told me if they didn't catch him pretty soon, I'd be an expert before this was over. "I didn't mean to make you mad. It's just that, the cops thought it was best if someone else wrote the story. I didn't want to get in trouble with them."

"Fuck the cops!" His rage-filled scream made me pull the phone away from my ear. "You listen to me, not those inept fools, got it?"

"Yes. Yes, I'm sorry. Maybe I can publish a follow up—"

"Don't bother. The moment's passed. Just make sure you write the article next time."

In my hung-over, terrified state, it took a few seconds for his words to register. When they did, coldness seized my insides, and my blood seemed to stop pumping.

"Next time?" I swallowed hard. "Please, no. Don't—"

"Of course there'll be a next time. And a next. And a next. That way, you can keep writing your stories."

I shook my head, even though he couldn't see the motion. "No. You're insane. If you hurt anyone else, I won't do it. I won't write about you anymore."

A soft chuckle that was somehow more chilling than his earlier rage made goose bumps break out over my flesh.

"You don't want me going back to see the old man, do you? Besides, it won't stop me. I'll just make them suffer more. Did the police tell you about the tooth? How I took it after she died?"

"Yes. They told me that."

He waited a beat, let my terror build a notch or two higher, then said, "Next time, I won't wait."

****

Lane and Tony sat in chairs across from Lieutenant Michelle Karakas's desk. Tall and broad-shouldered, she loomed over them, sending out her signature fierce glare.

Lane knew this look. It was the one that was crafted to make its recipients tremble in fear. Lane wasn't playing, and from Tony's relaxed posture—with his long legs stretched out in front of him and his hands folded on the back of his head—it wasn't working on him either.

She cleared her throat and began pacing back and forth, slapping a folder against her leg. "Another murder. This fuck head's at it again. You jokers think you can do better than the last team?"

"We'll catch him," Tony said.

"You will if you don't want to be bumped down to patrol." She stopped pacing and leaned her butt against the desk, crossing one booted foot over the other. "So, he called the Donovan woman, attacked her neighbor. That's where we need to focus. He's interested in her. That'll be the key to catching him."

Lane pushed aside the image of Monroe's pained expression as she'd sat next to Linus's bed—almost the same expression she'd worn when he gave her the news that he was staying with Catherine. He also pushed aside the fact that he was the biggest shithead on earth.

"We couldn't do a trace," Lane said. "He called from the victim's phone."

"No shit. If the guy was an idiot, he wouldn't have been killing for over twenty-five years and getting by with it. You got any leads at all?"

"Cameron Cooper, the suspect they were looking at on the first murders is out of prison," Tony said. "He has an alibi, a pretty strong one, for the night of the murder."

Lane added, "It's a long shot, but the mother of the boys who found the victim was dating a registered sex offender. I talked to him, but I don't think he's our guy."

"But you'll keep after him." Karakas lasered Lane with her stare, then gave it to Tony for a few seconds. "Both him and Cooper."

Tony inclined his head. "Right."

Karakas rubbed her hand over the back of her head, barely disturbing her short, mannish haircut. "You'll also stay close to the Donovan woman. If she gets another call, I want you there."

Lane's breathing slowed, but he forced his voice not to convey his emotion. "Lieutenant, I'm sure you know about our history. Mine and Monroe Donovan's. I don't think it's a good idea for me to be in contact with her."

"So, you're saying you can't keep your dick in your pants and do your job?"

Lane's face heated. "I'm not saying that. I just—"

"Do I look like fucking Dear Abby?"

Lane opened his mouth to speak, but she didn't give him the opportunity.

"We've got a killer who could possibly be the same cocksucker that murdered those girls twenty-five years ago—and some in between—and he's at it again. He's made contact with the Donovan woman, and you guys are going to stick to her like the pages of a girlie magazine. You think I give a fuck about your romance? Tell it to your therapist and find me my killer." Her lips curled in a grotesque semblance of a smile. "Or, maybe you want *me* to be your therapist. Is that it, Brody? You wanna cry on my shoulder?"

Lane shot a look at Tony. His partner's mouth quirked, and his cheeks expanded from trying to hold back a laugh. No help there.

"Maybe one of the other detectives could—" Lane started, but she cut him off.

"Maybe you can both do what the fuck I said. Get out of my office and don't come back until you have something for me."

She turned her back on them. They stood and exited her office, closing the door.

Tony snickered. "Your therapist. *Right*. She'd send a person into insanity if they were perfectly normal."

"Shit. Sticking close to Monroe. That's not going to be easy."

"Maybe you shouldn't have screwed her over like you did."

Lane scowled. "I did what I had to do."

"Yeah. She's too good for your sorry ass anyway." He looked back at Karakas' office. "You ever wonder where the other half is?"

"Other half?"

He cocked a thumb toward the lieutenant's door. "Of the ambiguously gay duo."

Lane cracked a grin. Razzing the lieutenant behind her back was a stress reliever. Doing so in her presence would be a death sentence.

His phone rang, and he looked at the caller ID to find

Monroe's number on the display. A little too anxiously, he flipped it open. "Monroe, is everything okay?"

Her voice sounded winded, panicked. "Lane. I probably shouldn't have called you. Maybe I should have called Tony. Or 9-1-1. I just didn't know… I wasn't sure…" Her breath hitched, and Lane's heart tried to pound out of his chest. "I didn't know what to do or…" she trailed off, her babbling coming to an end.

"What happened, Monroe?" His pulse beat erratically as he waited for her answer.

"He called. The killer. He called me again."

****

Lane rested his hands on the desk beside Detective Lucinda Rochester as she carried on a chat session with the service provider of the cell phone the suspect had called from. Lucinda was a wiz at computers, at obtaining information in a fraction of the time he and Tony could.

She slid her chair slightly to the right, closer to Lane, where their shoulders occasionally touched as her fingers flew over the keyboard. Heavy perfume that always reminded him of nightclubs and forbidden sex wafted up. He could move away, but it would be too obvious. Of course, it wasn't like Lucinda wasn't highly obvious herself. She had been since they'd met, right after he'd transferred to Kansas City from St. Louis.

Several months ago, she'd lured him to an alley on the pretense of having something for him in a case he was working. She'd then attempted to give him a blow job. Resisting hadn't been easy. Lucinda was an extremely attractive woman, and he and Catherine hadn't had sex in a very long while, even before their marriage imploded. But at the time, he'd just met Monroe, had just

Alicia Dean

begun falling for her, and although he'd like to believe he'd stopped Lucinda because of his marriage vows, a part of him knew it was mainly because of his feelings for Monroe. Apparently, Lucinda was willing to give it another try.

"Here you go." Lucinda jotted the information on a sheet of paper and lifted it toward Lane. As he took it, she stroked her fingers along the back of his hand. He raised his eyes to her face. She smiled, then tilted slightly forward, giving him a glimpse of her impressive cleavage. Flipping back a lock of her long hair, she slowly ran her tongue over her upper lip.

He resisted the urge to roll his eyes at the blatant ploy. In spite of the slight shifting in his groin, she mostly left him cold. "Thanks." He snatched his hand away and straightened from the desk, looking over her head at Tony, who wore a shit eating smirk. "Got the address. Let's head over there and check it out."

Tony grinned. "If you want, I could check it out on my own, and you could stay here at the station."

The look Lane gave was meant to say *fuck you*, but his mouth said, "Nah. I'll go with you. No telling what we'll run into."

Lucinda stood and purposely brushed Lane's body as she slid away from the desk. "Good luck, you two."

"Thanks for your help," Lane said.

"No problem." A husky chuckle issued from her full red lips. "Just remember, you owe me one."

Lane cleared his throat and gave a quick nod, then he and Tony headed to Beacon Street.

****

The house was a yellow two-story. Except for the color, it looked identical to the others on the street. The

78

neatly mowed lawn was a replica of the other neatly mowed lawns on the block, each holding one Amur Maple tree directly in the center of the yard.

They climbed from the car, and Lane stood back while Tony knocked. A thin woman with bright red hair answered the door. Drying her hands on a dish towel, she frowned at Tony, then looked over his shoulder at Lane. "Can I help you?"

"Hello, ma'am." Tony flashed his shield, and the woman's expression went from confusion to concern. "I'm Detective Tony Webber and this is my partner, Detective Lane Brody. We'd like to ask you a few questions if you have a moment."

"Questions? What about? What's happened? Is it Justin?"

"Justin?"

"My son. Did something happen to Justin?"

"No, that's not why we're here," Lane assured her quickly. It didn't appear she was going to invite them in. Unless she or Justin was the murderer, they didn't really need to come in. They just needed to find out what the hell the deal was with the cell phone. "Does someone in your home own a cell with the number 234-5867?"

She frowned. "That's Justin's phone number. Did you find his phone?"

Air deflated from Lane's chest. "His phone is missing?"

"Yeah. He was out with friends last night at the Power and Light District. He doesn't know if he lost it at the restaurant, or at one of the bars they went to, but it's gone."

Shit. Their guy had found—or stolen—the kid's phone.

"No, I'm sorry." Tony's voice sounded as letdown as Lane felt. "We didn't find the phone. A call was made from it by a suspect in a case we're working, so I assume he has Justin's phone."

Had Justin's phone, Lane silently corrected. No way would he keep it on him. They'd done a trace and pinged it to towers in the North area of Kansas. The asshole wasn't stupid. He wouldn't use a phone they could trace back to him.

"We're going to need your son to provide us the name of every location he visited last night," Lane told the woman, trying not to sound as frustrated as he felt.

He just hoped the next time the son of a bitch called Monroe, it was this same scenario—from a phone that belonged to someone still living.

****

I struggled through work on Monday, then forced myself to meet Asia at the Melting Pot for MPM. Our other co-workers couldn't make it, so it would just be the two of us. In my present mood, that suited me just fine.

It was important to follow the same routine, to pretend a psycho wasn't out to hurt the people I loved, and that the only man I'd had serious thoughts about a future with hadn't just shattered my heart. Of course, the lesson here was, don't make plans for the future with a man who's pledged his future to another woman.

Lane promised that once Catherine was better, he'd continue divorce proceedings. God knew how long that would be. Was I really besotted enough to wait around until that time came? *If* that time came?

"Hey, Roe, get with it, girl. You've barely touched your mojito."

Asia's voice drew me out of my musings, and I

forced myself to smile at her. "Sorry. You're right. I was just thinking about poor Linus."

Asia knew Linus had been attacked, she just didn't know the details of who or why. I'd been to the hospital to see him that morning before work. While he was feeling much better, the bruises on his sweet face were heartbreaking. The hospital was releasing him in the morning. I worried about him being home alone, but he swore he could take care of himself. I didn't remind him he hadn't done such a great job a few days ago.

I downed half of the delicious cocktail and felt marginally better when the alcohol warmed by bloodstream. Dipping a chunk of bread in the cheese sauce, I worked on forcing myself to enjoy the evening.

Asia leaned close to be heard above the music. "Are you okay? About Lane?"

She hadn't been pleased when I told her what happened. From the beginning, she'd been pushing the two of us together, but now she was angry enough to gut him with one of the fondue skewers we were using.

"I'm okay."

"We need to get you back out there. Find a man who'll rock your world and make you forget about Mr. Sexy Hot Mess Asshole."

I chuckled. "I wasn't exactly 'out there' before. It's not like I'm trolling for dates. After all, the one before Lane was Adam. My track record isn't particularly stellar."

Asia rolled her eyes and gave an exaggerated sigh. "Jesus. You don't have to settle for assholes or nothing. We can find you a good man."

I shrugged and took another sip of my mojito. Ugly truth squeezed my lungs. *I didn't want another man.*

"This thing with Lane could be temporary. If Catherine improves rapidly, he'll go through with the divorce," I defended weakly.

Asia's gasp made me turn to look at her. Her eyes were wider than the gold hoop earrings dangling from her ears. "Are you fucking nuts, girl? You're gonna hold out for a married man who doesn't have the balls to leave his psychotic bitch of a wife?" She harrumphed in disgust. "You'll let life pass you by while he plays nursemaid to his bat shit crazy wife."

She was right, and I was almost as surprised as she was that the words came out of my mouth. I'd been pissed at Lane and hadn't intended to give him even another day, let alone any longer. Now I was talking as though I'd wait around no matter how long it took.

Making one more feeble attempt to defend myself, I said, "It's not like I'm giving anything up. There's no one in the picture anyway."

"And there won't be until you cut Lane Brody loose."

I released a resigned sigh. "You're right." Reaching out, I squeezed Asia's forearm. "I won't wait around on him. But it's not that he doesn't have the balls to leave her. He made a commitment, and he feels obligated to see it through. His father abandoned him when he was small. It's ingrained in him to remain steadfastly loyal." My arguments were laughable. When had I turned into someone so needy? So desperate?

"Huh-uh." Asia tut-tutted, shaking her head and frowning. "Stop defending him, Roe. You're better than that."

Tears burned my throat, and I took another drink to force them back. Again, she was right, I was better than that. So why was I mooning like a pathetic loser?

****

Two hours and four mojitos later, I stood on the sidewalk outside the Melting Pot, sucking in gulps of fresh night air as I waited for a taxi. I left my car in the parking garage, not wanting to drive after drinking so much. Asia had offered me a ride home, but my house was in the opposite direction of hers, so I decided to take a cab. I declined her suggestion to wait with me. I'd had all the girl chatter I could handle for one night. The high of the booze was settling into a maudlin mood, and I wanted to be alone.

I glanced down the street. Not a vehicle in sight. It was, after all, eleven o'clock on a Monday. The Plaza didn't do a lot of business this late on a week night. I looked at my watch. What was taking the cab so long? I'd been waiting out here for half an hour.

Suddenly so weary—or drunk—that I didn't feel I could stand for another second, I weaved my way over to one of the benches on the sidewalk and plopped down to wait.

No sooner had I sat than I heard the sound of running footsteps. I whirled toward the noise in time to see a man barreling toward me from around the corner. I jumped to my feet, terror squeezing my larynx closed so I couldn't call out for help.

I backed away, but he was on me in no time. Part of my mind knew I should take note of his description—-in case I lived to provide it to the police—but I was so shocked, so confused and terrified, that I could only register the basics—dark clothing, ski cap, medium build, and mean-looking eyes. He grabbed my blouse and jerked me toward him. Something sharp pressed into my stomach. A knife. *Oh my God, he's got a knife.*

"What—what do you want?" I managed to stutter.

"Give me your money, bitch."

I fumbled in my purse, fighting back the urge to vomit. I'd faced a demented murderer last year and hadn't been any more terrified than I was now. Maybe because I knew the killer on a personal level. This guy was a stranger, and I had no idea what he might do.

My fingers trembled violently as I fished around in my purse. The knife loomed in my peripheral, seeming five times its actual size. The thud of my heart reverberated in my ears, and my vision was impaired by my tears.

"Hurry, bitch," he hissed.

I nodded vigorously, my fingers finally landing on my wallet. I listened for the sound of the taxi. Would it even matter? Would the driver see what was going on and keep driving? Would his appearance panic the man and cause him to plunge the knife into my stomach? The thought spurred me to hurry, and I yanked out a handful of bills, thrusting them at the man.

"I only have around fifty bucks," I gasped out from my paralyzed throat.

He scowled, but before he could take the cash from my hand, a movement behind his shoulder caught my attention. I watched in wide-eyed surprise as a stranger grabbed the assailant from behind and spun him around.

Now the knife was pointed at my potential savior. The guy was unfamiliar. A good Samaritan, but no one I knew. A new fear surfaced. What if the mugger killed the man who was trying to save me?

"Run, lady. Call the cops," the man panted as he and the attacker circled one another. I fumbled in my purse for my cell, but no way would I run and leave this man to die for his good deed.

I punched 9-1-1, and just as the operator answered, the assailant said, "Hey, dude. What the fuck?" then moved toward the newcomer.

It happened so quickly, I wasn't sure how it came about, but suddenly, my rescuer was the one with the weapon. There was a brief struggle where the men were in a boxer's clench. I couldn't move, couldn't speak. I could only watch as though I'd paid for a ringside seat.

The attacker went still, suspended on his feet for a few moments before he toppled to the ground.

"Hello?" the 9-1-1 operator said. "Is anyone there?"

Teeth chattering from shock, I finally stuttered into the phone, "Please send someone. There was an attempted mugging." I gripped the phone tighter as I continued, "A man's been stabbed. I think he's dead."

Chapter 6

My rescuer's name was Bartholomew Holland. He owned a coffee shop in The Plaza and had just closed down for the night when he saw me struggling with the man.

Bart sat next to me in the lobby of the police station, rocking back and forth, staring at his hands in horror, even though the blood was already cleaned from them. We'd been at the station all night. It was now nearly five in the morning. Bart had been questioned thoroughly, as had I. Now, we were just waiting to hear we were free to go.

"I can't believe it," Bart whispered, pushing his glasses up his nose with the back of his wrist, as if afraid to touch anything with his hands. "I can't believe I killed a man."

He'd said it half a dozen times, and just like each time before, guilt squeezed my chest. I couldn't believe it either. Couldn't believe he'd done it for me.

I reached out a hand and patted his shoulder. "I'm sorry. I'm very, very grateful, but I'm so sorry you had to go through that."

He lifted his head to stare at me. His hazel eyes watered behind the lenses of his glasses. "I'm not blaming you. I'm just glad I was there."

I smiled. "Me too. You're a hero."

His face colored a light pink. "I'm no hero. I just

reacted." A frown creased his mouth, and his hands trembled. "Heroes don't kill people."

"Please, don't torture yourself. It was self-defense. You saved my life, then you had to protect yourself."

He nodded, locks of his sandy brown hair falling over his forehead. He didn't seem convinced. I was afraid the guilt would stay with him for a long time. Maybe forever. But in my eyes, he was a hero. He'd risked himself to save a complete stranger.

Suddenly I knew exactly what my next article would be over. The heroic acts of a stranger. I'd leave out names, unless he wanted me to publish his, but his deed wouldn't go unrecognized. Of course, I had to run it by Adam, but there was very little that Adam refused me.

"Monroe, are you okay?"

I jerked at the sound of Lane's voice. I'd wondered if I'd see him before I left, half-hoped I would, half-hoped I wouldn't. I nodded and stumbled to my feet. For the first time since the attack, tears pricked my eyes. I blinked them back and withstood the desire to fall into Lane's embrace, to let him soothe the fear and sadness away. Not much use in that, since he himself had caused me sadness.

"I'm fine, thanks to him." I laid my hand back on Bart's shoulder. "He saved my life."

Bart stood, and Lane stuck his hand out. Bart stared at it for a moment, then looked at his hands again, as if unsure that they were safe to come in contact with another human. Finally, he reached out and briefly shook Lane's hand before releasing it.

"I heard what happened," Lane said. "Thank you. I understand they're not going to hold you."

Bart nodded. "I guess they decided it was a clear cut

case of self-defense."

"Definitely. And they ran a background check. Michael Finlay was a career criminal. Mostly petty stuff, but he isn't likely to be missed by many people."

"Do you think he could have something to do with the murders?" I asked. "He wanted money, but I don't know. It's kind of odd given what's happened lately that I'd be randomly targeted."

"We're checking that out too. My gut feeling is that it was random, but if there's a link, we'll find it."

"Murders?" Bart lifted his brows, and his already pale face whitened further.

Damn. I'd said too much. "I—I wrote a series of articles about unsolved murders." Bart stared at me intently. I lifted my shoulders in a casual shrug. "Then the girl who was killed at Riverside Park. I just thought maybe someone didn't like that I…" I trailed off, too tired and distressed to offer a better explanation. To even finish my thought. I turned to Lane. "One of the officers is supposed to take us back to our cars. We need to find him and see if we're free to go."

"I'll take care of it," Lane offered. "I'll make sure they're done with you, and I'll run you to your cars."

I locked onto his ocean gaze, and the same thrill that always washed through me was there again. "That's okay," I said. "No need to trouble yourself."

"No trouble." His husky voice, however, indicated he was highly troubled, but not by the inconvenience. "I'll be right back."

I offered Bart a half-hearted smile. "We'll have you out of here soon."

He nodded. "I'm just glad you're okay. I can take you home when we get our cars if you'd like. I'm sure you're still pretty shaken up."

"No more than you. I'll be fine."

He nodded again, but I detected a hint of disappointment in his expression. Poor guy probably didn't want to be alone right now.

"I tell you what," I said. "It actually would make me feel better if you saw me home. You can follow me and maybe come in for a cup of coffee?"

Pleasure replaced his earlier disappointment. "I'd like that. Maybe for just a little while."

"Great."

Lane reappeared. "We're good to go. My car's right outside."

We followed Lane out to his Crown Vic. I insisted Bart sit in the front while I slid in the back. Being so close to Lane was just too difficult.

When Lane pulled next to my Malibu in the parking garage, he climbed out and escorted me to my door.

His gaze searched my face, the torment evident in his eyes. "God, I nearly went crazy when I found out what happened to you."

"What nearly happened," I corrected. "Bart stopped him from hurting me."

Lane nodded and glanced back to where Bart sat in the passenger seat. "Do you need anything?" he asked when he turned back to me. "Want me to come by and make sure you get home okay?"

I smiled without humor. "Thanks, Lane. But your days of protecting me are over. I don't think you should be seeing to my needs." I was still hurt, and I wanted him to hurt too. It was mean, but I didn't care. "*Any* of my needs."

His flinch was so subtle I almost missed it. A shutter

came over his expression. "Unfortunately, you'll have to see me from time to time. The lieutenant asked Tony and I to stick close to you. In case nutbag calls again."

I gave a disbelieving laugh. "Well, you can't be around twenty-four/seven, and we have no idea when or if he'll call."

"True. But the odds are better we'll catch him if we keep a close eye on you."

I nodded. "Sure. Okay. But for now, I'm fine. I can see myself home. I'll be sure to call… Tony, if I hear from him again."

Lane's mouth drew back in a grimace. "Right. Okay." He stood silently for a few moments. He glanced back at his car, then to me, lowering his voice. "Listen, about us." He hesitated, frowning, as if searching for the right phrasing. "I don't expect you to wait for me, but I want you to know that I'm going to hurry this process through as quickly as I can. I won't let Catherine keep me in her clutches the rest of my life."

I hated myself for the glimmer of hope his words gave me. "You'd better get Bart to his car. He's had a long night."

He studied me for a few more seconds, then stepped back, watching as I climbed in my Malibu and locked the doors.

He and Bart drove away, but I waited in the garage for Bart to appear so he could follow me home. For a brief moment, I questioned the advisability of inviting a stranger to my house. But if the guy had wanted to hurt me, it wasn't likely he'd have risked his life to save me. I owed him a great deal. The least I could give him was a few minutes of my company and a cup of coffee.

****

Bart roamed my living room, checking out my eclectic furnishings, pausing to ask questions about one piece or another. It was my guess that he preferred to discuss anything rather than the event that had brought us together.

He was especially intrigued by my Jesse James collection, which wasn't unusual. Most guests were either amused or put off by it, but they were all intrigued. He took a sip from a bottle of Coke—ironically, he didn't like coffee.

"This is pretty awesome. I don't know a lot about Jesse James, but just the fact that you have all this old historical stuff is amazing."

"I know. I've always been fascinated by Jesse James, and I couldn't believe it when I found out my neighbor was a descendant, and he had so many relics." Thoughts of Linus sent a twinge of distress through me. He would be going home today, and he was doing well, but the fact that the bastard had gone after him was chilling.

"So, you said something at the station about writing articles. Is that what you do for a living?" Bart asked. "I'm not keeping you from your job, am I?"

"I'm a crime writer for The Northland Chronicle. You're not keeping me from my job. I'm taking the day off."

I'd called in to work, and what I really needed was to fall into bed and sleep the day away, but I didn't want to be rude to Bart, or send him off to wallow in his thoughts.

He lifted his brows. "Really? Pretty crazy that you write crime and were a victim of one."

I didn't tell him that it wasn't the first time I'd been

a victim. We didn't need to unearth all of our deep dark secrets. Other than the interview for the article I would write—if Adam allowed it—and maybe a 'thank you' fruit basket, I doubted Bart and I would have further contact. Was a fruit basket an appropriate thank you for the person who saved you from a knife-wielding maniac? I'd have to check the proper etiquette for that one.

"You know what? It's also kind of crazy that you own a coffee shop, and coffee is one of my very favorite things in the world."

His lips curved in the first full-on, genuine smile I'd seen from him. He had a nice smile that showed dimples and white teeth. It made him look almost handsome. Actually, now that I studied him—finally clear-headed and no longer a blubbering mess—he wasn't bad looking at all. Not that I was in the market for a relationship so soon, but a girl could do worse than a good-looking savior who owned a coffee shop.

He finished his Coke, and I took the bottle from him. "Would you like another?" I asked.

To my relief, he shook his head. "No, thanks. I won't take up any more of your time. I'm about dead on my feet, and I imagine you are too. My employees are taking care of the shop today. I'm going home to pass out."

"Sounds like a great idea. Think you'll be able to sleep?"

That gloomy expression came over his face again, and he pushed his glasses up his nose and shrugged. "Hope so. What about you?"

"I might have nightmares, but I think I'll pass out as soon as I'm prone."

He laughed. "Good." He leaned forward and placed

a quick kiss on my cheek. I didn't step back. He'd caught me by surprise. "Can I call you and check on you?"

I was reluctant to give him the wrong impression, but I'd need an opportunity to interview him about the article, if Adam approved it. "Sure." I gave him my phone number and opened the door.

"Take care of yourself, Monroe. I hate to sound cliché, but I wish we'd met under better circumstances. I like you."

I smiled. "I like you too. And if I was going to meet anyone under those circumstances, I'm glad it was you."

He blushed and stepped out onto the porch. It was close to six a.m., and the sun was starting to chase away some of the morning fog. After Bart climbed into his car and drove away, I closed the front door.

I thought I wanted to be alone, wanted to sleep, but the silence I normally enjoyed had taken on an ominous undertone. I checked all the doors and windows, making sure they were locked securely. I lay down, but every time I closed my eyes, I saw the assailant's face, felt the prick of the knife in my stomach.

****

Lane shuffled through the Murder Book, past the photos that, even after all his years of police work, were hard to look at. His eyes strayed to the television in the corner of the room where the Royals were playing the Yankees. He was so preoccupied with the dead girl and worry for Monroe that he couldn't even be bothered that the Yankees were up by two.

He perused the autopsy report. The coroner had found evidence that the killer had used a blindfold. Whether it was out of concern the victim would get loose and later ID him, or a method to instill an extra dose of fear, he wasn't sure.

The girl hadn't been raped. That was different from the older cases. Monroe's friend, Katie, hadn't been raped either. Were these two murders committed by the same guy and the others by someone else? How the hell had they not caught him in all this time? Was he that smart, or were they just that damned stupid? He gritted his teeth as he continued to sift through the file, a ball of frustration sitting heavy in his gut.

His mind drifted to the attack on Monroe. Was it a random robbery or did it have something to do with the murders? Michael Finlay… Cameron Cooper… Johnny Price. There were reasons to suspect them all, yet equal reasons that none of them were good candidates.

"Need help?"

Lane looked up as Lucinda's throaty voice penetrated his consciousness. "I need to catch this mother fucker."

She rested her hip against his desk and flipped through the pages of the book. "You really think it's the same guy? Twenty-five years is a hell of a long time to get by with murder."

Lane shrugged. "Zodiac, BTK. Wouldn't be the first time."

"True. Too bad this asshole doesn't help out law enforcement by sending a letter taking credit for the deaths like BTK did."

He didn't want to think about the fact that some killers, like the Zodiac, were never caught. "Yeah. Too bad."

She laid a hand on his forearm where it rested on the desk. Her red-tipped fingers slid down and slowly caressed his wrist. "Maybe there's something I can do to make you forget for a while."

He tugged loose from her hold. "We've been through this, Lucinda. Nothing is going to happen between us."

She shrugged, lifting her hand to stroke his face, leaning in close. "I thought you might change your mind after what happened with your little girlfriend. You're stuck with a mental patient for a wife, and now the piece of ass you had on the side—"

He gripped her wrist and tossed her hand away, pushing back from his desk and shooting to his feet. "If I need anything from you, I'll let you know. But don't hold your breath."

He stalked away, then got halfway across the station house and wondered what kind of a damn fool he was. He hadn't had sex in so long, he'd lost track. Lucinda was right. He was stuck with a wife in a mental hospital, and he and Monroe damned sure wouldn't be having sex now. He desperately needed a fuck, but the unfortunate truth was, if he couldn't have Monroe, he'd rather do without.

****

He watched as the girl headed from the movie theatre toward her car. It was well past midnight. At her age, she shouldn't be out so late, especially not alone. Lucky for him, someone wasn't keeping an eye on her.

His soft-soled shoes noiselessly covered the distance between him and his prey. She turned as he approached, her hand already tugging open the door of her Volkswagen. He snaked one arm around her waist, and clamped his other hand over her mouth. She couldn't scream, but she struggled like a person having seizures. He clamped harder, holding her mouth and nose closed until he felt her go limp. She wasn't dead. Just unconscious. He couldn't kill her yet. He had things to learn about her.

He dumped her in his trunk and drove the short distance to the abandoned high school just south of the river. Funny how easy it was to grab her like that. No one around. He loved it when a plan came together.

He parked next to the back door, climbed out of the car, and went around to the trunk. The girl lay still. So far, so good. He lifted her, tossing her slight weight over his shoulder—along with the duffle bag he kept handy—and carried her inside.

Once he had her blindfolded and secured to the rings he'd installed in the wall of one of the classrooms, he held smelling salts under her nose. She woke with a gasp, crying out, her head whipping around in panic.

"Who are you?" Her voice quavered with terror. "What do you want?"

Why did people always ask who he was? Like he was going to politely introduce himself. That wasn't really the important question, anyway. The important question was what would happen next. She'd learn the answer soon enough.

He sat cross-legged on the floor in front of her. "We're going to have a chat. That's all I want right now. Tell me a little about yourself. Your name, where you go to school, your favorite hobbies. Do you have a boyfriend?"

She whimpered, tears flowing from beneath the blindfold. Her blonde hair was matted to her head with perspiration from her struggles and her ride in the trunk. Her lip trembled when she spoke. "I-I don't know… what do you want? Please just let me go. Don't hurt me."

Her head fell back, and she let out a deafening scream.

"Shh, Take it easy. Calm down and answer my questions. If you want me to let you go, you'll have to tell me what I want to know."

Hope lit her voice. "Then you'll let me go?"

"I promise."

The relief on her face amused him. What made her think he was telling the truth? He'd just kidnapped her off the streets, blindfolded her, and tied her up. Yet she trusted he'd keep his word. The gullibility of people was astounding. He nearly laughed, but right now wasn't the time to indulge his humor.

"My-my name is Mindy Wainwright." She drew in a deep breath, then sputtered out a few more uninteresting facts.

"Tell me things that you remember about your childhood. Are your parents divorced?" When she nodded, he asked, "When did they split?"

She frowned again. "Four years ago. Why?"

He reached out and gripped her cheeks between his fingers, squeezing until she yelped in pain. "I ask the questions, not you. Just be a good girl and answer them, okay?"

She nodded vigorously, and he released her.

"Okay, let's keep going."

She shifted, trying to scoot further against the wall, even she was already tied to it. Her shirt rode up, and a silver ring glinted in her belly button. With one finger, he gently lifted the ring to study it. Her stomach muscles tightened as she flinched.

"When did you get this done?" he asked.

Once again, the confused frown. "Uh. On my fourteenth birthday. Two years ago."

"So, 2010." He nodded in satisfaction. "That will do."

The ring was just large enough for his pinky. He linked a finger into the silver hoop and yanked as hard as he could. Her scream cut through the air and reverberated around the walls. But no worries, no one could hear her.

He wiped the blood off the belly button ring with his handkerchief. "Okay," he said. "Now, I'll let you go."

Slipping the wire from his pocket, he whipped it around her neck before she could make another sound.

Chapter 7

After work on Wednesday, I met Josie at Arlo's Diner. Arlo's served greasy cheeseburgers, Coke out of old-fashioned Coke glasses, and their free jukebox didn't have any songs newer than the early 90's. Josie had been waiting tables there for the past few months. Life was falling into place for her, finally. She was clean, she had a job, and Matt—her abusive, drug supplier boyfriend—had disappeared.

Josie had gone back and forth with him for years, but one night, he'd attacked me, enraged because he thought I was coming between him and Josie and that I was helping the police locate him so they could question him about a murder. If I'd known where to find him, I'd damned sure have told the police, but I didn't. As far as coming between him and Josie, he'd done more to drive her away by hurting me than anything he'd done during their entire tumultuous relationship. I couldn't be happier. It had been worth getting my ass kicked to see Josie doing so well.

I slid into one of the red plastic upholstered booths, and in moments, Josie appeared at my table. Her Arlo's uniform—black pants, pink blouse, and a pink frilly apron—was extremely un-Josie like. I hid a grin.

"Hey there." She plopped down in the booth and slid a glass that I knew held Diet Coke in front of me.

I frowned and glanced around the diner. "Won't you

get in trouble? You're on the clock, right?" I couldn't help but worry she'd lose her job. Everything good in her life seemed tenuous. How long would she have to be clean before that feeling dissipated?

She waved a hand dismissively. "I don't have any tables right now, and Jason doesn't mind if I take a break."

Apparently, I worried about her job security more than she did.

I lifted a brow. "So, what's up with you and my brother? You've certainly been getting cozy lately. Has he asked you out?"

Her cheeks reddened. "No. Not yet. But, he has been kind of… I don't know… flirty." She slumped down in the seat. "Hell, I might have to ask him out."

"Maybe you should."

She shook her head. "I don't know if I'm that ballsy."

"Oh, you are." I laughed.

She grinned back and took a sip of my soda. Wrinkling her nose, she said, "Yuck. I don't see how you can drink that diet crap."

"Love Rollercoaster" blared from the jukebox. I was about to mention how the song took me back to our childhood, but the words died in my throat when I saw Josie's face. Her skin was drawn, her flesh as white as a frog's belly.

"Josie, are you okay?"

She jerked as if shaking out of a trance. "I'm okay," she said softly, but her voice held a tremble. "Just thinking."

"About Katie?"

In spite of the twenty-five years that had passed

since her death, Katie's ghost was a constant companion in mine and Josie's friendship. If she'd lived, we might have drifted apart. Her death sealed us in a way that nothing else could have.

Josie's lips crooked in a humorless smile. "You remember how freaked she was about this song?"

The faint sound of a girl screaming could be heard at the beginning of the song, and over the years, multiple rumors circulated about the source of the scream. They all had to do with a woman being murdered while the band was recording, but the method and identity of the victim changed with the various accounts. None of the rumors proved true, but Katie was spooked by the whole idea of it, and she refused to listen to the song. But then, everything spooked Katie. The irony that she'd died a violent, tragic death wasn't lost on me.

I patted Josie's hand where it lay on the tabletop. "I remember."

Josie had taken Katie's death harder than anyone. I wasn't sure why, other than the fact that Josie was a little mischievous—sometimes almost mean—and liked to play on Katie's fears, took delight in scaring her. She'd actually been taunting Katie only hours before her death. That had probably festered inside her ever since. It wouldn't be an easy thing to live with. Josie had only been twelve herself, so she shouldn't carry guilt after all these years, but she carried something, and I suspected it had a lot to do with why she'd become a drug addict.

The front door opened. I looked up to see Lane walk in. He wore faded jeans and a blue chambray shirt, tails hanging out in his usual careless style. My fingers itched to run through the dark strands of his windblown hair.

I linked my fingers, squeezing my hands together,

and swallowed hard to squelch the urge.

Josie's face split with a wide smile. "Lane! Hi."

She stood when he approached our table. In spite of being my oldest and best friend, she was extremely friendly with the man who'd broken my heart.

They hugged, and she shot me a sympathetic glance over his shoulder that somewhat appeased my ire.

Lane released her and glanced down at me. "Hi, Monroe."

I nodded stiffly. "Lane."

Tension so thick I could almost taste it settled around us. I was sure he could feel it, too. Why didn't he just leave?

He shoved his hands in his pockets and glanced around, seemingly searching for something to say. He cocked his head toward the jukebox as "Love Rollercoaster" wound to an end. "You know the history of this song? About the woman screaming?"

Josie sat back in her seat and looked up at him. "We were just talking about that."

"Did you know that it was actually the keyboardist? He was doing some kind of warm up, vocal exercise and made a screeching noise. They decided to leave it in the record. The band kept quiet about the true story, because the rumors helped their sales."

Josie's eyes rounded, her voice awed as if he'd revealed the meaning of life. "I had no idea. I always wondered what actually happened."

I rolled my eyes. *Seriously?* All the shit going on lately, and Lane stood there spouting his little nuggets of meaningless crap?

"Care to join us?" Josie asked.

Lane looked at me. The expression in my eyes must

have told him I'd prefer he declined.

"No, thanks. I just stopped to grab a coffee." He took his hands from his pockets and crossed his arms over his chest. "Speaking of coffee." He impaled me with a glare. "I understand Bart Holland was at your house."

"The guy who saved you?" Josie responded before I could. "Roe, you barely know him."

I glared at my traitorous friend. She, who'd slept on the streets, hung out in drug dens, and consorted with the dregs of society was lecturing me? And taking Lane's side? Since the night he'd found her in a drug-induced state and brought her to me to care for—rather than taking her to jail—she acted as though he were some kind of god-like being. Didn't my broken heart count for anything?

"Can we continue this in private?" I said to Lane through gritted teeth. It wasn't that I didn't want Josie to know what was going on. I just didn't want the continuing battle to be two against one.

Josie shrugged. "Sure. I need to get back to work anyway, but just so you know, I'm on his side. You don't even know the guy."

"Thanks, but I think you made it pretty clear where you stood on the issue." I smiled sweetly but I was certain my glare conveyed my true feelings.

She stuck her tongue out at me and slid from the booth. Lane settled in the spot she'd vacated. He tapped his fingers on the tabletop, a muscle in his jaw jumping, but remained silent.

"What?" I finally demanded, unable to stand the quiet any longer. "And anyway, how did you know?"

"We had him come back in for some follow up questions, and he literally gushed about how great you were to him. How you invited him over, didn't want him to be alone after what happened, called him a hero." He emphasized the last word with a dose of sarcasm.

"You don't think what he did was heroic?"

Lane hissed out a breath through clenched lips. "Yeah. It was. He risked his life to save you, and I'm thankful for that. But come on. You took him home with you? Are you insane?"

"Uhm, the guy saved my life, just so he can kill me?"

"Stranger things have happened. I'm a cop. I see all kinds of crazy shit. Besides, maybe he didn't want to kill you, but there are plenty of other ways men hurt women. You shouldn't take that kind of risk."

My response was delayed when Josie brought us coffee and slices of coconut pie. She took away the Diet Coke I'd barely touched.

"Don't mind me," she said, her eyes twinkling. "Thought you guys might need some sustenance for whatever's going on here."

"Thanks." Lane picked up his cup and gave her a wink before she departed.

He shoveled a forkful of pie into his mouth, but I ignored mine. I did, however, take a long, soothing drink of the coffee. Not as strong as what I made at home, but not bad.

I wrapped my hands around the warm cup and stared at Lane across the table. Keeping my voice low, I said, "I have a gun. I know how to take care of myself."

"Jesus, Monroe. You shouldn't put yourself in situations where you need to use a gun. Can't you just be more cautious?"

"Sure," I bit out. "I can do that. But don't you think

you should concentrate on rescuing one woman at a time?" I didn't mean to, but I allowed tears to choke my throat. Pissed at him and myself, I pushed out of the booth. "Catherine should be your concern, not me."

Ignoring the pained expression in his eyes, I stormed out the door.

****

Lane tried to concentrate on one of the many television screens hanging on the wall of the Blitz. Each showed a different MLB game—an opportunity for hours of entertainment—but all he could think about was his encounter with Monroe. He tilted the Heineken bottle to his lips and let the beer flow down his throat. Maybe it would push thoughts of Monroe out of his mind.

He snorted a laugh. "Yeah right," he muttered. There wasn't enough beer in the world.

"You talking to yourself now, man?"

He looked up at Darion, who stood behind the counter with a bar towel slung over his shoulder and his large arms crossed over his ridiculously large chest. Darion was his friend, but he was also Monroe's friend's husband. Why hadn't Lane chosen to drink at home instead of coming into the Blitz? He'd known Darion would be here. He owned the bar and was here every night.

Maybe it was because, as pathetic as it made him, Lane didn't want to be alone.

"Just thinking aloud," Lane finally said. "Give me another." He slid the bottle back to Darion's side of the bar.

"You want to forget, you gotta use something stronger than beer. That's for pussies." Darion's teeth gleamed in his black skin as he smiled. Grabbing a bottle from the shelf behind him, he poured a shot of Jack Daniels and sat it in front of Lane. "Drink that, then I'll keep pouring until you forget what an asshole you are."

Lane scrubbed his hands along the sides of his face and scowled at Darion. But he picked up the bourbon and downed it. He shook his head, his fingers tightening around the empty glass.

For God's sake. Were Josie and his mother-in-law the only people in the world who understood his decision? Probably, since he didn't fully understand it himself. But couldn't they all see how he was suffering for it? Couldn't someone cut him a little fucking slack?

He hadn't been to visit Catherine yet. He dreaded that almost as much as he'd dreaded telling Monroe he wasn't leaving his wife. He had absolutely zero feelings for Catherine. If he hadn't known it before, he knew it now. Every time he was near Monroe, or heard her name, his blood heated, and his heart sped up like a lovesick teenager's. When he thought of seeing Catherine, of staying married to her, his gut clenched with the urge to vomit.

Without speaking, Darion refilled the glass. Lane picked it up and tossed the liquor down his throat. Maybe this mess wouldn't drag out long. Maybe he could see Catherine through to some kind of stability, then get the divorce done and over with. Maybe by then, Monroe wouldn't have found someone new. Wouldn't hate him so much she'd never give him a second chance.

"You have a lot of goddamned nerve!"

Lane whirled at the angry female voice. He caught the edge of the bar with his hand, afraid he'd topple from the stool. Those two shots, along with the three beers he'd already consumed, were fucking with his equilibrium.

Asia stood glaring at him, hands planted on her hips. She looked over Lane's shoulder at Darion. "Thank you for calling, baby."

Lane glanced back at his 'friend.' "Yeah, thanks, *baby*." He snorted in disgust. "What happened to bros before—" He stopped himself from delivering the line that was sure to be the end of him. Asia looked ready to rip something in two, and he didn't want that something to be him. It wasn't the kind of thing he would normally say, but his head was spinning, and his words weren't coming out the way he intended.

Darion lifted his hands, palms up, and shrugged. "Sorry, dude. She cooks for me and sleeps with me. She's a little higher on the totem pole."

Asia settled on the barstool next to Lane. Fury came off her in waves. Darion set a glass of white wine in front of her.

She sipped some of her drink, then slapped the goblet down so hard, he expected the delicate stem to snap in half. Her dark brown eyes shot fire. "Monroe has waited all her life for the right man to come along. What a pity that *right man* turned out to be you."

He opened his mouth, but she lifted a hand, silencing him before he began.

"She deserves better than you. Deserves someone who truly loves her, deeply and forever, so much they'd do anything in the world for her."

Lane sucked in a breath, and a lump rose to his throat. Around the stone that crushed his heart, he managed to say, "I love her like that."

Asia narrowed her eyes and studied him. Her features softened, and when she spoke again, her voice had gentled. "Maybe. But do you love her enough to let her go?"

****

I knocked on Adam's half-open door. He looked up from his desk, his green eyes sparkling when he saw me.

"Monroe, come in." He stood and held out a hand to a chair across from his desk. I sat, and he did the same, his brows creasing. "Are you okay? I mean, after the mugging?"

I nodded. "Thanks to Bart Holland, I'm fine. He's actually why I'm here."

"What about him?"

"I'd like to do an article on the attack, on his saving me. I don't know if he would want me to use his name, but I'd like to write the article, if that's okay."

Adam leaned back in his chair and tapped a pen against his chin. "Might not be a bad idea. People eat that hero shit up. Seems like all the stories we print have a less than happy ending. This would be uplifting."

"That's what I was thinking."

He flashed a white-toothed smile. "Good to know we're on the same wave length on some things."

I didn't answer, uncomfortable when his comments turned personal.

His voice lowered. "I miss being on the same wave length in other ways, Monroe."

"Adam, I don't think we should—"

"I heard Brody is staying with his wife. Don't you think we could give it another shot? At least try? We could take our time, ease into it."

I took a deep breath and let it out slowly. If Adam continued to bring up the topic of 'us,' I might have to leave my position. Maybe if I told him that, he'd back off.

Instead, I said, "That's never going to happen. I'm not rejecting you because of Lane. It's because our relationship was a freaking disaster. Because you cheated on me and cast me aside like used goods."

He flinched. "I know. I kick myself every day over that, Monroe. But I'm a changed man. I swear. Tabitha has been trying to get me back. Even though her dad owns the paper, and she could cause me to lose my job, I won't go back to her. Ever. Even if there's no chance between me and you. I'm done with women like her. I need someone decent and kind and loving. Someone like you."

I clasped the hair on top of my head, then let it fall from my hands. "You'll find her, Adam. It just won't be me."

His eyes hardened, looking like chips of emerald glass. He stood and came around the desk, leaning over me with a hand on each arm of the chair. "Nothing I ever do will be enough for you, will it?"

He was so close, I could barely breathe. The tendons in his forearms bunched as he gripped the chair. I leaned away, as far as I could get from him. "Adam? What the hell? Back off."

He blinked, and the angry expression cleared from his face. "Sorry. Jesus, Monroe." He straightened away from me. "I'm sorry."

I stood and hurried to the door. Would he keep it up until I had to leave? I loved my job, but I wouldn't continue to put up with Adam's aggressive behavior. Which, judging from his little display, was escalating.

"You can do the article, Monroe," he said. "And again, I'm sorry."

"Thanks." I nodded without turning to look at him, then quickly left his office.

An hour later, I was at my cubicle going over my article for the next issue when my cell rang. Mindy Wainwright showed on the caller ID. I didn't know a Mindy Wainwright, but I answered.

"I have another surprise for you," the hateful, familiar voice said.

Dizziness assailed me. I latched onto the edge of my desk. "What have you done?"

Was Mindy Wainwright his latest victim? *Please God, no.*

"I don't think the police have even found her body yet. You can tell them where I left her. In her hand, they'll find a penny dated 2010 along with her navel ring. You'll probably make the connection, but 2010 was when she got her piercing. The police might not tell you that, but you'll put it in the article, right?"

Bile clogged my throat. "Please, no. Please tell me you didn't hurt another girl."

"Monroe, Monroe, Monroe. We have this thing going now, you and I. Perhaps you aren't enjoying it as much as I am, but you have to admit, it's exciting. I bet you've never connected with another human on this level. You might as well start cooperating, because you're in this until the end. Tell them to look in the southwest region of the woods across the street from Jesse James' home." He chuckled. "I thought you might like that added touch. I'll talk to you soon."

My stomach heaved, and I raced to the bathroom, barely making it to the toilet before I vomited. Cursing my weakness, I stumbled to the sink to wash my face and hands. I punched Tony's number into my cell, rinsing my mouth with water and spitting as I listened to the phone ring.

"Tony," I blurted tearfully when he answered.

"Monroe, what is it? What's wrong?"

"You need to look in the woods across the street from the James house. In the southwest section." I sucked in a shuddering gasp of air. "I'm afraid you'll find another victim. I think her name is Mindy Wainwright."

"Ah, Jesus." I heard him give instructions in the background. He sounded out of breath, on the move, when he came back on the line. "He called you? He killed another girl?"

"It looks that way." My voice had lost its panic. Now it sounded dead. As dead as Mindy Wainwright surely was.

Chapter 8

Lane bit back a curse, clamping his jaw so tight he thought his molars would shatter. The girl was just where the bastard said she'd be. Lying in the weeds. Dead eyes staring at the heavens.

Through the trees and across the street was the Jesse James Museum. Several feet behind that was the home where the outlaw had been born. Tourists wandered from their cars into the museum, pointing and talking, unaware that—within spitting distance—a girl had been discarded like yesterday's trash. A young life cut short for no more reason than she'd caught the eye of a monster.

The girl was Mindy Wainright—the ME had confirmed that based on the driver's license he found in her billfold. An autopsy would provide a more definite ID, but there was no logical doubt as to the identity of the victim.

Keaton bent over her, studying the ligature mark around her neck. He lifted her shirt a few inched above her jeans, revealing her navel and the dried blood that had leaked from it. He opened her clenched hand and retrieved a penny and a silver belly button ring. That explained the dried blood.

Rage gnashed at Lane's insides. They had to stop this mother fucker. No one was that clever, that invincible. What the hell were they doing wrong?

"Shit," Tony muttered. "Karakas was right. We need to stick to Monroe, maybe be around next time he calls."

"Maybe we should just catch the son of a bitch before he does this again," Lane bit out.

Tony looked at him, brows raised. "You have some magic trick up your sleeve I don't know about? Last I checked, we were *trying* to catch him."

"Fuck. I don't know. He can't keep doing this bullshit. Two girls in less than a week. It's been three years since the last one. Is Monroe spurring him on? Did her goddamned articles start this sick cocksucker up again?"

"Hey, hey." Tony narrowed his eyes. "You're not blaming Monroe, are you?"

Lane let out a weary sigh. "No. I'm not blaming her."

But maybe he was, just a little. And he was blaming himself, and the entire police force, including the ones who worked the case twenty-five years ago. Mostly, he was blaming the dickbag murderer.

"We'll follow up on Cooper and Price," Tony said. "Keep a closer eye on Monroe. Maybe if we're with her when he calls again, we can get her to draw him out. Get her to agree to meet him somewhere."

Lane jerked his gaze to Tony. "I'm not putting her out there as bait for this psycho piece of shit."

"Cool your jets, dude. I didn't say she would actually meet with him. Maybe we can get her to convince him she will."

Lane shook his head. "Only a dumb son of a bitch would fall for that. And regardless of what kind of monster this guy is, he's not a dumb one."

A hoarse bellow behind him made Lane turn. Two

of the cops guarding the perimeter had a young man in their grip. He struggled against their hold, kicking and flailing, screaming, "Let me go, you assholes. Let me see her."

Lane caught Tony's gaze. By unspoken agreement, they made their way to where the boy had almost broken free from the cops.

"Hey, man. Take it easy," Lane said. "You can't come through. This is a crime scene."

The boy was tall and thin, with a soul patch and long blond hair. Red, wet eyes met Lane's. "Is it her? Is it Mindy?"

Lane's chest tightened. No one should have known. No one other than Monroe. "How did you hear about this?"

"*Is—it—her?*" The kid enunciated each word, his mouth tight, his face twisted with anger and grief.

Lane crossed his arms and stared steadily at the boy. "I'll talk to you if you talk to me. Who are you, and how did you know?"

"I'm Kemp. Mindy's boyfriend. A f-friend of mine is a cop. Mindy's been missing since Tuesday. When he heard you'd found a bo—" He snuffled and choked back a cry. "—body, he called me. Is it her?" His eyes pleaded with Lane to say *no, it's some other girl. Your Mindy is fine.*

Lane wished he could.

Although it was against protocol, Lane said, "It's her."

"Oh God." Kemp fell to his knees, and the cops released him. "Oh God, how? Who? What happened?" He covered his eyes, sobbing into his hands.

"We need you to answer some questions for us,"

Tony said, gentling his voice. "When was the last time you saw Mindy?"

The boy rose to his feet and made to push past the cops. "I need to see her."

Lane reached out and gripped the teen's arm, feeling tremors so strong, they shook his fingers. "You can't go over there. Trust me, you don't want to. You've got to give us some answers so we can find the bastard who did this, okay? Can you do that for us?"

Kemp sucked in a deep breath, then slowly nodded. Lane released him.

"I saw her Tuesday. She was going to the movies with her girlfriends, then coming to my house." His mouth trembled, and tears resurfaced in his eyes. "She never showed up. Her friends had no idea what happened to her after they left the theatre."

Lane frowned. "You haven't seen her in two days, and you didn't say anything? Did you tell her parents?"

He wiped his eyes and shook his head. "Not until today. I told her mom. She was pissed."

"Yeah. Wonder why," Tony muttered. "How come you waited so long?"

"She wasn't supposed to spend the night with me. Her mom thought she was staying at Cindy's. I didn't want to get her in trouble."

Lane barked a bitter laugh. "Looks like your plan failed. She found a whole hell of a lot of trouble."

The boy flinched, and Lane almost regretted his words. But, if the dumb kid had told them she was missing the first night, things might have turned out differently. She might still be alive.

Yeah, right, and pigs might fly out of my ass.

Tony spoke to the two cops still flanking the boy.

"Take him to the station. We'll want a statement from him. We also need to hold him, make sure he doesn't speak with anyone until we've notified next of kin."

After they led him away, Tony sighed and ran a hand over his head. "We can let the techs finish up here. Let's go tell the parents their child has been slaughtered like an animal."

****

Gable called on Thursday morning and asked me to help at the shelter. I wasn't sure if it was because he wanted to get my mind off all that had been happening, or if he thought I needed to do something selfless rather than wallowing in self-pity. Either way, I agreed. I didn't want to sit at the house alone.

They'd confirmed the killer had been telling the truth. A young girl, Mindy Wainwright, had been found dead. The thought of writing the article about her death made me physically ill, but the thought of what would happen if I didn't was unbearable.

"Here you go, sis." Gable grinned, handing me a mop. "Lunch ended a few minutes ago. You made it just in time for clean-up." He wore rubber gloves and an apron over his priestly garb. I laughed at the sight of my manly brother looking like some kind of sanctified Mr. Clean.

I dipped the mop in the bucket and started on the floor. Around me, people engaged in various activities from reading, to sleeping, to playing cards. Most looked street-worn, with the sallow features and thin frames of drug addicts and alcoholics. Others looked like average people, those you might run into at a supermarket or in the work place. Their shell-shocked, shameful expressions indicated they never thought they'd end up in their current position.

Across the room, a young couple with a little girl sat at a table playing checkers. Occasional laughter rose from the group. Happy sounds that seemed incongruously out of place. How could they be happy in their situation?

Maybe because they had each other.

Thoughts of Mindy Wainwright filtered through my mind. Maybe they realized things could be much, much worse.

"I have another volunteer today." Gable's words cut through my reverie. "Someone I think you know." He nodded toward a corner of the room. I followed his gaze, shocked to recognize Paxton dusting a book shelf.

"What's she doing here?"

"I guess she got into some trouble. Tony asked if she could help out here. Probably thought it would do her good to see she doesn't have it as bad as she might think."

"How's that working out?"

Gable shrugged. "I think *volunteer* was the wrong word. She's not exactly Mother Teresa. Judging from her attitude the past few hours, the message isn't sinking in."

Knowing Paxton as I did, I had to agree. I rested my mop against the bucket. "Excuse me."

I walked over to Paxton, and she turned at my approach. Her brows rose, but other than that, there was no reaction. She was probably a little too cool to show much of one.

"Hey, Paxton. How's it going?"

She rolled her eyes. "How does it *look* like it's going? I'm stuck here at this crappy place. Figure it out for yourself."

"There are worse things."

"Yeah? Like what?"

I shrugged and looked around. "Being homeless."

She frowned, but didn't respond. Turning her back to me, she continued with her task.

Okay... got it. Don't want to chat.

I went back to my mopping. I'd been polite, said hello. I didn't have to hang around and deal with the attitude.

For the next hour as I worked, I covertly eyed Paxton from time to time. She unenthusiastically finished the shelves and a few other tasks. I watched closely as she approached the table where the little girl who'd been playing checkers earlier was now alone, coloring. I suffered a brief moment of unwarranted angst, but breathed a sigh of relief when Paxton smiled and joined the child. She picked up a crayon and started on the other page of the open book. For the first time, Paxton's expression was relaxed, no longer defensive. Like she didn't have to be constantly on guard.

"Her parents both went on a job interview," Gable said at my shoulder. "I thought it would be good for Paxton to keep an eye on her."

I smiled. "So, you're the one who matched the two of them up. You weren't afraid Paxton would traumatize the poor child?"

His mouth quirked in a grin. "Sometimes you just gotta trust God."

My gaze went back to the two of them. The girl leaned back in her chair, laughing so hard, she had to hold onto her stomach. Wow. Paxton had a human side after all.

"I have about a half hour," I told Gable. "What else

do you need me to do?"

"Could you go in the storage closet and get some bedding? We'll need to change out the sheets and blankets on the cots."

"Be right back."

I made my way to the storage closet at the end of the hallway off the main room. Inside, I searched the shelves until I found the one that held the sheets and blankets. I loaded my arms down and headed to the door.

I'd only taken a few steps when a figure appeared in front of me. I halted, letting out a small scream. Squinting in the semi-gloom, I recognized Cameron Cooper.

"What the hell are you doing here?" I demanded, although my heart was pumping so fast, I could hear it thrumming in my ear drums.

"You need to leave me the fuck alone."

Anger was slightly overshadowed by a wash of fear. "Leave you alone? What are you talking about?" An idea formed, one that I didn't like. "Are you here because of Paxton? Are you following her?"

"You heard what I said. You printed my name in those damned articles of yours. Named me as a suspect."

He moved toward me, and I forced myself not to back away. Lifting my chin, I said, "You *are* a suspect, dumbass."

His face reddened, and his fists bunched at his sides. "I ain't never wanted to hit a woman so bad in—"

"No, usually, you just want to rape them. *Correction*. Not women, young girls." I wasn't sure why I was saying such incendiary things, but I couldn't help myself. My anger was overtaking my sense of self-preservation. "I'll give you five seconds to get the hell out, then I'm calling the police."

He leaned forward, pushing his face close to mine. Somehow, the barrier of soft blankets didn't feel all that secure. "Better watch yourself, bitch. If you know what's good for you." His breath reeked of stale alcohol, and his blood-shot eyes flashed with fury.

I forced my voice to remain steady. "Five… four… three…"

With a string of muttered curses, he jerked the storage door open and disappeared.

Setting the blankets down on a nearby shelf, I pulled my cell from my pocket. Lane and Tony were tied up with the murder, so I dialed the station. They transferred my call and Detective Lucinda Rochester answered. I told her I'd seen Cooper, and she assured me she'd send someone out to look for him.

"I'm certain I'll see Lane before you will," she drawled. "So I'll be sure to let him know."

Was I imagining it, or was there a hint of smug malice in her tone?

****

The Wainwrights were divorced. The father lived in Nebraska, so Tony and Lane went to see the mother. A woman opened the door—fortyish and pretty, except for her red nose and watery eyes.

"Ms. Wainwright?" Dread curdled Lane's gut as he waited for her response.

She looked at Tony, then her eyes locked onto Lane's. The expression in them said she knew they were cops. Her trembling lip and the way she crumpled against the door frame said she knew why they were there.

"You found her? You found my Mindy?"

"I'm afraid so, ma'am. Can we come in?"

She swayed, nearly going to her knees. Lane stepped forward and took her gently by the arm, leading her into a living room where he settled her onto the edge of a cream-colored sectional.

"How?" Her bleak eyes pleaded with them to tell her that her daughter's death hadn't been horrible. That she hadn't suffered. Victims' families always wanted to know the answer to that... or at least, *thought* they wanted to know. "How did it happen?"

Lane sucked in a fortifying breath, but it didn't help what he was about to say. "She was murdered."

A sob tore from the woman's throat. She bent forward over her knees, then rocked back, shaking her head from side to side. "Oh God, no. No, not my baby. Not my Mindy."

Tony plucked a tissue from a box on the coffee table and pressed it into her hand. She wiped the moisture from her cheeks, but more immediately took its place.

"We're very sorry, ma'am," Lane said. "We'll do whatever we can to find the person who did this to her."

She turned her tear-streaked face to him. "Was it the same as the other girl? The girl found in the park? Do you think it was the same guy?"

Tony and Lane exchanged looks, then Lane slowly nodded. "We think it might be."

She barked a laugh that bordered on hysteria. "Did you promise *her* parents you'd find him too?"

The words landed like a punch to Lane's gut. Helpless frustration coursed through him. They *had* told Charity's parents the same thing. That's what they always said. Truth was, too many times it was an unintentional lie. Since the bastard had been at it for a quarter of a century, what the hell made them think they'd catch him now?

"We'll do our best, ma'am. I promise."

She sniffed and nodded. "I know. I'm sorry. I'm sure you're doing all you can." She went quiet, and her face grew pensive as she stared out the large picture window next to the sectional. Lane doubted she was admiring the rows of poplar trees and the perfectly manicured lawn. "You know, Mindy had already suffered enough in her life. She was a happy, well-adjusted teen, considering what she'd been through. Now, she had to die like this. Before she had a chance to really live."

Knowing the woman needed to talk, Lane nodded sympathetically. "The divorce?"

Ms. Wainwright shook her head. "No. Not only that. The divorce was mild compared to what happened when she was five."

"What happened?" Tony asked.

Mindy's mother hesitated, her lips pinched together. Her expression darkened.

She finally spoke, the words sounding like they came from some hollow place deep inside. "She was molested. By a man who lived down the street from us in the old neighborhood. My husband was never really the same after that. He wanted to kill the bastard, but the law took care of it and sent him to prison." Her eyes widened and she turned to Lane. "Oh, God. I heard he was released. They have to tell the victims' families, you know." Her breathing sped up, and she shot to her feet. "Do you think he's the one who killed my little girl?"

"Who?" Lane stood also. "What's his name? We'll follow up on it."

The woman nodded. "You do that. I heard he's back

in the area. His name is Johnny Price."

****

I sat on the sofa, exhausted from my day at the shelter, but not so exhausted that my mind would shut down. Mindy Wainwright's image kept surfacing, even though I had no idea what she looked like. Her face was the same as that of all the others. Innocent and trusting. Helpless... victimized... terrorized.

I held a pillow to my chest, thinking of what her family must be feeling now.

Was it my fault the psycho was killing these girls? If I didn't write the articles, he'd make them suffer more. If I did write them, it seemed to be fueling some kind of sick fantasy of his. No matter what, I couldn't win.

"Can I get you anything?" Lane's voice startled me, although I hadn't exactly forgotten his presence. He was here to more or less babysit me. He and Tony had come over to share the news, and Tony left to question a suspect. Poor Lane. I guess he'd drawn the short straw. He was probably as uneasy about us being alone together as I was.

"No, thanks. I'm fine." I shifted my legs beneath me and hugged the pillow tighter. "I'm not sure why you and Tony are shadowing me right now. It's not likely he'll call yet. Not until he kills again." I hated the fatalistic words, but I believed them. He was far from done.

"He's called to gloat afterward. Maybe he will tonight."

"Maybe. He'll probably wait until my article comes out tomorrow." I turned to face Lane. "I have to write about the penny and the ring, you know that, right?"

He nodded. "It's not likely he'll let that trip him up anyway. And if you don't, he'll be so pissed, there's no telling what he'll do."

I had no desire to write his stinking articles. I felt like the puppet of some macabre puppeteer. But I also had no choice.

The phone rang, and my heart stuttered. With shaking hands, I picked up my cell. I smiled when I read the caller ID. Bart. He hadn't called since that day he left my house. Relieved, I answered. "Hi there. I wondered if you'd call."

At Lane's lifted brows, I shook my head.

"I thought I'd give you a few days to rest up." Bart's voice was warm and tender, strangely comforting. "How are you?"

"I'm doing okay. Much better. How about you?"

There was silence, then he said, "I'm not sleeping that well. Nightmares won't let me. I'm sure that guy had a family. I keep wondering how this has affected them."

"You can't think like that. He put himself in that position. If you hadn't done what you did, you might have been killed."

I shot a look to Lane. His mouth was drawn in a frown. He'd figured out who I was talking to. *Good.*

He stood and paced away, looking out my window that faced the graveyard.

"I wondered if you'd like to get together," Bart asked. "Maybe have dinner?"

His hopeful voice made me say cautiously, "I *would* like to talk to you. I'm not sure about dinner, but my boss said I could write the article. I'd like to interview you."

"Sure. Yeah." His voice held unmistakable disappointment. "But we could eat while you're interviewing me, right? It wouldn't be a date."

I laughed. "True. Just because we have a meal,

doesn't mean it's a date." I'd lowered my voice, but I saw Lane's shoulders tense. On one hand, I childishly wanted to make him jealous, on the other, I didn't want him to think I could so easily pick up with another man. Even though he was bound to another woman.

"Just so you know," I said to Bart. "I'm not ready to date anyone right now. Things have been a little too… crazy lately."

"Hey, hey. Slow down. Someone thinks pretty highly of themselves. I said a meal. I didn't propose." He chuckled, but I could tell it was to cover his embarrassment.

"Right, then. A meal and an interview. When?"

"Tomorrow night? You could come over. I'm not a bad cook."

"At your house?" I shot another glance at Lane. He stood stock still. "I'm not sure…"

"It would give us privacy for the interview, and I don't know about you, but I'm not ready for a lot of socializing in public right now. I promise I won't poison you. Or take advantage of you. As long as you promise not to take advantage of me."

I smiled. "That's only fair. It's a deal."

"Okay. I'll see you tomorrow at seven." He gave me his address, and we said goodbye.

When I disconnected the call, Lane returned to the couch. His mouth was still tight. He stared down at me, his eyes wounded, the pain making them look like blue crystals.

"I'm not going out with him, Lane. I'm interviewing him for an article about his rescuing me."

Lane shrugged. "It's none of my business what you do. I worry since you don't know him that well, but you're free to see whoever you'd like."

I frowned. This didn't sound like the man who was *temporarily* staying with his wife until she was stable enough that he could divorce her. We hadn't talked about holding out for a future together, and my reaction to his news hadn't exactly been calm understanding. But there'd been hints that we'd someday find our way back to each other.

"It won't bother you if I see other men?" I narrowed my eyes.

"Of course, it bothers me," he snapped. "I care about you."

Dampness pricked my eyelids, but I blinked it back. "It's good to know you *care* about me. And that you're giving me permission to see other men. How magnanimous of you."

"Look, I was wrong to expect you to even consider waiting 'till I get this mess straightened out. You're right. I waited too long to tell you I love you." He shook his head. "I want you… I admire, you, but if I really loved you, I wouldn't stay with Catherine."

I nodded, unable to speak, knowing if I did, the threatening tears would surely fall.

****

He poured a bowl of cereal, then sat down at the table and unfolded the newspaper.

His heart raced. There it was. On the front page.

With a trembling finger, he traced her name. Monroe Donovan…

He lifted the spoon to his lips and shoved in a bite of cereal, unable to tear his gaze from the paper.

Her photo was there, in the corner just under the headline. A tiny photo, but large enough that he could make out her haunting dark eyes, her sensuous smile. He glided his finger over the picture slowly, pretending he could actually feel her silky skin. He swallowed hard. *Get it together. You must stay in control.*

If he didn't, all his caution for the past twenty-five years would be for nothing. His only regret was that he couldn't reveal himself to her. He longed for the time when their eyes met and she knew who he was. There would be shock, then horror, then he could see it... her exquisite features softening into acceptance. Afterward, she'd acknowledge her love for him.

She might outwardly appear horrified by his deeds, but he could read between the lines in her articles. He intrigued her, fascinated her. The thrill she experienced from the things he did was almost palpable.

Shoving another bite of cereal into his mouth, he carefully re-read every word she'd written about him.

God, it was good to be back.

Chapter 9

I was nervous about going to Bart's home. Lane was right. I didn't really know him. However, he'd saved my life, and it was an assignment. I'd gone to strangers' houses plenty of times before on assignment. This was no different. Other than the fact I had a strong feeling Bart was attracted to me. I could handle it, though. It wasn't like he was going to rape me.

Besides, if I stayed home, I'd do nothing but think about Mindy. About how it felt to see her name—and the other girls'—on my cell phone. Knowing the creep was holding something that had no doubt been precious to them, almost an extension of themselves.

I pushed the thought aside when Bart opened the door. He smiled, stepping back and waving his arm for me to come inside. His home was enormous, with marble flooring in the foyer. The living room was furnished with tasteful, expensive pieces. I just barely managed to keep from gaping. The coffee business must be lucrative.

"Your home is lovely. Did you do this yourself or use a decorator?"

"I hired someone. I'm an idiot when it comes to décor." He motioned to a burgundy suede chair. "Have a seat. Would you like something to drink? I have wine, beer, cocktails, soda, tea—you name it."

He seemed so eager to please. I found it endearing. "Wine, please."

"Great. I'm making Steak Oscar. Cabernet Sauvignon goes best with it. Will that be okay?"

"Perfect."

The smell of dinner wafted through when he disappeared into the kitchen. I'd never had Steak Oscar—didn't know what it was—but it smelled heavenly.

I wandered around the room, looking at photos on the mantle. There was one of Bart, staring into the eyes of a pretty woman with long blond hair. He looked maybe ten years younger. They were both smiling, their faces alight with love.

I turned when I heard him enter the room. He halted mid-stride, his face pale, a glass of wine in each hand.

"Are you okay?" I asked.

He nodded slowly. "I'm sorry. I just saw that you were looking at…" His words choked off, and he cleared his throat. "The photo of me and Sylvia. It's been in that same spot ever since I moved here, but I've become so used to it, I hardly notice it anymore. Seeing you looking at it…" He took in a deep breath and shook his head. "I'm sorry. I don't mean to be rude."

Coming fully into the room, he handed me a glass of wine.

My stomach clenched with sympathy as I watched the myriad of emotions cross his face—none of them pleasant ones. "She must be someone very important to you."

"Was. I mean, she is, but she's no longer with me." He took a sip of his wine, staring at the photo like it was the Holy Grail.

I didn't know if she'd left him or died, so I stayed silent, waiting to see if he'd reveal more. I took a drink from my glass. The wine was a little dryer than I normally liked, but it wasn't bad. It tasted as costly as his furnishings looked.

After a few moments of silence, he continued, his voice strangled with sentiment. "I lost her right after we became engaged. She was my whole world. She died in a car accident, on her way to look at wedding dresses."

"I'm so sorry," I whispered.

He nodded. "It's been nearly twelve years, but it seems like yesterday. I think about her every day. I haven't been out with another woman since she—" He broke off, his face coloring. "I'm sorry. I've revealed too much. That must make me seem pathetic."

It was a little odd, I had to admit, but it struck me that it was also the height of love and loyalty. For him to stay true to a woman who'd been dead for twelve years said a lot about the depth of their love. Unlike Lane's feelings for me.

I pushed away my bitter thoughts. It also occurred to me I was… envious.

Placing my hand on Bart's arm, I said, "I think it's sweet. She was a very lucky woman."

He smiled down at me, tears making his hazel eyes shimmer behind the lenses. "Thanks, Monroe. You're very kind. Compassionate." He patted my hand, and I removed it from his arm. "Dinner's ready. Want to eat, and then we'll do the interview?"

"Works for me. I'm starved."

I was pleasantly surprised to learn that Steak Oscar was beef tenderloin with crab meat, asparagus, and Béarnaise sauce. It was delicious.

Halfway through the meal, Bart said, "I read your article this morning." He frowned. "You're a great writer, but I don't see how you can… God, I don't know. The horror you have to deal with. The details. That's why I've never really read the newspaper much. Until I met you, that is." He flashed a smile. "I guess I'd rather bury my head in the sand and pretend the world is a better place than it is."

"It's not easy," I admitted. I'd printed the information about the penny and the girl's mutilated navel. The media had already dubbed the maniac The Penny Killer. Mine was the only article with that detail, but the television news had run with it.

Suddenly, the food didn't taste as good as it had at first. I managed to eat a few more bites, then after finishing off with a chocolate soufflé, we settled in the living room for the interview.

First, he filled me in on his background. How he'd been raised in a small town outside of Denver, graduated high school, worked hard, ended up in Missouri six years ago, then decided to open his coffee shop. There was no mention of Sylvia. Once we reached the part about the mugger, he downplayed his role. It was what I expected and hoped. His modesty would only add to the impact of the article.

After he'd answered all my questions, I stood. "I think I have enough. Thank you for agreeing to the interview. And for a lovely dinner."

He lifted my hand and placed his lips gently on the back. "Thank you, Monroe. I can't think of the last time I've enjoyed an evening so much." He didn't say, but the haunted look in his eyes made me think it had been when Sylvia was alive. "Can I call you sometime?"

This was what I'd been afraid of. I wasn't ready for a relationship. But he was kind. And he'd saved my life.

We could at least be friends. I offered a smile. "I'd like that."

****

Lane's neck muscles tightened with anger as Keaton examined the dead girl. The autopsy suite smelled of chemicals and death. Lane always declined the mentholatum that helped disguise the smell, but often regretted it—he wished he didn't feel the need for the full experience.

"We found traces of a white powder and unidentified fibers." Keaton narrated through the mask he wore over his mouth. "We've sent those off for evaluation. There were also traces of saliva on her stomach. It wasn't enough that we think he licked her or anything like that. It might have just been spittle that flew from his mouth in his efforts to detach the navel ring."

"Was the ring removed postmortem?"

Keaton's eyes hardened. "No. He took it while she was alive. Painful as hell for the poor girl."

Tingles of fury raced over Lane's arms. He balled his hands into fists, wanting to get ahold of the bastard. He'd seen a lot of cruelty over the years, but he'd never gotten used to it. The fucker was purposely making these young girls suffer. How the hell did he get off on that? And why had he gotten by with it for so long?

Not much longer, asshole, he vowed. One way or another, he'd stop this mother fucker. The guy couldn't be that slick, that intelligent. He'd screw up at some point, and Lane would be there when he did.

The best way to catch him would probably be to use Monroe, he grudgingly acknowledged. Even knowing it to be true, the thought made his gut seize. If anything

132

happened to her…

He looked down at the blue-white flesh of the victim… at her innocent young face… her permanently dead gaze.

He didn't want to risk Monroe's life, but he couldn't let this son of a bitch continue to kill. Monroe was insistent on helping, and Karakas would use whatever means they had at their disposal. If endangering Monroe was what it took, Lane would reluctantly go along. But it would be the single hardest thing he'd ever done.

****

I was working on the Bart article when my doorbell pealed. I looked through the peephole. My heart dropped back to its normal rhythm when I recognized Tony and Paxton. I hated this constant hanging-over-the-precipice feeling.

"Tony? Is everything okay?" I asked as I opened the door.

He blew out a breath and rolled his eyes toward his daughter. "I would have called, but Cadence has been on my phone and Paxton's is dead. We were heading out of town, and Paxton pitched a mother of a fit. Cadence has a tournament in Wichita. Paxton doesn't want to go. I didn't want to leave her home alone, so I thought I'd see if you would mind—"

"I don't need a baby-sitter, for chrissake. I'm fifteen." Paxton crossed her arms over her chest, and her lip curled mutinously.

"After the stunt you pulled, there's no way in hell I'm leaving you alone overnight."

I was as surprised at being asked to babysit as she was at needing one. I wasn't sure what she'd done, but it apparently had Tony in a snit. "Sure. Yeah. She can stay with me. How long will you be gone?"

"Just until tomorrow evening. You're a life saver, Monroe."

"What should I do when I work?"

"I'm okay with her staying by herself in the daytime. Just not overnight, you know. Teens. And then, well, there's the psycho who's mutilating young girls."

"You're not worried—since he's calling me—that he might zero in on her?"

Tony's face lost its color. Before he could speak, Paxton said. "Yeah, good call, Dad. Keep me safe in the lair of a crazed killer."

"I hadn't thought about that," Tony said, ignoring his daughter. "But Lane promised he'd keep an eye on you. She would probably be safer with you than anywhere."

"True. Just to be extra cautious, I'll take her to work with me."

"Great," Paxton bit out. "Bring your kid to work day. How fucking cliché is that."

"Watch your mouth," Tony snapped. "I don't know what your mother lets you get by with, but you won't use that language around me, and you'll show respect to my friends."

"Friends?" Paxton's brow lifted. "You mean you're not doing her? If not, she'd be the only woman I've seen you around that you're not."

"Come on, Paxton," I intervened. "That's no way to treat your dad. You're not impressing anyone with that attitude. You can either chill here with me while he goes, and at least pretend you appreciate it and are having a good time, or you can get in the car with your father and hang out watching your brother's tournament all weekend. Your choice, but I won't take that attitude from you either, so you'd better put a lid on it."

Paxton stared at me, eyes wide. "I thought you were cool."

"Yeah? I thought you were out of grade school."

****

Lane couldn't breathe. Never had Catherine's hospital room seemed so small. He stood in the doorway watching her for a few moments while she sat in an easy chair, reading. Where her beauty had once sent his heart into overdrive, it now left him cold. He knew what was underneath that beauty, and even before the murder, it had been ugly.

She turned and saw him, her face lighting with a brilliant smile. "Lane!" She stood and set the book down on the nightstand, then moved gracefully toward him. When she reached him, she wrapped her arms around his neck and pressed her lips to his. He rested his hands lightly on her waist, but pulled back from the kiss.

She stared into his face, her brows drawn. "What's wrong? Are you angry with me?"

He stepped away from her and moved further into the room. "I'm not angry, Catherine."

"Then what's the matter?" Her blue eyes shimmered with tears. "No one will tell me why I'm here. I've missed you so much. I couldn't wait to see you, and now you're being cold to me. Please tell me, Lane. What happened?"

His shoulders tightened with tension. As tempted as he was to tell her exactly what had led up to her being where she was, the doctor had made it clear they had to proceed cautiously.

"You had a bit of a—breakdown. You haven't been

well."

Her brow furrowed. "I feel okay. I just want to go home. How long have I been here?"

He knew she'd asked that question of Miriam several times—and received an answer. He wasn't sure if it was part of her game, or if she really didn't remember.

"Almost three years."

A slender hand flew to her mouth. She shook her head and backed away until her knees hit the bed. Sinking onto the mattress, she shook her head more violently. "No. That's not possible. Surely I'd have gotten better during that time. Why can't I remember? Did something happen to cause my breakdown?" She slid her hand from her mouth. "You seem angry with me. Did you do something to cause me to lose it, Lane?" She sprang to her feet. "Did you cheat on me?"

Lane's mouth quirked at the irony. "No, Catherine. I didn't cheat on you. You know you've had problems your entire life. We were having marital difficulties. My job was a constant stress for you. I think it all just got to be too much." None of that was a lie. He'd just left out the part about the cheating and murdering.

"Why are you angry with me, then?" Her tone softened, and she once more approached him, running a finger down the front of his shirt. She lowered her voice. "I miss you, Lane. Miss our lovemaking." Her hand wrapped around the back of his neck, and she pulled his mouth down to hers. Against his lips, she whispered, "Make love to me, Lane. Please. I want you so bad."

His entire body tensed, and anger made his throat close. He stepped away. "That's not a good idea, Catherine. The doctor said we need to work on helping you to get better. Helping you remember. I don't want anything to hinder that."

Her lip curled in that vicious way he recalled all too well. Her gaze locked onto his. "Don't bullshit me, Lane. There's someone else. I can see it in your face."

Paper thin flesh stretched over her cheek bones. Her face darkened with fury, turning her expression into that of a bitter, heartless woman. How could he ever have thought her beautiful?

Monroe's soft brown eyes and smooth skin, full lips with the dimple in one cheek came to mind. He swallowed as he spoke the lie. "There's no one else, Catherine."

Really, it wasn't a lie. There wasn't anyone else, because he didn't have Monroe. He was married, yet he was more alone than he'd ever been in his life.

****

That night, Paxton and I watched *Jersey Shore*. The show was so annoying, it took all my willpower not to claw my eyes out, but Paxton wanted to watch. And, what she'd said at the carnival was true. As lame as it was, I wanted to bond with her. Besides, even if I clawed my eyes out, I could still *hear* the show, and that was worse than seeing it.

"You hungry?" I asked.

She shook her head. Hesitantly. As if it weren't quite true.

"Are you sure?" I persisted. "Have you had dinner?"

"No." She shrugged. "But I don't need to eat. I had lunch."

Man. Someone had really done a number on her about her weight. I could definitely feel her pain. "I'm going to eat a salad and some fruit. If you want, I can fix you some too. I'm not that hungry, either, but if I don't eat something at mealtimes, I seem to end up overdoing it later. You know, pigging out on junk food and stuff."

Her eyes lifted to mine, her face showing interest. "Yeah. I could eat a salad or something."

Feeling as though I'd scored a victory, I went into the kitchen and made us both a salad. I cut up strawberries, tangerines, and bananas and lined them up on the plate next to the salad. When I returned to the living room, Paxton's gaze was riveted to the Jersey Shore crew and their drunken antics. I'd called Tony to make sure it was okay that she watched the show. He said her mother let her, so he didn't have a problem with it. I half hoped he'd say no. But then again, I wouldn't have known how to entertain a fifteen-year old without it.

When the second episode finally drew to a close, she turned to me. "I'm sorry my dad stuck you with me."

"I wasn't *stuck* with you. I'm glad you're here. It sucks being on my own all the time. I like the company."

"I'm sure you've got a boyfriend or something you'd rather be with."

Her off-hand words were like a shard to my heart. "No. There's no one."

"I thought you were hooking up with Lane."

"He's married."

"I thought he was getting a divorce."

Although the last thing I wanted to do was talk about Lane, I sucked in a deep breath and said, "I thought he was too."

Paxton lifted her brows. "Did he dump you?"

Her young face held sympathy and understanding. I'd been fairly discreet about mine and Lane's relationship, but she seemed to need to be needed. To feel like her opinion mattered. To have attention paid to her.

"He did," I said. "I should have known better. A married guy and all."

I went on to tell her a condensed, surface version of what had happened with me and Lane. She and I ended up talking halfway through the night. She told me about a guy at school that she liked and how she knew he'd never even look at her. I assured her she'd have plenty of guys after her. All she had to do was be patient, not try too hard, and not settle. I didn't want to disillusion her by telling her she might never find the right guy. Let her have her hopes and dreams while she was young.

After the boy talk, I asked her what she'd done to get into trouble.

She huffed out a breath. "Snuck out of my window."

A chill raced over my spine. "At night?"

"Two a.m."

"No wonder your dad's pissed. You realize there's a guy out there snatching young girls, right? Like I told you at the river? That these young girls *never* make it home alive?"

Sniffing, she nodded. "That's what Dad said. I could have been killed."

"Exactly."

"I told him that would give him more time with my brother."

"Paxton! That's an awful thing to say. Your dad loves you very much."

She nodded unconvincingly. I looked at the clock. It was nearly two a.m.

"You ready for bed?" I asked.

She nodded again. I showed her to the guest

bedroom and waited until she was settled in.

I stared at her from the doorway. She looked half her age with her face snuggled into the pillow. During the course of the evening, I'd noticed a change come over her. She'd gone from a sullen, spiteful teen to a mature, concerned young lady.

Affection squeezed my throat. Maybe she just needed someone to make her feel like she mattered.

Chapter 10

The article on Bart came out in Sunday's edition. I was proud of the results. I'd managed to convey his heroism and modesty without coming off cheesy. Normally, seeing my name on a byline excited me, especially when I knew it was a good article. But all I could think about now was the insane murderer and the fact that he was calling me. I could barely concentrate on Sunday dinner. My nerves were on edge like they'd never been before. Each time a phone rang—anyone's phone, even if the ringtone sounded nothing like mine—I jerked like I'd been shot.

"Good grief, Monroe." My mother's sharp voice cut across the dining room. "What on earth is wrong with you? Are you starting to do drugs with that Josie? I've never seen anyone so jumpy."

I took a deep breath and counted backwards from five. Instead of saying, *"Actually, mother, a psychotic killer is slaughtering young girls as a gift to me, then calling to brag about it,"* like I wanted to, I said, "For one, Mother, Josie's been clean for six months. For another, if I were going to do drugs, don't you think I'd have started well before I was thirty-seven?"

She grunted, her mouth turned down in her 'Disapproval of Monroe' expression. "I'd have thought you'd done a *lot* of things before you were thirty-seven. Just goes to show, what do I know?"

This time, I counted backwards from ten.

"Monroe," Naomi's soft voice intervened. "Want to help me change Sierra's diaper?"

"I'd love to." I smiled gratefully at my sister-in-law and followed her into the guest room that had been turned into a nursery.

Tonight, I was going to babysit Sierra while Naomi had drinks with friends. She seldom did anything on her own, and Coburn was working this evening. Mom had wanted to watch the baby, but Naomi chose me. I was looking forward to an evening of playing with my niece, even though two-month-old babies couldn't do a whole lot. I found it entertaining just watching her sleep. Besides, I had scored a small victory over my mother, and that was always a plus.

Naomi laid Sierra on the changing table, and she immediately began kicking her tiny feet and waving clenched fists. I laughed, staring at her in adoration.

Deftly, as if by second nature, Naomi unsnapped Sierra's pink, duck-covered onesie. She removed the wet diaper, then replaced it with a dry one.

Without raising her head, she said, "Monroe, can we talk?"

I lifted my brows. I liked my sister-in-law, but we'd never been close friends, never engaged in bonding/girl talk. My stomach tightened in concern. "Sure. What is it?"

She looked at me, then back down to her task, but not before I saw moisture in her eyes. Her voice lowered to a hoarse whisper. "Do you think Coburn is cheating on me?"

I was shocked into silence for several seconds. For so long, in fact, I was concerned I'd raise her suspicions.

Shit. Not what I expected. I didn't *think* he was cheating on her. I knew he was. Last year, I'd discovered him going into a hotel with some blond woman. I hadn't said anything to him, or anyone else.

"What makes you ask that?" I evaded the question with one of my own.

She sniffed and rubbed the back of her hand across her nose. "I don't know. I just get this feeling. He seems… distant. Doesn't really want to be home much. I mean, he adores Sierra, but when he's home, she's his entire focus." Her pale skin colored, the freckles nearly fading into the pink. "We haven't had sex since before she was born."

I was sure my face turned red too. I didn't want to discuss my brother's sex life, or lack thereof. I also didn't want to admit what I'd seen to Naomi. It wasn't that I wanted to protect my brother. Coburn needed his ass kicked. He was hell bent on hurting his wonderful wife and precious child. Someone should let him know he'd better learn to keep his dick in his pants.

"Do *you* think he's cheating?" I asked not wanting to talk around the subject but unable to find a better way to address the problem. It wasn't what I had intended. It was too much like lying.

She shrugged, rubbing her hand gently along Sierra's belly, her eyes taking on a faraway expression. "I don't want to believe he is."

For a moment, I was tempted to tell her the truth. She deserved to know. My cheating piece of crap brother should have to face up to his wife, face up to the consequences. But Naomi always seemed so fragile. I wasn't sure how she'd handle knowing.

"Tell me this. Would you really want me to tell you

if I knew something? I mean, really want to know or would you prefer to keep the picture-perfect life you've always had?"

She sniffed. "Honestly? I would want to stay ignorant, never know the truth. Trouble is, that doesn't always work, and if it is the truth, I'd rather know now, so I'm not blind-sided and I can figure out what to do."

My next words weren't exactly a lie, more of an evasion tactic. "Look, Coburn loves you. He loves Sierra. I can't imagine he'd ever cheat on you."

She nodded, but didn't look convinced. "If he did, I'd leave him. I'd take Sierra and go back to Chicago."

A wave of fear gripped me. Naomi had fled Chicago because of her dysfunctional, abusive family. "You left Chicago because you couldn't take that environment, couldn't take being around your family. You'd really subject Sierra to that?"

"I wouldn't want to, but what choice would I have? I couldn't take care of her myself, and if I divorce Coburn, I couldn't stay here, watching him with other women."

I picked Sierra up from the table and laid her on my shoulder, rubbing her fine, soft hair with my chin. The motion soothed me. Her sweet smell kept me from unleashing on her wimpy, needy mother the way I wanted to. Kept me from grabbing onto her scrawny shoulders and shaking some sense into her.

"My family would be here for you. We love you and Sierra. We'd take care of you. And you could get a job."

"I don't know how to do anything. I couldn't make enough to support us, even with child support."

How could she be so helpless, so dependent on a man? I couldn't let Naomi take my precious niece into that den of insanity she called a family. It was time Coburn and I had a little chat.

I smiled reassuringly and patted Naomi's arm. "Don't worry. It won't come to that. You need to keep your family together, and I know that's what Coburn wants."

"I hope so. If I ever find out there's another woman, I'd leave this place and never look back."

****

Sierra was lying in her carrier next to me on the couch, sleeping. Her long lashes lay on her soft pink cheeks, and her lower lip was tucked in—a cute little habit she had when she slept.

The television was on—a Reds and Cubs game— but I had the sound muted, not wanting to disturb her sleep.

The doorbell pealed, and I cringed, but she didn't stir. Easing the carrier down on the floor, even though I knew she couldn't fall off the couch, I hurried to the door before the bell rang again.

Through the peephole, I saw Lane. I opened the door, staring at him for a moment without speaking, willing my traitorous heart to return to its normal beat.

"Is everything okay?" Lane asked, breaking my dazed stare, his brows drawn into a puzzled frown.

"Fine. Yes. It's just that… I'm babysitting. Sierra was sleeping."

He peeked over my shoulder and a grin lit his face. "Sorry," he whispered. "Did I wake her?"

I stepped back, shaking my head. "No. She's still asleep. Come on in."

He came inside, and I shut the door. Still speaking in a hushed tone, I asked, "What brings you here?"

Lane wandered over to where Sierra lay and squatted down beside her carrier. "She's adorable," he whispered. "I can't get over how small she is."

I smiled. "Babies are supposed to be small, you know."

He rose to his feet and turned to face me. "Well, yeah, I know that. I mean, I'm a cop. We check these details out."

I laughed softly. In spite of the fact that he'd broken my heart, it was good to be with him. Just being around him made me feel safe… cherished. Even though he'd pledged to cherish another woman.

"You didn't answer my question. Why are you here?" I still spoke quietly, but this time it came out sounding a little rude.

He moved from Sierra back over to me, looking down into my face.

He stood so close that if I moved forward half an inch, my breasts would touch his chest. Just the two of us—other than a sleeping baby—in my semi-dark living room, speaking in soft tones, proved to be a little more than I could handle. I stepped back, taking a deep breath as I waited for him to answer.

A pained expression crossed his face, but he didn't mention my putting distance between us. "It's been a few days since he's called. The lieutenant thought I should stick by you for a bit. Tony will be over later to stay with you."

"You guys aren't watching me round the clock now, are you? That's ridiculous when you could be using that time to chase down leads. Like Cameron Cooper. Detective Rochester gave you my message, right? You talked to him?"

"We're looking for him. And no, we're not watching you round the clock. The lieutenant had a hunch. She just wants us to keep a close eye on you for the next twenty-four hours or so. She'll let you have a breather then."

I clenched my hair in a fist on top of my head. Not only was a psycho murderer trying to establish a bond with me, but Lane was a painful reminder of a bond I'd lost. "God. This has got to be over soon. We need a plan to draw him out."

I dropped down onto the couch, and Lane settled in the easy chair. He rubbed his hand over his chin. "The last thing I want is to put you in danger."

"Everyone's in danger until this maniac is caught."

"Yes, but he's not stupid. He'll recognize a ploy. We've been tossing around ideas at the station."

"And?" I waited expectantly.

Lane's blue eyes hardened to sapphire gems. I could sense his reluctance as he began to speak. "We haven't come up with anything concrete yet. As I said, he's not stupid. If you simply pretend that you're starting to shift to his side, he'd never believe it."

"Right. But we could play on his ego, somehow. On this connection he feels we share."

Lane nodded. "That's what we concluded. We don't have all the details worked out, but we figured one thing you might try is suggesting he let you interview him. Tell him you don't want to do it over the phone, but you understand why he wouldn't trust that you're not tricking him. Maybe set up a Skype chat. Tell him he can disguise himself and pick the time and tell you where he'd like you to be."

"What good would Skyping do? Can't he Skype from a public computer that couldn't be traced until later?"

"Yeah. But we're hoping he'll give something away. Hoping something in his mannerisms, the background noise, some clue will help us zero in on him."

I pursed my lips as I considered the idea. "That's not very likely. Surely there's a way to get close to him. Physically, and not through a computer."

"I don't want you close to him, Monroe. The guy's a fucking monster."

I drew in a deep breath. "I know. I don't want to be close to him either. But I refuse to be responsible for another innocent life lost. If he doesn't call today, I'll write an article for tomorrow's paper that will make him reach out to me." My heart pumped as inspiration hit. "Maybe that's what we can do to trip him up. I can put something in my article that will draw him out in the open."

The idea was just starting to develop. I paused, letting it all come together in my head. "I could mention a certain place I like to go to think about the murders. I could go there and wait. The police could stake it out, and he might show up." Excitement made my voice rise. "Or I could put something subtle in the article that makes it seem like I'm subconsciously starting to enjoy the game, like I don't want him caught. If he starts to believe that, he might agree to meet me. Somewhere remote, of course. Somewhere he'd be assured that—"

"Are you out of your mind?" Lane's hands gripped my upper arms. "I'll agree to use you as bait to an extent, but we're not putting you in some remote location where you'll be easy pickings for a serial killer."

I jerked away. It was too late for him to play the protector. I didn't need anything from him. Not anymore.

"I appreciate your concern, Lane. But you're looking at it from a personal perspective. I'm sure your Lieutenant would see it my way."

****

Lane gritted his teeth. She was right. Karakas would see it her way. But then, Karakas wasn't risking the life of the person she loved most in the world. He cast that thought aside. He had no right to love Monroe. He let out a frustrated breath. Too bad his heart didn't know that.

"We'll figure out something," he said. "Hopefully, a safe way to catch this bastard before he kills anyone else."

Monroe nodded and skirted around him, settling onto the couch beside her niece's carrier. A squeaking sound, then a cry indicated the baby had awakened. Monroe lifted her from the carrier and held her close, smoothing a hand along her back. "Are you hungry, my precious girl? Mommy left you a bottle. Hold on one second and Auntie Roe will get it for you."

She rose and disappeared into the kitchen. He heard the microwave ding and a few moments later, she and the baby returned. His eyes misted, and he had to turn away at the sight of Monroe with the infant. He could see her like that with their child. With her big heart and loving nature, she'd make an amazing mother. He'd wanted children with Catherine in the beginning, but after he started to see her true nature, he'd changed his mind. No way would he have wanted a woman like her taking care of his children. And that was before he knew she was a cheating murderess. But Monroe? Oh yeah. He could definitely see her as the mother of his children.

Don't think like that. It's over, you jackass. You made sure of that.

He shoved his hands deep in his pockets, turning back, watching in utter stillness, utter silence while Monroe fed the baby, cooing and murmuring jibberish that were the sweetest sounds he'd ever heard. Just when he thought his heart could take no more, the doorbell rang. He let out the breath that had constricted his chest.

"Would you get that?" Monroe asked, looking at him for the first time since her niece had awakened.

"Yeah. Sure." He went to the door and glanced through the peephole. He opened it when he recognized Monroe's brother.

Coburn's brows rose. "Lane," he said, extending his hand. "I didn't expect to find you here."

Lane shook his hand. "I'm working on the Penny Killer case. I had to go over some things with Monroe."

Coburn nodded and moved past Lane into the room. Monroe stood, but didn't hand the baby over.

"There's my number one girl," Coburn gushed, reaching out to take the baby.

Monroe handed the child to him, her face set in grim lines. "I'm glad you came to pick her up. We need to talk."

Coburn glanced at Lane with a frown, then turned back to Monroe. "I assume you mean in private? Is something wrong, sis?"

"I don't care if Lane hears. I trust him."

Lane's heart warmed. She might be furious with him, she might think he was a no good piece of shit for abandoning her, but she trusted him. That was something.

"What is it?"

"Sit."

Coburn laughed, but it came out a tad on the nervous

side. "Okay." He settled onto the couch and put his daughter on his shoulder, patting her back. "I'm sitting. So talk."

Monroe stared at him steadily for a few seconds. "I know you're having an affair."

Coburn said, "What?" with the kind of laughing disbelief of the guilty. "I don't know what you're talking about."

"Cut the crap. I've known for several months. I just didn't say anything, because I figured it was none of my business."

"So—if it were true—why is it suddenly your business?" Coburn's head tilted at a defiant angle. Out of all of Monroe's brothers, Lane liked him the least. He didn't know why, maybe it was his smooth arrogance that set his teeth on edge.

"Because, Naomi asked me today if I thought you were cheating."

Coburn jumped to his feet so fast, Lane was afraid he was going to drop his child. "What? Why would she ask that?"

"She's seen signs lately. The details aren't important. What *is* important is that you do whatever it takes to keep your marriage together; preferably, stop doing that blond bimbo of yours. If that's not possible, then you'd better get better at hiding it. If Naomi finds out you're cheating, she'll leave the state and take Sierra to Chicago." Monroe paused to draw in a shuddering breath. "She'll go back to her fucked up family. To the people who abused her and drove her away. Is that what you want for Sierra?"

Coburn's face drained of color, and his voice lost some of its arrogance. "No. No, of course not. That

151

would kill me."

"Then you'll stop this affair? Stop fooling around with other women?"

"You don't understand. I have women throwing themselves at me all the time. And honestly, I don't love Naomi anymore. I'm not sure I really ever did."

"Have you ever loved anyone but yourself?"

Without answering her question, he said, "Naomi is so busy with the baby that she… Ah, hell, even before she became pregnant, she wasn't very…" He sighed. "Yeah, yeah. Okay. I'll stop."

Monroe's mouth twisted in derision. She'd obviously heard the same insincerity in his voice that Lane had. "Bullshit. You're not going to stop. Are you that self-centered that you'd endanger your child? Drive your family away?"

"Naomi won't find out," he said, his voice lacking conviction.

Monroe shook her head. "You're an idiot. I swear, if you cause us to lose Sierra, cause her to be put in harm's way, I'll never forgive you. Even Mom won't be too pleased with her *perfect* son."

"I'll handle it," he snapped. Snatching up the carrier, he placed it on the couch, then nestled his daughter inside, strapping her in. "It's my marriage. My business. I'll take care of it my way."

Monroe's mouth tightened, but she didn't respond. She crossed her arms over her chest as her brother strode to the door.

"Here, let me get that for you." Lane opened the door, stepping out onto the porch behind Coburn. "I'll help you to your car."

"Thanks, man."

Lane shut the door behind them, then waited while Coburn strapped Sierra into the back seat.

Once the baby was inside, Coburn turned to Lane and rolled his eyes. "Women! Am I right? Hell, almost every married man I know cheats. Bitches need to lighten up."

Glancing back at the house, making sure they were out of sight of the window, Lane grabbed Coburn's shirt front in both hands and slammed him back against the driver's door.

"Hey!" he yelped. "What the fuck is your problem?"

Putting his face close to Coburn's, Lane spoke softly. "My problem, asshole, is that you're a piece of shit. You're cheating on your wife, risking losing your family, and you're hurting Monroe. Every one of those things pisses me off."

"What the fuck business is it of yours?" Coburn demanded, his face red as he clawed at Lane's hands.

"I love your sister, and that makes it my business."

Coburn managed a disbelieving laugh. "Well then you're a goddamned hypocrite. Last I heard, you were married too."

Anger seized Lane's insides, boiling through his blood. "Yeah, I'm married. That's why I'm not with Monroe, you dumb motherfucker." He released him with a final shove and stepped back. "Just know that if your wife finds out you're cheating and she takes the baby away, you'll have me to answer too."

Coburn straightened his shirt and brushed a hand over his hair, trying to arrange it back to its former perfection. "Maybe I should kick *your* ass for what you've done to my sister."

Lane gave a bitter laugh. "Trust me, there's no way

you could hurt me any more than I've hurt myself."

****

I looked up from the still silent TV when Lane stepped back through the door. "You were out there a while."

He shrugged a little too nonchalantly. "Male bonding."

"Right," I said slowly. "You and Coburn bonding. I can see that happening."

His grin made me wonder what had occurred, but I didn't ask.

"So, what should we do for the next hour?" He glanced at the TV. "Looks like the Reds are getting blown out. Want to get out of the house?"

"Tony will be here in an hour?" I tried to hide the disappointment that I shouldn't be feeling.

"Thereabouts."

"Let's take a walk." As wound up as I was, an hour alone with Lane in my tiny house would either have us fighting or making love.

I pulled on a jacket, and Lane held open the door so I could precede him outside. Without conscious thought, I headed to the cemetery at the end of my road. As odd as it was, that's where I found solace. It wasn't the cemetery where Katie was buried, but for some reason, it still made me feel close to her. Made me feel like I'd find answers to the questions that had haunted me for twenty-five years.

Lane walked silently next to me, not commenting when we ended up at the graveyard and I strolled along the path, sometimes stopping and reading a headstone. I'd read most of them, if not all, during the time I'd lived in the neighborhood. My favorite was a large angel statue, similar to Katie's. This was the grave of a grandmother, though, not of a young girl who hadn't yet reached her teens.

"Did you know that Hugh Hefner bought a plot next to Marilyn Monroe?" Lane asked. "He said he did it because he wanted to be buried next to the most beautiful woman in the world."

I turned to him, suppressing an unexpected grin. The many insignificant facts he knew never ceased to amaze me. "I did not know that. You'd think I would, having been named after her."

"Well, now you do." After a few moments, he said, "You never really told me exactly what happened the night Katie died. Do you want to talk about it? I know the details in the police report, but I never heard exactly how it came about. Never heard your version, what you went through."

I sucked in a deep pull of the cool night air and lowered onto a bench beside the grave. "It was terrible," I said softly. I felt Lane settle on the bench next to me. "It was the worst day of my life. It's been a quarter of a century, but I remember it like it was yesterday."

Chapter 11

Summer, 1983

Light from the bulb on the back porch seeped in around the edges of the tent flap. The spark of fireflies flickered on and off. We'd stood flashlights upright inside coffee cans to illuminate the inside of the tent. The glow shone on Josie and Katie's faces, lending an eerie cast to their features.

"Every Breath You Take" played on the boom box, and I leaned over to turn up the volume.

"Come on, Roe," Josie said. "You can't let go of the board. We all have to concentrate together."

"Take a chill pill," I said, scooting back to the Ouija board and once more placing my fingers on it.

"Okay. Here we go. Is everyone concentrating?" At mine and Katie's nods, Josie spoke, her voice hushed and solemn, "Is the legend about Jeremiah really true?"

I heard Katie catch her breath and knew she was scared. She hadn't wanted to mess with the Ouija board in the first place. We waited in silence, hands poised lightly on the planchette. A slight quiver started at the tips of my fingers. Or was that just my imagination?

A shiver skittered up my spine. I liked a good scare as well as anyone, but I didn't want to actually conjure evil spirits.

When the planchette began to move, I told myself

Josie was making it. But I wasn't sure.

Gradually, the planchette made its way upward. It slowed, then stopped on 'yes.'

Katie jerked her hands away. "I don't want to play anymore."

"Quit being a big baby," Josie said, rolling her eyes. "It happened, like, fifty years ago."

"It was thirty," I said.

I knew the story well. It had taken place in 1953 behind the woods of my house, just beyond where my friends and I were now.

Jeremiah Bodecker had been ten years old when he was murdered. His mother had beaten him to death. Then, fearing her husband would come home from work and discover what she'd done, she took his body out to the woods and dumped him in the well.

When Jeremiah's father came home, she told him Jeremiah had run away. That night, unable to sleep, imagining she heard her son's voice in the house, the woman got out of bed and went into the woods to make sure the boy was still in the well. She never returned. A few days later, a hunter found her body. She lay in the bottom of the same well where she'd thrown her son. Her throat had been torn out. Also in the well was a pair of cowboy pajamas, just like the ones Jeremiah had worn. His body, however, was never found.

Some claimed that at the well, on a still night, the screams of a woman and the laughter of a little boy could be heard. I had been out there several times and never heard anything.

"Come on, Katie. Put your hands back on it," Josie begged. "We all have to do it for it to work."

"I don't want to."

"It's okay," I told her. "It's just a silly board. Let's see what it does."

Katie sighed, slowly reached out, and placed her fingers back on the planchette.

Josie made her voice trembly and low—or as low as a twelve-year old girl could. "Is Jeremiah's ghost still walking the earth?"

"Stop it!" Katie squealed. She scooted back on her butt and put her hands behind her back. "We are *not* doing this."

"Quit spazzing," Josie said. "You're such a dweeb sometimes."

"Call me what you want," Katie said, her voice tremulous with tears, "but no more Ouija board."

Josie sighed. "What if we ask it something different?"

Katie frowned and twisted her mouth, considering. "Nothing scary?"

"Nothing scary," I promised. "I'll ask this time."

"Okay."

When we all had our hands on the board again, I said, "Does Brandon Weiher like Katie?"

"As if!" Katie cried.

"Shh," Josie said. "Let the board answer. You know you think he's fine."

Katie went silent, her cheeks pink.

Slowly, the planchette moved to 'yes.'

Josie squealed, "He does like you."

"Does not. These things are bogus. Besides, they're evil. My parents would kill me if they knew I was using one."

"They are not evil." Josie rolled her eyes. "You are the most paranoid spaz in the universe."

I opened a package of cherry pop rocks, tilted my head back, and filled my mouth. The candies fizzed against my tongue.

"Give me some," Josie said.

I passed the package to her, and Josie emptied it into her mouth. "What should we ask it now?" I said.

"Hm," Josie picked up her Dr. Pepper. "How about—"

"Don't do that!" Katie reached out and grabbed Josie's arm, causing Dr. Pepper to slosh from the opening in the can.

"Why not?" Josie scowled, wiping the soda from her fingers onto her pants. "Look what you did."

"It can mix with the pop rocks and cause your stomach to explode."

"You're such a tard." Josie rolled her eyes again. "That story's totally bogus."

"Is not," Katie said stubbornly. "It totally happened."

"Oh my God. You think *everything* is going to kill you." Josie pinched a section of Katie's neon pink parachute pants in her fingers, tugging on the fabric. "Oooh, Katie, better not wear parachute pants. I heard the plastic gives off toxic fumes that gets in your skin and eats you *alive*." Her voice rose with the last word.

"Shut up." Katie reached out as if to shove her. Josie rocked back to avoid Katie's hand and ended up falling backward—the same results she'd have gotten if Katie had made contact—giving off a whiff of Sweet Honesty perfume.

Still on the ground, she stretched her arms above her head and rummaged through her backpack. When she sat up, she held a pack of Lady Eves in her hand.

"What are you doing?" I asked.

"Duh." The eye-roll again. "Smoking."

"No way."

"Way."

"Are you spazzing? Smoking in my back yard?"

"Chill. Your parents aren't home."

"They could come home early. Or my brothers could narc. Then I'd be grounded. We're supposed to go see *Flashdance* this weekend, and I won't get to."

"Fine. Whatever." Josie huffed out a sigh and put the cigarette back in the pack. "Hey, let's ask the board one more thing."

"What?" Katie said cautiously.

"Come on." Josie motioned with her hands toward the board. "Everyone."

Once more, we placed our fingers on the planchette, and Josie said, "Of us three, who will die first?"

"Josie!" I said. "Cut it out."

"No, come on. I mean, Katie's all paranoid about every little thing. Let's see if she has a reason to be."

I looked at Katie. Her eyes were wide, her mouth tight with fear, but she nodded. "Let's see. I wanna know."

"It doesn't mean anything," I insisted. "It's a stupid game."

Katie looked back down at the board. "Ask again."

Josie did. I once more felt the planchette move beneath my fingertips. I wanted to stop it, but couldn't make myself do it. It was as if my hands were being controlled by something other than me. I couldn't exert any more pressure than I was, nor could I let go.

As I watched, the planchette slowly moved toward the right side of the board, toward the letters at the top. J

K L M. All three of our first initials were in that group. A chill moved over me, and I shivered.

"When the Doves Cry" now played on the radio, but I could still hear other sounds that should have been drowned out by the music. Locusts. Dogs barking. A distant siren. Josie and Katie breathing. My own heart pounding like a drum.

The planchette moved, ever so slowly, until it hovered, then stopped. The letter 'K' was visible through the lens.

This time, Josie was the one who jerked her hands off the board. "Who did that?" Her face was even paler than normal, and her eyes were wide.

"Didn't you?" I asked, barely able to get the words out past the lump in my throat.

Josie shook her head. We looked at Katie. Her face was tight, but she wasn't crying, wasn't speaking. Hadn't moved her hands off the board.

Gently, I took Katie's wrists and pulled her hands away from the board. I placed them on her lap.

"I don't know about you dweebs, but I need a cigarette." Josie gave a nervous laugh and picked up the pack. "Let's go to the well and smoke."

"Are you juiced?" I asked. "We're freaked out enough as it is."

"It's just a stupid story. Come on," she said to Katie. "You can use the air."

Katie shook her head. Her blonde hair seemed to give off sparks in the glow of the flashlights. "I'm staying right here."

"You're such a chicken shit."

Katie shrugged. "Go on without me."

"Come on, Roe," Josie said. "We'll go and leave

baby Katie here."

"Will you be okay?" I asked Katie.

Katie slowly nodded.

"I'll go, then. We'll be back in a little while."

"Okay," Katie said, reaching over to turn up the radio.

Although the well was probably no more than thirty feet into the woods, it seemed to take hours to get there. I was familiar with the trail that led to it, but I'd never been out there at night. Never noticed all the sounds the woods held… the furtive scratching—was that an animal? The way the wind, even on a still summer night, seemed to moan through the trees. Or was that a woman's cry?

We reached the well, and Josie leaned her butt against it while I stood a few feet back. A rope, minus the bucket, hung in the center of the well. The bricks had started to crumble and wear away from years of disuse. I didn't want to get any closer than I was.

Josie lit a cigarette, took a drag, and passed it to me. I put it between my lips, then jerked it out of my mouth. "Gag me," I said, using the tail of my shirt to wipe Josie's sticky watermelon lip gloss off the butt. "You could have cleaned it off."

"Whatev," Josie said, rolling her eyes and taking the cigarette from me.

We smoked quietly for a moment before Josie said casually, "Does Mitch have a girlfriend?"

"What's it to you?"

She shrugged. "Just wondering."

"Ha! You like him."

"Do not."

"Do so."

Another shrug. "So, does he have a girlfriend or not?"

"He has tons of girls who like him. I don't think he's going out with any of them."

"Doesn't matter," Josie said, taking another puff of the cigarette. "He thinks I'm just a kid."

"Yeah. He's such a dink. I'm only three and a half years younger than him, and he acts like he's so cool. Like he's all grown up."

We finished the cigarette, and Josie dropped it down the well. "Ready?"

We started to head back, but I reached out a hand to stop her and asked the question that had been weighing on my mind. I wasn't sure that I wanted to know the answer, but I had to ask. "Hey, Josie."

She turned to me.

"I was wondering... did you do that? The thing with the Ouija board?"

She looked at the ground. "You mean with the 'K?'"

"Yeah."

Josie shook her head, lifted it to look at me. "I didn't. I was hoping you did."

A chill raced through me. "No," I said, my voice strained. "And I don't think Katie did either."

Silently, we made our way back to the tent. Our steps were more hurried, but it seemed to take even longer than the trip out had.

Katie sat in the middle of her sleeping bag, tears shimmering in her eyes.

"What's wrong?" I asked, dropping to my knees beside her.

"Your brothers are tools."

"Gabe and Mitch?"

Coburn was in college now, although he was home for the summer. But I knew Katie wasn't talking about him. Cobe was anything but a tool. He was mature... reserved. He excelled at everything, including carrying a 3.90 average. It wasn't likely he'd done anything to upset Katie.

"Yes," she cried. "They were hassling me, calling me a titty baby."

Josie laughed, but I gave her a glare and put an arm around Katie. "Don't let them get to you. Me and Josie shouldn't have been giving you grief either. We're sorry. Hey, let's play Uno or Trivial Pursuit."

"L-a-a-m-e," Josie said, drawing out the word so I'd know just how lame it was.

"No." Katie rubbed a hand over her nose and sat up. "I want to go out to the well."

"What?"

"I do. I don't want to be a titty baby."

"We just came back from there."

"Come on," she begged. "It won't take long."

"Katie, I'm tired, we just went. Maybe another time. Besides, you don't have to do that to prove you're not a titty baby."

"I'll go with her," Josie spoke up.

I felt Katie shiver beneath my arm.

"No," I said firmly. "We're all staying here."

The tent flap opened, and Gable stuck his head inside. "You noids doing okay? Mom says I'm supposed to baby sit you."

"Get bent," I said. "You shouldn't have been messing with Katie, dickweed."

"She shouldn't be such a spaz. You better not say shit to Mom and Dad, or I'll tell 'em about the smokes."

"Be a narc then. See if I care."

"I'm not a narc, shit-for-brains." He shot me the finger. "Hey, me and Mitch are going hunting. Think you babies will be okay while we're gone?"

"Screw off," Josie said, giving Gable the finger in return.

Gable laughed, letting the flap fall shut as he left.

"Now we for sure can't go," I said. "The boys are hunting, and we can't be out in the woods while they are."

"Now who's the chicken shit?" Katie said, but she sounded relieved.

We changed into pajamas and climbed into our sleeping bags. For a while, we lay in the dark, talking. At some point, I dozed off, but wasn't sure if I was the first or if my friends had already fallen asleep.

Sometime later, I felt someone shaking my shoulder. I blinked one eye open. Katie knelt beside me.

"Gabe and Mitch came back," Katie whispered. "Let's go out to the well."

"No way. Go to sleep and leave me alone."

"Come on, please. I want to prove I'm not a baby."

"Katie, no one thinks that," I mumbled, letting my eyes drift shut. "Go to sleep."

I dozed off once more, but woke with a start, not knowing how long I'd been asleep. I sat up quickly. Something had woken me, but I wasn't sure what.

Josie was sitting on her sleeping bag, the light from the edges of the tent illuminating her silhouette. She rocked back and forth, small sounds like sobs emitting from her.

"Josie?" I whispered. "What's wrong?"

She shook her head, not speaking.

"Josie," I said more loudly. "What's going on?"

She looked at me, but her eyes didn't seem to really be seeing me.

"Nightmare."

"Must have been a bad one. You look freaked."

She nodded, but her gaze moved past me. Her eyes were round with fear, her mouth working, but no sound came out.

I looked around the tent to Katie's empty bed roll. "Where's Katie?"

Without moving her gaze, Josie said, "She's not here?"

"No duh! She must have gone to the well alone. Let's go get her."

"No. You go."

"Josie, come on. I don't want to go out there by myself."

Josie nodded slowly, but didn't move. I tugged on her arm, and she reluctantly rose.

In spite of the summer temperature, the air was cool. I wrapped my arms tightly around my body as we hurried to the well.

When we reached it, there was no sign of Katie. "Katie!" I called out. No response.

"Where could she be?" I asked Josie.

Josie didn't answer. We searched, calling out her name, but didn't find her.

"Shit," I muttered.

We went back to the tent. Still no Katie.

A lump of fear rose in my chest. "We have to wake Mom and Dad."

Josie nodded. She'd barely spoken since I woke, and I was starting to get ticked off.

We went inside and into my parents' bedroom. They weren't happy about being roused from sleep. When I told them what had happened, their irritation turned to concern. They jumped out of bed, my mother wearing a yellow nightgown, my father wearing only brown pajama pants. In spite of my worry over Katie, I was embarrassed at Josie seeing my father's bare chest and big belly.

Josie and I waited in the house while my parents went outside. It seemed to take an eternity for them to return.

When they came in, their faces were white with worry. My father called the police. By now, my brothers were awake. It was three in the morning, and the neighborhood suddenly came alive as if it were the middle of the day.

Squad cars lined the streets. Neighbors formed search parties—some fully dressed, some still wearing pajamas. Mitchum, Gable, and Coburn joined in the search, but Josie and I were instructed to stay in the house. One young girl had already been endangered. The other two must be protected.

We didn't speak while we waited. I cried silent tears. Josie rocked, that same look of shell-shock on her face. I wondered if her nightmare had been about Katie, some kind of omen, or if she were just feeling guilty about the way she'd teased her.

Unable to stand it any longer, I went to the back porch to wait, watching through the trees at the bobbing glow of flashlights.

Just before dawn, a not-quite-human wail sounded from the woods.

A neighbor, Mrs. Compton, had found Katie's body.

Katie wasn't at the well, but she was close. I didn't know how we'd missed her, but I was secretly glad we had. Especially when I learned how she'd been found.

Her body was partially nude. She'd been strangled, and her head was crushed from where she'd fallen on a rock. Or where the killer had hit her with it. The police never determined which.

****

Monroe's face was pale in the moonlight, half-shadowed by the overhanging trees, but Lane could still see a shimmer of tears glistening on her lashes. Twenty-five years, and she still grieved for her friend. Apparently, still carried guilt about her death. And now the man who'd likely killed Katie was taunting Monroe.

Lane wanted to reach out, to pull her into his arms. It seemed like such a natural thing to do. Seemed so right. How would she react? How would he feel after deciding to stay with Catherine? Would he feel like a cheater, just as he'd accused Coburn of being?

He settled for reaching out to brush a tear off her cheek.

She turned sad eyes to him and gave a wan smile, wiping the rest of the tears away herself. "Jesus," she said with a shaky laugh. "I've been quite the crybaby today."

"I'd say you've earned it." He tried to keep his voice steady, but he was drowning in desire for Monroe, drowning in the pain of losing her, and he was unsuccessful.

His phone rang, and he snatched it off his belt and flipped it open. "No matches on the DNA," Tony said.

"Fuck," Lane bit out. "Cooper, Price, and Finlay are all in the system. It should have come back if it belonged to one of them."

"I know. That bites the big one. Hey, I'm heading over there now to relieve you."

"Thanks." Disappointment rose up to stifle anything else Lane might have said. He disconnected the call. "Tony's on his way."

Monroe nodded and rubbed her hands along her arms. "We'd better head back."

"Listen, don't worry. We'll catch this guy. I promise." He didn't know why he made the promise, what made him qualified to make that declaration, but he wanted to make some of the fear and pain leave her eyes.

She nodded. "I hope so. We need to settle on a plan that will lure him to me."

"You could get killed." He didn't say it with much conviction. It was likely their best shot.

Her warm cocoa eyes latched onto his. "You'll protect me."

He smiled, his heart chipping just a little more. "I'd die to protect you."

She sucked in a sharp breath as tears sprang to her eyes. She stood and headed toward the cemetery exit, and he had to hurry to catch up.

They didn't speak on the walk back. Had he offended her? Caused her more pain?

When they reached her porch, before she opened the door, he said, "Monroe, answer something for me."

She halted and looked up at him. "What?"

"Have I totally killed your feelings for me?"

Her lovely mouth twisted in a bitter smile. Her voice husky, she said, "I only wish that were true."

He squeezed his eyes shut briefly. God. He couldn't do this. He couldn't stay away from this woman. Not unless he stayed *completely* away. Every time he was around her, his body hummed with wanting her. He lifted a hand to tuck a strand of hair behind her ear. His fingers lingered on her cheek, slowly working their way down, curving behind her neck. Without conscious thought, he nudged her toward him.

She didn't resist. Her gaze dropped to his mouth. He closed his eyes, giving in to the temptation, to the insanity and wrongness of it all, and touched his lips to hers. She was soft warmth, sanctuary and light. Her lips molded to his, her mouth opened to his searching tongue. For a few brief moments, all the darkness in his soul dissolved.

"Are you doing CPR?"

Lane groaned and jerked away at the sound of Tony's voice.

His partner stood on the bottom porch step, arms crossed over his chest. When neither Lane nor Monroe responded, Tony said, "I mean, 'cause I know you're not kissing her. Not when you decided to stay with Catherine."

Lane released a frustrated breath. Monroe stepped away, her face coloring beneath the light of the porch. He looked into her eyes and saw passion, along with pain.

Damn, damn, damn. How was he going to be around her and not touch her?

Chapter 12

Tony stayed with me for a few hours, but when midnight rolled around and no calls came, he left, cautioning me to lock the doors, and to be careful. He hadn't mentioned Lane while he waited, but I had a feeling the warning was two-fold.

Not twenty minutes after Tony left, my cell phone rang. The display showed a blocked call. *It was him.* He hadn't called in all the time I'd had a watchdog. Did he know when I was alone? Was he spying on me? The hair on the nape of my neck tingled at the thought that he was monitoring me. Watching the private moments of my life. The people I knew coming and going. If he was doing that, he definitely wouldn't fall for any kind of sting with the police involved. I would have to come up with something on my own.

"Hello." I noticed my voice no longer trembled when he called. I was still frightened, but no longer for myself. I wasn't the one he wanted to harm. I was his reason for doing what he did. If he hurt me, who would he present his gifts to?

"Who's this guy you wrote the article about? He's not taking my place in your affections is he?"

"I was attacked, and he saved my life. If you read the article, you should know that."

He ignored my sarcasm. His voice came back on the line filled with anger, but not toward me. "I know. I was

171

enraged when I learned about that. If he hadn't killed the guy, I would have."

I grunted a laugh. "Well, it's not like it's a big deal for you to kill someone. For you, it's as easy as breathing."

He once again ignored my mockery. "I like the article you wrote about the girl. What a unique twist. You should have been there. It was priceless."

Nausea roiled in my stomach. I closed my eyes, pushing away the thought of what Mindy Wainwright must have felt—the pain, the terror—just before she died. Trying to infuse nonchalance into my voice, I said, "I have an idea. Let's meet. You want me to get to know you. You say we have a connection. Let's get together."

There was a pause. "I'd love to reveal myself to you, but then it will be over for both of us. I'd have to stop, and you wouldn't have anything else to write about."

"You don't have to reveal yourself. We don't have to meet face to face, or get close to one another. We could go somewhere secluded. You could meet me there, but we can keep our distance."

He chuckled. "Monroe, Monroe. I'm not an idiot. You'd bring the cops."

I sucked in a deep breath and took a chance. "I'm going to be honest with you here. The cops did want to set up some kind of sting operation, but I know it won't work. You're too smart. And no, that's not flattery. You wouldn't fall for that either. I don't know you, but you must be smart to evade capture all these years."

"So, why are you telling me this?"

"Because, it's not going to happen now. And I was hoping since I was honest with you, you'd do me a favor."

"Anything for you, Monroe." His voice lowered with the intensity of his declaration. "Short of turning myself in."

"I want to interview you. We could do it at the cemetery. It's my best place to think anyway." I had to be out of my mind to be making such a foolish plan, but now that the scheme was spilling out, I couldn't stop. "I'd like for you to meet me there, but if you won't do that, and I wouldn't blame you for being afraid, just call me while I'm there. We can have a nice long talk away from the cops, where they can't trace the call. Can't listen in. I want to learn about you. I want to write the article of the century. How many people can say they've interviewed and written a story about an active serial killer who's still on the loose? It would be huge."

Suspicion clouded his voice. "Come on, Monroe. I know you care more about the girls than you do fame. What's your angle?"

"You're right. I do care more about the deaths. I'd rather the police stopped you. I'd prefer they found you and gave you the punishment you deserve. But, until that happens, and since it hasn't happened, I might as well get what I can from the situation."

"So, you're telling me where you'll be. Alone. Vulnerable. Aren't you afraid of me?"

"No. I'm not. You wouldn't hurt me. You said you would have killed that guy for hurting me. I hate what you're doing, but I know you mean me no harm."

He was silent for a few moments, then he said softly, "You have no idea what that means to me. Let me think about it, and I'll get back with you." I heard a catch in his voice. "I'd love to have a face to face. I've wanted this moment, Monroe. Yearned for it. To be with you in person, for you to see me for who I really am. We'll work this out. I'll be in touch."

Hand shaking, I lowered the phone from my ear and punched the End button. He sounded eager... touched. This was really going to happen.

Dear God. What have I done?

****

Bart called me on Monday morning. He was pumped about the article. Said he was flattered, but I made him out to be a bigger hero than he was. For a moment, I wondered if the humility were a ploy. Come on, at some point, a guy's going to puff out his chest and beat on it like an ape, roaring about how he saved the little woman. No one was that modest.

"Can I see you again? I don't want you to think I'm taking advantage of your gratitude, but I haven't been able to stop thinking about you."

"I don't know, Bart. I just got out of a disastrous relationship, which followed an even worse one. I'm not ready to date again. Not for a long while."

"I'm not either. I swear. I can't think about another woman in that way yet. But, you're fun. You're sweet and funny. You make me laugh, and it's been way too long since I've laughed. All I'm looking for is friendship. I promise."

"I don't know..."

"How about if I throw in free coffee for life?"

I laughed. "You do know the way to my heart. I tell you what, Josie and I are going out to our cabin this evening. It's on Lake Viking. It might be fun if you come along." I'd decided to forego MPM and hang out with Josie. She and I hadn't been spending enough time together, and I didn't want to invite her to our Happy

Hour. Not only were she and Asia not exactly BFF's, Josie was better off not being around people who were drinking.

"That sounds like fun. And with your friend there, you can be sure I won't take advantage of you."

"Great. Meet me at my house this evening around five."

I called Josie when I hung up and told her Bart was coming along.

"What? You've already replaced Lane? What's wrong with you?"

I sighed. "Josie, he's not a replacement for Lane, number one. Number two, Lane replaced *me*. And three, we're just friends. The guy saved my life. He gets no credit at all for that?"

"Well, he gets credit for that. But does it mean you have to hook up with him?"

"I'm not hooking up with him. How about you just meet him? Give him a chance. You're not mad that I invited him, are you?"

"No, that's fine. It's a good thing, actually. I need to get a read on this guy. See if I'll allow him in your life, or if I'll have to destroy him."

Laughing, I hung up the phone. When I arrived home from work, Bart's car was in my drive, but as usual, Josie was late. I invited Bart in and offered him a drink. He once again wandered around my house, looking at my Jesse James collection as he sipped on his Coke. Josie finally showed up, and I introduced them.

Bart smiled and reached out his hand. Josie stared at it for a moment before taking it. "Thanks for saving my friend's life."

Bart blushed. "Sure. I'm just glad I was there."

"Me too."

After that, they didn't utter another word to one another. The awkward silence left it up to me to keep the conversation going during the hour long trip to Lake Viking.

Bart's eyes widened when we drove up the path to the cabin. "Wow. This is great. It belongs to you guys?"

"Yes," I said. "It belonged to Josie's family, and now it's ours."

He climbed out of the car and looked around. "It's right on the lake. It's beautiful. The water's so blue."

I grinned. "It is. We love it out here. Let's get our stuff in, and I'll show you around."

I gave him a tour of the cabin, then led him outside. "Want to walk down to the water?"

"I'd love to."

We started down the path. I kept chatter running about how we'd acquired the lake house and how it was Josie's, but I paid for the upkeep, so she gave me half ownership. The most interesting story I could have told was that—at this very lake house—I'd been held by a psycho who nearly killed Adam and his girlfriend. Instead, I'd helped them escape, and he'd killed himself. Suicide by cop. Lane and Tony had been outside when he ran out. I never learned which of them killed him.

But, I didn't tell Bart all the details of that horrifying, painful incident. I didn't know him well enough.

A light breeze ruffled my hair, bringing with it the scent of nature—raw earth and the Carolina allspice that bloomed along the path. I loved it out here, the foliage burgeoning with different hues of green, ribbons of blue sky peeking through the trees above our heads, the gentle lapping of the water.

We were nearly to the lake—Bart walking slightly behind me—when I heard a high-pitched, girlish scream. I whirled, my jaw dropping in shock when I realized it came from Bart. He was frozen on the path, his eyes glued to the ground. His mouth was still open in a circle, but now he'd gone silent.

"Bart?" I took a step toward him. "What is it? Are you okay?"

"No," he squeaked out. "Stay back. S-s-snake."

I looked at the ground. A rat snake slithered across the path and into the grass. I almost laughed, but the terrified expression on Bart's face and the greenish cast to his skin convinced me to hold it back. "It's okay, Bart. It's gone. Besides, it's just a rat snake. They're harmless."

His body shuddered, and his teeth clacked noisily. "I don-don't care. Snakes—" He shook like a wet dog. "They give me the creeps."

"It's okay," I said more softly now. I approached him and rested a hand on his arm. "Let's go back to the cabin. It's okay."

His eyes found mine, and he blushed, groaning. "Oh, Jesus. You must think I'm the biggest wimp in the world. I can't believe I freaked like that in front of you." He shook his head. "Shit."

"No. I don't think you're a wimp. We all have our fears. Really. Don't be embarrassed."

He smiled gratefully. "Thanks, Monroe. See why I like you so much?"

"You know, though, snakes for the most part are harmless. My neighbor actually has a corn snake as a pet. Rambo is the gentlest thing you've ever seen. I've taken care of him on occasion when Don has gone out of town."

His cheeks paled. "God. I can't imagine having one of those hideous creatures as a pet." Another shudder ran over his body. "I'm sorry. They just freak me out."

"Hey, a lot of people are afraid of snakes. No biggie." I took hold of his arm. My hand vibrated with the trembles coming from him. "Come on. Let's go fix some dinner. We brought steaks to grill."

He managed a wavering smile, but his voice still shook when he spoke. "I'm a pro with the grill. Let me do the steaks."

"Sounds good. Neither Josie or I are great at it."

We arrived back at the cabin, and Josie was kicked back on the couch, smoking and watching *Dexter* on TV.

"Josie, you said you wouldn't smoke in here when other people come."

"It's okay," Bart said. "It doesn't bother me."

Josie shrugged. "I'll put it out if it does. I mean, I wouldn't want to cause you any… distress."

Her mouth quirked, and I knew. She'd heard Bart scream. I flicked a glance at him, but he didn't seem to get that she was mocking him. Of course, he didn't know Josie like I did.

"Bart's going to grill the steaks. I'll get him started, and you and I can make the salad and potatoes."

"Super."

I showed Bart where to find the grill and charcoal on the back deck. After I'd seasoned the steaks, I took them out to him, along with a beer. He thanked me with a wink, then turned back to the grill.

When I went back inside, Josie was in the kitchen chopping lettuce. "Did you wash your hands?" I asked.

"Yes, Mother." She rolled her eyes.

I was a little obsessive about clean hands. I knew she'd likely washed them, and I certainly knew she was an adult, but I'd seen countless adults who didn't wash their hands, and the thought made me cringe. I'd known Josie for most of my life, but it was habit to ask.

"So, what was she screaming about earlier?"

I couldn't help it. My mouth twitched. "*He* saw a snake."

"Ooooh. Was it like an anaconda or a rattler or a cobra?"

I took out potatoes and rinsed them, then began scraping them with the potato brush. "It was a rat snake," I said quietly.

"Did you say a *bad* snake or a rat snake?"

I scowled at her. Lights of amusement danced in her green eyes.

"I mean," she went on. "Because, if you said a *rat* snake, they're harmless. Totally, completely harmless, which would make him a pussy."

"Josie!" I shook my head. "He has a fear of snakes, okay?"

She shrugged. "Whatever. But I can't imagine Lane screaming over a snake, can you?"

I slapped a potato down on the counter and turned to glare at her. "I realize Lane saved your ass that night when he brought you to me instead of to jail, but doesn't the fact that he betrayed me and broke my heart count for anything? Or are you just concerned about how people treat *you*?"

Her amusement turned into a flinch, and I immediately regretted the outburst. She put the knife down and came over to me, then took my hands in hers.

179

"You know it matters to me how people treat you. I know Lane hurt you, but he thinks he's doing the right thing. You don't know this guy. But you know Lane. He's a good man. Not because of what he did for me, but he just is." She tugged on my hands, leading me over to the table. We sat, and she stared at me earnestly. "When you run with the people I ran with, when you've seen and done what I've seen and done, you develop instincts. I don't know Bart, but something about him puts me off. I'll admit it might be because I know Lane. I know that he's loyal and honest, and he loves the hell out of you."

I barked a bitter laugh. "Right. He showed me how much he loves me."

"I hate that he's staying with Catherine. Believe me, I do. But I understand. His conscience would eat him alive if he didn't try to help his wife, if he didn't honor his commitment. He could have lied to you. He could have pretended to start divorce proceedings and strung you along, all the while playing devoted husband to the bitch. He didn't do that, though. He was honest with you."

I nodded. "He was honest," I reluctantly admitted.

"You guys haven't slept together, right?"

I shook my head.

"He could have at least gotten in your pants before he told you he was staying with her. But that's not his style. He's honorable."

I let out a long sigh of acquiescence. "Yes. He's honorable."

She grinned. "And harmless reptiles don't make him scream like a little bitch."

Chapter 13

Although the cemetery was normally a place of refuge, tonight as I entered the gates, my knees shook so badly I could barely walk. The weight of the pistol in my pocket was little comfort. I wasn't sure what I was up against, or if he'd even show, but I knew the man was evil, and I was more frightened than I'd ever been in my life. He'd called with his plan the night before. As instructed, I went to the bench at the head of the third row of headstones. I sat on the cool wrought iron. It was a warm June night. My shiver had more to do with the situation than the weather.

Just as he'd said, an earpiece lay in a box on the bench. I attached it to my ear. He'd said to wait for an hour while he observed me, making sure I was alone. A shudder rippled along my spine. Was he watching me now? Was he near? An hour was a long time to sit alone, in the dark, with nothing for company except thoughts about a maniacal killer.

As instructed, I hadn't alerted the police. He wouldn't show himself if I did, but if he came, I was prepared. I would take him in myself, and if he endangered my life, I'd shoot him. *If you're going to own a gun, be prepared to use it.* My brother, Mitchum, had told me that when he taught me to shoot. I hadn't had to use one yet, but I was sure, if it became necessary, I could pull the trigger. *Reasonably* sure.

I'd worked up the bravado to appear alone because I knew if he wanted to kill me, he'd had ample opportunity. He'd been to Linus's. He knew when I was alone in my house. He was watching me. He could take me out any time. But that wasn't what he wanted from me. Not yet.

Wind moaned through the tree branches, the only sound to penetrate the eerie stillness. I waited. Then waited some more. I wanted to walk around, study the headstones and free my mind, but I was told to sit… and wait. So, that's what I would do.

I drew in a long, deep breath and let it out slowly. To pass the time, I thought of Sierra's sweet face. I tried not to dwell on the dead girls or Lane. I didn't need anything else to screw with my mood.

"Monroe, I'm quite pleased." The voice filtered from the earpiece, seeming to reverberate through the graveyard. I gasped, jumping to my feet. I spun around in all directions, but I saw nothing. Not a light, not a movement of any kind. Where the hell was he?

"Hello?" I called out, my voice trembling as much as my hand that closed over the pistol in my pocket. "Where are you?"

"I thought we might have a little chat from a distance before we meet face to face. I have to be absolutely certain you're alone."

"How will you decide if I am?"

"I already scoped out the area. I'm relatively sure you didn't bring the police. I was here an hour before you."

I experienced a quick and unreasonable irritation at his making me sit here for all that time when he'd already checked the place out.

"So, what now? I'm cold. I'm tired." I'm not sure where the courage came from, but I forced a note of sarcasm into my voice. "And quite frankly, I'm bored. I expected more from you. I expected a story."

"You'll get your story. A story that will make you famous."

"Are you here? Nearby?"

"That's my little secret for now. We'll talk first, see how it goes."

He said it as though we were on a date.

"Okay, I'll start. How old are you? Where are you from? Where did you go to school?"

A gravelly laugh came to my ear. "Monroe, come on. Do you think I'm that stupid? Do you think I'd answer questions that can lead the police to identify me? Don't insult my intelligence, or you'll upset me. You don't want to upset me, do you?"

I swallowed loudly. "Why? Why are you killing these girls?"

A sigh came from the speaker in my ear. "It's a compulsion. I can't explain it any more than I can explain why the sun comes up in the morning. It just is."

"How did you start? What made you kill your first victim?"

He was silent for several seconds. "I've never told anyone this story." His voice was charged with emotion. "You're the one I want to share it with, Monroe. The only one. I don't want you to print this part, okay? Can you do that for me?"

He was pleading with me? He had all the control, and he knew it. I wouldn't do anything he didn't want me to. Other than kill him, if I got the chance.

"I promise. I'll only print what you want me to."

"I was twelve years old. My parents' marriage wasn't perfect. I knew that, but I never knew how serious their problems were until that night." He paused, but I waited without speaking. "I thought my dad was gone. I went out to the pool area. I liked to catch frogs by the pool and…" He laughed. "I know this will sounds cliché. A serial killer who tortures animals, but I liked to pull their legs off. Watch them spasm in pain. Watch them die."

Bile rose in my throat. "You're right. That's cliché."

"So, I'm not perfect. Anyway, I heard a noise in the pool house, and I went to investigate. I was afraid someone had seen me at my… hobby. As it turned out, I wasn't the one who was caught that night. It was my father. I found him in the pool house. Naked. With my babysitter, Angie." Tears choked his voice. "She was sixteen, and I had the biggest crush on her. It might have even been love. Although, what a boy of twelve knows about love, I'm not sure. They were standing, my father behind her.

"Angie saw me first. I met her beautiful green eyes, and she shrieked, lifting her hands to cover her breasts. I went into a rage. I rushed into the pool room. Threw myself on them both, fists flailing. My father easily got loose, tugged me off of Angie. She was crying. Her lip was bloody, and her eye was already starting to swell. Enraged, my father beat the living shit out of me."

I flinched, picturing the scene. Although I knew what kind of monster he'd become—what kind of monster he was, even at twelve—I couldn't imagine what that was like for a young boy. "That must have been very difficult for you."

"Not as difficult as what came later. I ran into the

house, bleeding, crying. My mother was inside. That asshole was fucking my babysitter with my mom in our house. I told her what happened. She didn't react. No reaction at all. Not a word. She cleaned me up. Checked my injuries to make sure I didn't need to go to the hospital. Then she put me to bed. I couldn't sleep. I don't know how long I lay awake, but finally, I fell asleep. The next morning, sore and aching, I climbed from my bed and went down to the kitchen. My father sat at the table, his face haggard, his expression etched with fury."

I wanted to take the ear piece from my ear. Didn't want to hear any more of this disturbing story, especially since it elicited just the merest touch of sympathy. After a brief pause, he continued.

"I'll never forget that day. Every detail is indelibly imprinted on my mind. The day that toppled my world. My father rose to his feet and came toward me. The look on his face was like nothing I'd ever seen. It was as though he wanted to kill me. But he didn't touch me. Instead, he said, 'I hope you're happy, you little fuck. Your mother killed herself last night.'"

I couldn't control my gasp of horror. I was glad I was sitting. All the feeling left my body. He was right. This would make a hell of a story. But I couldn't print it. He'd told me not to. But he didn't tell me I couldn't tell the police. He wouldn't know if I did. It might help them find him. If I wasn't successful in taking him in tonight.

"I'm sorry," I said. "Truly, I'm so sorry. I can understand how that could screw with a young boy. How you must have suffered."

"I knew you'd understand. I'm telling you, Monroe, we have a special bond. A connection like nothing I've ever known."

185

A shudder of revulsion rippled through me at his voice, the voice of the person who'd killed Katie, speaking to me as though we were lovers.

"Why did you kill my friend? Why did you kill Katie? She was only twelve years old, for God's sake." It hit me then that she was the same age as he was when the incident with his father took place. The other victims were a few years older… the babysitter's age. Was Katie his one kill that represented killing his childhood like his father had?

"I didn't."

"What? She was just like the others. Of course you did."

"No. She wasn't like the others. I'm telling you, I didn't kill your friend. That was someone else."

I nodded, although I didn't believe him. He would say that. Now that he was enamored of me, he wouldn't want me to think he'd killed someone close to me.

"Will you reveal yourself to me now? I want to meet you. You know there aren't any cops around. Please."

After a brief pause, he said, "Okay. I want to see you too. Face to face. With all secrets out between us. Stand and walk forward. When you get to the fifth row of graves, go right. Keep walking. You'll see me. I'm sitting on a bench next to the last headstone. I'll be waiting for you, Monroe."

With as much dread as anxiousness, I stood, walking unsteadily along the route he'd told me to take. Each step seemed to take me closer to my doom. The wind picked up, its howl echoing my trepidation.

My heart stalled when the bench came into view. There he was, sitting just where he said he'd be. I slipped my hand into my jacket pocket.

Would he wonder why I'd worn a jacket on a balmy night? No. Surely he wouldn't think about that. My footsteps picked up, although I wanted them to slow down, wanted to run the other direction. I pulled the .22 from my pocket when I was no more than six feet from him.

"Okay, stand up. Nice and slow," My voice quavered more than I would have liked, but I figured the weapon in my hand would balance out my fear. "On your feet. Now."

"What?" the voice sounded young. Younger than the Penny Killer could be. If he'd been killing for twenty-five years, even if he started at twelve, he had to be close to forty. This guy sounded like a teenager.

He came slowly to his feet.

"Hands up," I commanded. "Where I can see them."

"Hey lady, you got the wrong guy. I don't want any trouble."

Something wasn't right. I knew instinctively this wasn't the man I'd been speaking with. "Who are you? What are you doing here?"

I moved closer. In the dim light, I could make out a young face and longish hair peeking from beneath a gray beanie. He wore baggie jeans beneath a baggier Slipknot T-shirt.

"My-my name is Brandon Charles. This guy paid me fifty bucks to sit here. He wouldn't tell me why, and I didn't ask. I didn't know this shit was going down. What are you going to do to me? Please don't kill me."

"Damn it to hell," I bit out.

The voice in my ear said, "Monroe, I'm disappointed."

I gasped. I'd almost forgotten about the earpiece, so

intent was I on my mission.

"I thought we'd established a trust. You were going to shoot me?"

Tears welled in my throat. *Fuck, fuck, fuck.* "You son of a bitch," I choked out. "You could have gotten the boy killed."

Boisterous laugher rang out. "You know who I am. Know what I've done. Do you think the loss of some punk's life would affect me at all? This was a test, and you failed. You didn't bring the cops, but you were going to betray me. You realize there'll be consequences, right?"

"Lady, who are you talking to?" The boy still had his arms in the air. "What are you going to do to me?"

"Stay right there. I'm calling the police. They'll want to speak with you." Into the earpiece, I said, "Fuck you." I snatched it from my ear and dropped it to the ground. I should probably give it to the police to check for prints, but this guy wasn't stupid. He wouldn't have left his prints on it. Besides, mine were all over it. I crushed it beneath my feet so I couldn't hear his hateful voice again.

I took my cell from my pocket and dialed Tony's number.

Chapter 14

Tony sent a patrol officer to take the kid into custody since he couldn't get there quickly enough himself. He was none too pleased at my holding a gun on a possibly dangerous individual and didn't want it to continue any longer than necessary.

I watched the red and blue flashes of light shoot along the night sky as I waited. Tony arrived shortly after the patrol car, stalking toward me, his face set in anger. Dread over the confrontation curled through my stomach but was overpowered by relief that Lane wasn't with him.

"What the hell were you thinking?" he demanded as he halted in front of me.

"I was thinking that I might catch the Penny Killer," I said just as sharply. I refused to be intimidated. After all, the bastard was using me, wasn't he?

He ran a hand over his almost nonexistent hair. Even in the meager light of the cemetery, the irritation in his face was evident. He shook his head. "You could have gotten yourself killed—"

"Monroe? What the hell?" The flesh on my arms tightened as Lane's voice cut through our conversation. I'd been so intent on Tony, I hadn't noticed him arrive. I turned to him.

The rage on his face made the expression on Tony's seem benevolent. He rushed over to me and gripped my upper arms. His eyes looked like hard sapphires as he stared down at me, a muscle in his jaw ticking. "Are you out of your mind?"

"Like I told Tony, I was trying to catch this guy. Something none of you have been able to do so far."

A smirk curled his lips. His grip tightened on my arms. "Really? All alone? A psycho who's slaughtered young girls for twenty-five years, and you..." His eyes raked over my body. "*You* were going to take him down?" He screwed his eyes shut, then opened them and muttered, "Jesus Christ, Monroe. Not only could you have gotten killed, now there's no way in hell any sting operation we set up will work. You screwed that up royally."

I jerked loose from his hold. Anger choked my voice. "It wouldn't have worked anyway. He's watching me. He waits until you guys leave to call. Even tonight, when it was just me, he didn't show himself. So how the hell did you wonder cops think you were going to trap him?"

Tony had been standing by, watching our exchange in silence, but now he spoke. "Now we'll never know, will we?"

All the strength left my body. Had I really ruined their chances of catching this guy?

No. He wouldn't have fallen for their trap. No way. He was so cautious, even after watching for an hour and assuring himself there were no cops around, even with the chance of coming face to face with me, he'd stayed hidden in the shadows like the coward he was. I'd tried and failed, but I wouldn't let Tony and Lane make me feel guilty.

"Look. I'm spent. I need to go home. Maybe you

guys should get my statement instead of tag teaming me with the reprimands."

Lane snatched a notebook out of his pocket. "So, shoot." He lifted his head and quirked a brow. "That's a euphemism, Annie Oakley. It doesn't mean I want you to draw your weapon."

I bit down on my annoyance. "I spoke with him. Through that earpiece." I pointed at the ground where I'd thrown the device.

Tony took a plastic bag from his pocket and squatted, then slipped it inside.

"He told me what happened in his childhood. What made him start his killing spree." I relayed what he'd said, in detail.

After I mentioned his catching his father with the babysitter, Lane and Tony shared a look.

"What was that about?" I asked. "Does that mean something?"

They were silent for a few moments. Finally, Tony said, "The victims were found with their arms crossed over their breasts. I think we now have our reason for that."

A chill raced through me. He was killing his babysitter over and over. "He said he didn't kill Katie, but I'm sure that was because she was my friend. He wants me to like him."

Another look passed between them.

"What?"

"Nothing," Lane said. "Tell us what else he said."

I gave them a replay. I nailed it almost word for word. His story was branded on my memory, and there was no way I'd ever be able to shake it.

"That's it," I said. "That's all. Now, I'm going

home. You two have a suspect to question. He was hired by this guy to sit out here and fuck with me. Maybe you can get something out of him. As for me, I'm done here."

I stalked down the path, not turning when I heard footsteps. Lane caught up to me in seconds. "Monroe," he barked.

I didn't turn around, kept walking, didn't answer. He took hold of my arm and, although his touch was gentle, it was enough to make me stop.

I turned to face him. "What?"

He locked his gaze on mine. "Don't you realize what could have happened? I was reluctant to use you as bait at all, but the only reason I agreed was because we'd be here to protect you. You were out here tonight, all alone. Vulnerable. A perfect target for a maniac who's obsessed with you."

Some of my irritation left. He cared about me—even if he'd decided he didn't love me—and I was aware that he was speaking from his feelings for me. "I knew what I was doing. He doesn't want me dead, Lane. He would have killed me already. I was afraid, I'll admit that, but I had my gun. I can take care of myself."

He nodded. "In other words, you don't need me."

I gave a sad smile. "You have a wife who needs you. That's what matters." I jerked my chin toward the patrol car with its still flashing lights. "At least I got you a suspect who might have information. You should go talk to him. I need to go."

"Tony will handle him. I'm walking you home and seeing you inside. Do you actually think I'll let you go off on your own after you toyed with a killer?"

Too weary to argue, I nodded. Without another word, we headed to my house.

Lane went ahead of me, took my key, and unlocked my door. Once he'd searched the house and assured himself no one was hiding, waiting to ambush me, once he'd checked to make sure all the doors and windows were locked, he walked to the front door. "Lock this behind me."

"I will." I looked up into his face. "Do you really think a sting operation would have worked? Did I endanger more girls by what I did tonight?"

He smiled, his eyes roaming over my face. "No, Monroe. You did what you thought you had to do. You're right. This guy's too slick for a sting to work. Besides, it could have gone very wrong if he'd realized you brought the police. You might have been killed. We'll figure out another way to get him."

I knew he'd said the words to comfort me, whether he believed them or not. "Thanks, Lane," I whispered.

"Any time." He stood there for a few seconds longer. His gaze settled on my lips, and I thought he was going to kiss me. I wanted to believe I wouldn't let him, but I wasn't sure.

I would never know, because instead, he stepped back, onto the porch. "I'd better get back to the station. They should have the kid there by now. I'll let you know if we find out anything."

"Thanks."

"Lock the door."

"Yes. I know."

"Now," he said, still waiting on my porch.

I smiled and closed the door, then turned the deadbolt. Leaning against the door, I let out a deep sigh. How could my feelings for Lane overpower the close call I'd had with a murderer? But they did. All I could think about was the concern in his voice, in his blue eyes. And wish it was because he loved me as much as I loved him.

****

Lieutenant Karakas stormed into the station, her wide face puffy from sleep. She didn't pause until she stood in front of Lane's desk. "I'd charge your little girlfriend with obstruction of justice except then she'd be locked up and the cocksucker couldn't call her. What the fuck was she thinking?"

"She didn't feel that he'd—"

"Did you get anything from this punk?" Karakas cut him off, swiveling toward the interview room where, through the glass, they could see the kid at the table. "What's his story? Who hired him?"

So Karakas was even less pleasant at two a.m. than she was during normal daylight hours. At least she was off the topic of arresting Monroe, although being in jail would at least keep her safe.

"He doesn't know who hired him. It was all done through Craigslist. The money was left in an envelope, along with instructions. We've done a trace on the email address he used on Craigslist. It was set up at a library and has already been deleted."

"Fuck," she growled.

"Our guy left the envelope in a locker at a Grant's Gym. The kid was paid half, and the other half would be paid once the job was done. He was to pick it up that night."

"Let me guess. You already checked out the locker, and the second envelope wasn't there." It wasn't really a question, so Lane didn't answer. "Did he have the first envelope? Any prints on that or the earpiece? Any goddamned thing for me at *all*?"

"Monroe's prints were the only ones on the earpiece. The kid no longer has the envelope or the money. He has nothing we can use. Not a damn thing." He told her the story the Penny Killer had given Monroe. "We can put someone on checking suicides of females—mothers—during a specific time span. If this guy was killing girls twenty-five years ago, he should be at least forty or forty-five. That would narrow down the time frame. It would mean she killed herself thirty or thirty-five years ago. Of course, if he's sixty, that means it happened fifty years ago, so that's a wash."

"I don't need you to tell me things that are a *wash*," Karakas bit out. "I need you to tell me things we can fucking *use*."

"Right." Lane made his hands clench the arms of the chair so they wouldn't punch the lieutenant in the face. He'd never hit a woman. Never hit a superior. But he was on the verge of breaking that streak. Monroe had placed herself in serious danger tonight. They had a killer who was thumbing his nose at them while he continued to slaughter young girls. And Lane was fed up with getting his balls busted by someone who was more worried about covering her ass than she was saving lives. He gritted his teeth, reining in his temper. "He denied doing Katie Broussard. On one hand, it could be because he doesn't want Monroe upset with him. On the other, it could be that he didn't. Broussard was younger than the rest, her arms weren't crossed over her chest, and she wasn't raped. If her killer was a copycat trying to make it look like the same MO, since he didn't know about the arms crossed over the breasts, he wouldn't have known to pose her like that."

Karakas nodded. "We'll treat them like the same

case for now. We don't need two unsolved cases where the victims are young girls. Cut him loose. He's no good to us." She stomped toward her office, turning as she reached the door. Pieces of her short hair stood up around her head, and her eyes held a bleak look, an almost human emotion. "Find this mother fucker, Brody. Jesus Christ. Find him."

Lane leaned back in his chair, eyes closed, hands linked behind his head. Were they dealing with two suspects, or had this guy killed Katie too? Had her death been symbolic for killing his twelve-year-old self, and the others were symbolic of the babysitter, or had someone else done Katie?

They'd researched a link between the victims, especially the recent ones. Tried to find something they had in common. They'd come up empty. Other than the fact that they were all young, innocent, and now dead.

His mind wandered to Monroe. A yawning, aching void had opened in his chest the moment he decided to stay with Catherine. No matter how often he told himself he was doing the right thing, nothing could erase the guilt, or the despair. He just wanted to be near her, to absorb her soothing essence, her spark, her vitality. He lived in shadows, saturated in evil and tragedy. Only Monroe gave him peace, comfort, escape.

He grunted a humorless laugh. The tingle in his chest, the rush of blood to his groin every time she was near, the painful urge to touch her, taste her. Who was he kidding? What he wanted from Monroe was far more than comfort.

****

We moved the family dinner to Friday because Naomi and Coburn would be out of town over the weekend. Without Coburn, my mother didn't see much reason to cook… or exist.

I took Josie with me. Mitchum would be there, and since Josie hadn't made a move, I figured it was time for me to step in. A few days ago, I tried to feel Mitch out about his feelings for Josie, but he hadn't taken the hint. I didn't want to come right out and ask. He and I had never had that kind of relationship. He was stubborn and would retreat if I pushed.

Josie looked exceptionally pretty. She'd worn skinny jeans and a shimmery gold blouse that brought out the amber highlights in her green eyes. Her make-up was sparse. Her natural beauty amazed me, and I never understood why she hid behind the heavy, dark gunk she used to wear. But it started soon after Katie's death.

I managed to maneuver her next to Mitch at dinner. I could see peripherally that he seemed to pay a great deal of attention to her. Seeing them together warmed my insides. Made me feel hopeful in a world that was becoming increasingly hopeless—violent and insane.

I tried to concentrate on my family and not think about the Penny Killer. He hadn't contacted me since the night at the cemetery. Was he stalking his next victim? The dread that sat in my stomach said he'd wait until he had another victim before calling. And that thought terrified me.

After dinner, Mitch and Josie offered to get dessert and bring it to us in the living room. I sat on the sofa next to my mother, and she gave me her 'why can't you be more like your brothers' look. What now? I wanted to scream.

It didn't take long to find out. My mother wasn't one to suppress her feelings. "Your *friend* certainly is brazen."

The flesh on my face tightened with irritation. "What's that supposed to mean?"

"Her tawdry behavior at the dinner table. She was all over poor Mitchum."

"Are you kidding me?"

"Mother, come on." Gable, my hero, to the rescue. "They've known one another all their lives. She didn't do anything the least inappropriate." His lip quirked in a grin. "And Mitch didn't seem to mind at all. Matter of fact, if either of them were acting tawdry, it was your son."

My mother gasped. "Mitchum wouldn't—"

"With a pretty girl like Josie?" Gable cut her off. "*I'd* be tempted."

I didn't even attempt to hide my smile. I stood, needing a strong cup of coffee. "I'll go make a pot of coffee and see what's keeping the lovebirds so long."

I could have planted corn in the crevices in my mother's scowl.

I went into the kitchen, and my mouth dropped open at the scene before me. Mitch was feeding Josie a bite of chocolate cake, but didn't make it entirely in her mouth. He swiped a thumb along her cheek to wipe off icing. She giggled, and I halted in shock.

Josie giggling? She hadn't even giggled when we were children. Derisive laughter, yes. Giggling? Hell no.

I cleared my throat, and Josie saw me over Mitch's shoulder. She blushed when she met my gaze. *Yes*. Romance was definitely in the air.

"Excuse me, but I need coffee, and you guys have Mother in a tizzy."

Mitch cocked his head, giving a lop-sided grin.

"Then she'll be at stroke level when she learns we're going out this weekend."

I laughed, a rush of pleasure washing through me. At least something positive was happening in the insanity my life had become.

"That's fantastic. You guys better take what's left of the cake to them. I'll bring coffee shortly."

They left the kitchen, and I almost hummed while waiting for the coffee to brew. I took the pot into the living room. My mood lifted when I saw Josie and Mitch glued side by side. If possible, mother's expression had grown even fiercer.

As we were finishing dessert, and I was mentally devising my escape, Naomi set her cake plate down and turned to me. "Monroe, did you know Coburn and I are going away for a second honeymoon?"

I looked at Coburn. He gave me a sad, resigned smile.

"No, I didn't," I said.

"We're going to Paris the second week in July. We were hoping you and Mother Donovan could share in watching Sierra."

"I'd love to. I'm so happy for you guys. That's wonderful."

"Things *have* been wonderful for us lately."

"I'm glad." I almost felt sorry for my brother, stuck in a loveless marriage—but not completely. He'd committed to Naomi. They had a beautiful, precious child. As I knew all too well, sometimes we didn't get what we wanted in life.

Chapter 15

Monroe's brothers, Gable and Mitchum, sat across from Lane at the interview table. He hadn't called Coburn in. The eldest brother hadn't seen the girls that night, hadn't been around when the tragedy occurred.

"I appreciate you guys coming in on a weekend."

"Sure," Mitch said. "I'm not sure how much help we'll be. It's been so many years. We told the police everything we knew back then."

"I know." Lane nodded. "But since we've reopened the case, we'd like to interview old witnesses. You'd be surprised at how often something new arises. I have some questions about the night Katie was killed."

"Shoot," Gable said. "If there's anything at all I can do to help, I'd be happy to. This man needs to be stopped." His voice shook, and the skin beneath his eyes was tight. In spite of his calm demeanor, it was obvious the girl's death still troubled him—both of them. How the hell could it not?

Lane poised his pen over the notepad. "You guys were hunting the night Katie was murdered. Do you remember what time you got back home?"

"It was around eleven," Gable said. "We were supposed to be keeping an eye on the girls for our parents."

"Yeah," Mitch inserted. "Instead, we were screwing with them. Trying to scare them. From what Monroe and

Josie said, Katie might have ventured out on her own to prove she wasn't…" He paused, swallowed. "Wasn't a chicken shit like we called her. We were assholes back then."

Gable thumbed his eyes. A trace of moisture remained when he dropped his hands. "That's pretty much how I remember it."

Lane nodded slowly. "Did you see or hear anything at all while you were hunting? Anything suspicious? Any other people you might have spotted in the woods?"

Gable shook his head. "No. The woods behind our house were mostly used by us. I didn't see or hear anything that night."

"Me either." Mitch shifted in his seat. "I wish we could be more help. Trust me, I've thought about that night over and over again. Wondered what I could have done differently. Wished we'd stayed out longer. We might have been able to save her." He blew out a breath and shrugged. "Nothing comes to mind. Nothing at all. I've beat myself up over it for years, but still nothing."

Lane asked a few more questions, but they were hollow, useless ones. These guys obviously didn't have anything to offer. He was grasping at straws. When they finished, he stood and stuck out a hand. "Thanks again for coming in. I'll let you know if I have any other questions."

Mitch took his hand in a firm shake. "You're welcome. Happy to help."

Gable clasped Lane's shoulder. "Listen, I'll pray about this. I'll pray for God's blessings and His protection over these young girls. That He'll speak to you, help you catch this guy."

"Thanks," Lane said.

"It wouldn't hurt if you put in a few prayers yourself. If you ever need me… or God. We're here."

Lane snorted a laugh. "I don't think God listens to me anymore."

Gable's smile held a hint of pity. As if Lane were a lost soul, doomed for eternity. "Just because you turned your back on Him doesn't mean He's turned His back on you."

****

I knocked on Corrine and Vic Broussard's door. I hadn't visited them in months. Being around Katie's parents was hard. I hated looking into their faces, seeing my own grief and helplessness reflected there. But it was selfish of me to avoid it. So I knocked harder.

Corrine opened the door. Her face lit with that odd mixture of pleasure and sadness she'd honed to perfection over the years. Each time I saw her, I wondered if Katie would have looked like her had she lived. Corrine was blond and petite like her daughter had been, pretty in spite of the wrinkles and grief etched on her face.

Vic pulled me into a hug that wasn't as strong as it used to be. Once handsome and muscular, the years and sorrow had worn on him, making him seem feeble and older than his sixty-five years. They led me to the kitchen, where we always sat when we visited. That suited me just fine. In the living room, they'd left Katie's jacket hanging over the back of a chair since her death. After a quarter of a century, that struck me as a little unbalanced. In spite of my understanding that they were grieving parents, I preferred not to sit in the room with the reminder.

Corrine set a plate of homemade blueberry scones in

front of me, along with a steaming mug of coffee. I dutifully picked up a pastry, although I had no appetite.

"Monroe, sweetie." She settled on the opposite side of the kitchen table and took my free hand in hers. "Those pennies I found. I still have a strong feeling they have some kind of meaning. Are they some kind of message? And now, with that—that animal using them for his evil." Her voice broke and she shuddered. "Do you think Katie was trying to communicate with me? That maybe she can help find the man who killed her?"

A wave of helpless sympathy moved through me. "I'm sorry, Corrine. I want desperately to believe the same, but I think they were just complete coincidence."

Tears coursed down her cheeks. She released my hands and swiped the tears away. "I wanted them to be a message from Katie so badly that I think I convinced myself that's what they were. I'm just a foolish old woman."

A knot formed in my throat. I set my untouched scone on the plate, but took a drink of the coffee. "You are not. You're a mother who needs closure. Who needs to see her child's killer caught. I totally get that."

A smile tilted the corners of her mouth, but didn't reach her eyes. "You're a good girl, Monroe. Smart too."

She said the same words every time we spoke. Actually, all our conversations seemed to be duplicates of this one. Was she that consumed with her daughter's death and the past? Or was her mind starting to slip so that she didn't remember we'd already had the conversation? As always, Vic sat silently by, letting Corrine do all the talking.

I stayed long enough to assuage my guilt, then stood to go. I hugged them both, leaving with a heavy heart, with that twinge of remorse that I'd survived and Katie hadn't. That she'd been taken while under my watch. That I couldn't help bring the maniac guilty of her murder to justice.

I was only twelve, I excused.

It didn't help.

I stepped outside, drawing in a deep lungful of the evening spring air. The sound of a car made me turn. Lane's Crown Vic pulled to the curb. I waited, pulse pounding. He climbed from the car and approached.

"Lane? What are you doing here? Has something happened? How did you know where to find me?"

He hesitated as if I wouldn't like what he had to say. "We've been following you from time to time. Just keeping an eye out."

"Following me? You don't trust me?"

"No, for God's sake, no. It's not like that at all. We're not following you because we're suspicious. We're watching out for you. Looking for any opportunity to get a bead on this fucking psycho."

I nodded. I couldn't be angry at that. They could follow me night and day if it meant nabbing that bastard.

"So, what now?"

He shrugged and glanced around the neighborhood. "Beats me." His gaze landed back on my face. "Truth is, I'd planned to keep my distance. I didn't want to intrude on your privacy. And I know you wanted me to stay away from you." His voice softened. "But I don't think I can."

Tears surfaced in my throat. "I didn't *want* you to stay away. I needed you to."

"Because you hate me? Or because you don't?"

He waited, his cobalt gaze trapping mine, reeling me

in. I struggled to breathe, struggled to resist, but I swayed, gravitating toward him as if pulled by an invisible string.

The shrill ring of his phone stopped my forward momentum.

He huffed out a breath and snapped the phone open. "Brody," he barked.

I watched as he listened to the caller, a multitude of emotions chasing over his face.

"Ah shit," he said after a few seconds. "Is she okay?" He listened again. "I'll be there shortly."

He hung up, and I searched his face. "Is everything okay?"

He pursed his lips. "Johnny Price, Shelly Crane's boyfriend—the one who molested Mindy—just attacked another girl. They have him at the station. I need to go."

"Should I come with you? If he's the one calling me maybe I will recognize his voice. Maybe he's the killer, and you can prove it now."

"Don't get your hopes up. Too many things point to him not being our guy. But yeah, we will need you to see if you can identify him." He ran a hand through his hair. "Of course, the caller disguises his voice, but you still might hear something familiar. We'll process Price first, question him before we have you listen. We'll record it. I'll get back with you, okay?"

I nodded, trying not to let Lane's doubt cloud my hope that they'd finally found the right guy.

I watched him climb into his car and drive away, wondering what would have happened if the call hadn't interrupted us. Wondering if I'd have regretted it as much as I regretted the fact that I'd never know.

****

I went by Bart's coffee shop, even though it wasn't my usual spot, and it was a little out of the way. He'd been on my mind a lot. Not because of any attraction I felt toward him, but because of his tragic story, his risking himself to save me, and his ridiculous—yet admirable—sense of loyalty.

He was behind the counter, and he grinned when he saw me. "Well, this is a nice surprise." He pushed his glasses up his nose. "What brings you here?"

"The need for a great cup of coffee. You promised me free coffee for life, if you remember."

He placed a hand over his chest in mock pain. "And I thought it was my unwavering charm."

I leaned my elbows on the counter. "That's what made me come *here* for a great cup of coffee."

He laughed. "Nice save. What's your pleasure?"

"Being served by the owner. I'm honored."

"Don't get too high and mighty. I work the front a lot."

I smiled. "You can't just let me have my fantasy? I'll take a dark roast with a shot of espresso."

"Damn, woman. Do you have an iron stomach?"

"I'm a girl who likes her java strong."

He grabbed a cup and went over to a large stainless steel machine. The loud grinding of the espresso maker momentarily prevented the opportunity for conversation. After adding coffee to the cup, he slid it in front of me. I dosed it with a small amount of half and half, then took a sip. The coffee was good, but not as good as my favorite hangout. I lied and said it was better.

Bart and I chatted in between his waiting on customers. When I'd finished most of my coffee, he came back over to me. "Hey, listen," he said. "I'm heading out in a second. Want to go grab a bite to eat or something?"

"I have beef stew in the crockpot at home. Not exactly a gourmet meal, but you're welcome to come over for dinner."

The smile on his face warmed my heart. Lane could have had all of me, and he'd let it go. Bart was overjoyed at the thought of doing nothing more than sharing a meal. Why couldn't I muster even a smidgen of the feelings for Bart that I had for Lane?

****

Tony was interviewing Price when Lane arrived at the station. He watched through the window and listened in through the speaker.

Using his intimidating voice and posture, Tony loomed over Price. "Look, you little pervert. We got you. You might as well confess. You're a sick son of a bitch who hurts little girls."

His mouth drew in. "I might… like young girls, but I don't kill them. I'd never hurt them."

Tony pounded his fist on the table. "You think forcing yourself on them doesn't hurt them?"

Price looked up, lips trembling, but didn't speak.

"Then, maybe you sometimes get carried away. You get so worked up, you get violent. You murder them, Price. Isn't that the way it is?"

"No!" Johnny shouted. Even through the window, Lane could see saliva fly from his mouth, see his body quaking.

Pushing away from Price, Tony pointed a finger in his face. "You're in a shitload of trouble. I'm going to leave you here to think about how you want to play this. If you want to come clean, things might go easier on you.

If you make us work for the truth, you won't like the results."

Tony slammed out of the interview room. He walked over to Lane and pushed the sides of his suit jacket back, resting his hands on his hips.

"You want to take a run at him?" Tony asked. Frustration emanated from him in waves.

Lane shook his head. "He's not likely our guy." Price had been in jail at the time of at least one of the murders.

"Shit. I know." Tony crossed his arms over his chest. "We'll have to settle for sending him back for violating his parole, for assaulting that girl."

"I'll take the recording to Monroe. See if his voice sounds familiar at all. I'm sure it's a waste of time. Not only is he not our guy, the caller disguises his voice."

"Yeah. Waste of time, but at least you have an excuse to see Monroe again, right?"

Lane narrowed his eyes. "What I need is to stay away from her."

"Right." Tony gave a derisive smile. "But what we need and want are seldom the same."

Chapter 16

Bart and I were just sitting down to dinner when a knock sounded on the door. I opened it to find Paxton standing on the other side. Her face was drawn into a sullen frown.

"Paxton?" I looked past her out into the street. Tony's car was nowhere in sight. "What's up? Did your dad bring you?"

She shook her head. "He doesn't know I'm here. I had to get the hell out of there." She let out a bitter laugh. "Since I don't have any friends here, I had nowhere else to go."

"Thanks. Nice to know where I rate." I tried to infuse some humor in my tone, but she didn't seem to find it amusing. "How did you get here?"

She shrugged. "Walked."

"You walked all this way? Your dad will go nuts."

"Like he gives a damn."

"Come in. I'll call your dad and let him know you're okay. Of course he cares."

She paused uncertainly before entering.

I rolled my eyes at her hesitation. Had she walked all this way just to hang out on my porch?

She saw Bart and came to a standstill. "Who's that?"

"Bart Holland, Paxton Webber." I introduced them then picked up my phone to dial. "After I speak to your dad, we'll have a chat about manners," I told her. "I

209

won't have you being rude to my guests."

When Tony answered, I let him know Paxton had shown up on my doorstep.

"Shit," he bit out. "I was just taking Cadence to ball practice. I'll drop him off instead of watching, then swing by and pick her up. Sorry, Roe."

"It's no problem. I don't mind her staying here, but I figured you'd be worried."

"Hell. I thought she was in her room." Guilt mingled with the irritation in his tone.

"She can stay until you're done, if you want. I think she'd rather hang out here than watch Cadence's practice."

"You sure you don't mind? I appreciate it. That'll give me time to come up with a suitable punishment. I guess I can ground her."

"Ground her from what?" I asked, keeping my voice low. "She has no friends, nothing to do. What are you going to ground her from?"

His response was a frustrated sigh. "I'll be there in a little over an hour."

When we hung up, I said to Paxton, "You hungry?"

She nodded.

"You like stew?"

She shrugged. "It's okay." She turned to Bart. "Sorry I was rude. I'm just in a pissy mood. Nice to meet you."

I didn't tell him that 'pissy' was her *only* mood.

"Nice to meet you." Bart winked and dropped his tone conspiratorially. "No sweat. I get in a pissy mood sometimes myself."

She smiled, and it transformed her face. I saw the beauty she was destined to be. She should smile more often.

"Sit, and I'll get a bowl," I said. "You want something to drink? Diet Pepsi, Dr Pepper, tea?"

She sat in the chair next to Bart. "Tea would be good. Sweet tea."

I poured her a glass and joined them at the table.

While we ate, Bart elicited details from her that I'd had no idea about. She liked to draw and had aspirations of getting into graphic arts design. She liked classic rock and hip hop, but didn't care much for rap. She actually laughed a few times, and by the time Tony came to pick her up, her mood was loose and chipper. I raised my brows at Bart. He must have some kind of special gift.

After Tony left, Bart helped me clear the table. We were loading the dishwasher when the doorbell rang. Odd, I rarely had company, and this would be the third guest in one evening.

I looked through the peephole and lost my breath when I saw Lane standing on my porch.

****

Monroe opened the door, her chocolate brown eyes darkening with concern. "Hi, Lane. I wasn't expecting you. Did you find out something? Is he the guy?"

"I don't think so. We're still checking out a few things. Can I come in?" He pulled the tape from his pocket. "I brought a recording of—" The words died in his throat when Bart Holland appeared behind Monroe. He rested a hand on her shoulder—familiarly, possessively, like he had the right. A primal urge to smash his fist in the man's face rose. Lane just barely made himself resist.

"Hello, Detective," Holland said. "Is everything okay?"

Lane felt as though he'd been gut punched. His breath seized in his lungs, and he forgot what he'd been saying. His eyes moved to Monroe's face. Her expression held a hint of guilt and sympathy. Sympathy was the last thing he wanted from her. He didn't even want to think about the first thing he wanted. That was never going to happen.

"I just. I stopped by to…" He inhaled sharply, a jagged pain ripping through his mid-section. "I need to speak with Monroe alone."

Bart looked down at her, and she turned her face up to him. In Lane's imagination, he saw the bastard bending, saw Monroe lifting her lips to meet his, saw them sharing a passionate kiss as though Lane wasn't even there. But, in reality, she simply smiled her gut-wrenching smile. "Could you excuse us please? It won't take long."

Lane held back the words that surfaced in his mind. *How do you know that? How do you know how long I'll need you? Maybe I'll need you forever.*

He pinched the bridge of his nose between his thumb and forefinger, staunching the threat of tears. *Tears? Are you kidding me?*

Jesus Christ, he was a piece of work. He'd ended things with her. He'd chosen to stay in his fucked up marriage, and now he was acting like the wounded party.

"Thanks, dude," Lane said to Bart. He stretched his lips into a smile that felt as though it strained every muscle in his face.

"Sure. No problem. I'll take a walk."

"See you in a few," Monroe said.

After Holland left, Lane turned back to Monroe. He couldn't seem to speak. Instead, he stood there, staring at her, feeling foolish and sad.

"You wanted to talk to me?" she asked. "What is it?"

Somehow summoning words, he said, "I have the recording. Price's voice. I thought you could listen to it and…"

Her face lit with hope. "Yeah. Of course." She stepped back to allow him inside.

He inhaled a bit of her spring rain scent as he passed by. He must be some kind of fucking masochist.

"You and Holland are getting pretty chummy, it seems." His words sealed the loser/fool image he'd apparently been trying to cultivate.

"We're just friends."

Lane was grateful that she didn't add, *not that it's any of your business.* It wasn't, but he was still glad she didn't add it.

"I don't want to keep you any longer than necessary." He held up the recorder, making an effort to return to cop mode. "Listen closely. See if you can identify anything about his voice, his phrasing, anything at all."

Pathetic, he knew, but he held the machine purposely close to his body, so she'd have to get near him to hear, so he could continue to torture himself.

She listened, head tilted, nose scrunched in concentration.

When the tape ended, she shook her head. "Nothing. Not familiar at all."

"Damn," Lane bit out. "I can't say I'm surprised, though. Price has an alibi for at least a couple of the murders. For one of them, he was in prison. Can't get much more solid than that."

"I'm sorry," Monroe said. "I'm really sorry I had to

disappoint you."

Lane met her gaze, and knew she wasn't just talking about the tape. He lifted a hand and trickled a finger along her jaw line. "It's okay. Believe me. I understand."

Her full lips curved in a smile, and she gave a jerky nod.

He managed to hang onto his masculinity and tell her goodbye without his voice quivering. He managed to shake Holland's hand when he returned to Monroe's as Lane was stepping off the porch. He even managed to get inside his car without so much as a hint of a reaction.

But once he'd driven a mile down her road, he pulled to the side, dropped his head on to the steering wheel, and released the groan of anguish welling in his chest.

****

The girl had the curves of a woman, but he'd bet she was no more than sixteen or seventeen. She carried a book bag over her shoulder and walked with a little boy wearing a backward ball cap—her brother, he presumed.

She gazed down at the boy with rapt affection. "Okay, that was good, but you missed one of the words. If you can get them all right this time and make a hundred on your spelling test, I'll get you ice cream after daycare and play Madden with you."

The boy stopped walking and stomped his foot. "They're hard. Can I still get ice cream if I miss some, but you just don't play Madden with me?"

The girl laughed. She had a nice, tinkling laugh. Lovely blue eyes that sparkled in the morning sunlight. Maybe he should snatch the brother too. He'd bet the girl would be extra cooperative if he did.

"Hey," she said, removing something from the boy's

hand. "What are you doing taking this to school?"

"I like to play with Hot Wheels."

"You can't take toys to school. I'll hold onto it, and you can have it back after you get out of daycare." She dropped the car into the outside pocket of her book bag.

They moved on, the girl's voice fading as she said, "One more time. Spell 'boat.'"

The boy heaved a deep sigh. The man followed them from a distance. He was no longer able to make out their words, but could hear the murmur of their voices.

Before he could decide whether to snatch them both, they'd reached the daycare. Just as well, he'd have his hands full with one victim. Two would be too much. Besides, Monroe would be confused. Her articles wouldn't have the same tone if he killed a kid along with the teenager. Best to stick to his regular MO.

Excitement coursed through his veins as he approached the girl. What little gem would she offer him that he could pass along to Monroe? The anticipation was almost as much fun as the act itself.

Her wide eyes turned to his when he touched her shoulder. Before she had time to cry out, his hand was over her mouth, and he dragged her to his car. Good thing she'd cut through a quiet neighborhood. Snatching victims from a busy street was godawfully risky.

****

Lane shifted in the witness seat. He hated testifying at trials. Hated being put in the spotlight and having his integrity questioned. He'd rather run through hell wearing gasoline britches.

"What did you discover when you entered the apartment?" The prosecutor, Blain Collier, stood with his hands clasped behind his back as he waited for a response.

Lane leaned into the microphone. "I discovered the victim, Ms. Benson, crouching on the floor, her clothing ripped to shreds."

"Did she tell you what happened?"

"She was so hysterical, she could barely form words. Finally, she told me she'd been raped."

"Detective Brody," the Judge interrupted. "Please refrain from using the word 'rape.' It's incendiary."

Lane turned to the judge, his eyebrows raised in disbelief. "No disrespect, Your Honor, but rape is pretty damned incendiary."

The judge's forehead wrinkled in a scowl. "I'll cite you with contempt, Detective Brody, if you don't follow the Court's instructions."

Lane clenched his jaw and once more leaned into the mic. Enunciating each word, he said, "The victim had been brutally, horrifically, savagely forced to participate in violent intercourse, entirely against her will."

A murmur rose in the galley. The judge banged his gavel. "That will be enough, Detective."

Collier's mouth tilted in amusement. "No more questions."

To Lane's relief, the defense chose not to cross examine.

After Lane exited the courtroom, Tony called his cell.

"We have a missing girl," Tony said. "The mom called it in a few hours ago."

"And?"

"She's just about right for our psycho. Sixteen years old. She walked her brother to daycare this morning, and no one's seen her since. Mom was at work, and didn't know her daughter was missing until she failed to pick up her brother. We've put out an APB."

"Shit. Name, description."

Lane listened intently while heading to his car.

He slapped the phone shut, anxiety working at his gut. Teens came up missing all the time. Mostly it was something harmless, teens being teens. But he had a terrible premonition that this was a hell of a lot more.

Chapter 17

The girl cowered on the floor, trapped by her bindings. Tears dripped from beneath the blindfold, staining her purple blouse.

He ran his hands through the pile of pennies. Not a damn one from 2006. "Shit. I'm afraid I'm going to have to run a quick errand. You don't go anywhere, okay?"

She whimpered, and he grinned. What was it about the abject terror, the helplessness, that gave him such a rush?

He looked up at the blades hanging above her head. He'd let her see them before he'd covered her eyes. Nothing like a little intimidation to escalate the terror.

"Who'd have thought, out of all these pennies, I wouldn't have one from the year your brother was born? What's his name? Oh yeah, Jacob. Cute kid. Glad you took his car away from him. Makes everything click into place, like it was meant to be."

"You—you're the Penny Killer." It was an accusation, not a question.

"Bingo. I bet you're a straight-A student." He shoved the pennies back in the bag, purposely making as much noise as possible. Her trembling increased. *Nice.*

"I'll be back in a flash. Try not to miss me too much."

He secured both doors before he left. No way would anyone show up, and no way could she could get loose, but he hadn't enjoyed all these years of success without taking those extra precautions. Whistling, he slipped the keys in his pocket and headed to his car.

****

Lane cruised the streets, although he knew it was a fruitless venture. If their guy had her, she was tucked away somewhere no one would find her. Not until the bastard was ready for her to be found. He slammed his palm against the steering wheel. "Mother fucker," he muttered.

His phone rang again. Tony. Too much to hope they'd found her…

"Don't know if this means anything to you," Tony said, "But the autopsy report on Mindy Wainwright came back. Those fibers were asbestos, and the dust was chalk."

"Chalk? As in school chalk?"

"Could be. You think this guy is using a school? Since they're out for the summer, they'd be empty."

"Nah. He wouldn't be that stupid. Schools still maintain staff during the summer—lawn care, maintenance workers and stuff. Besides, asbestos hasn't been used since the 80's."

"Then where would it be coming from?"

Lane tapped his fingers on the steering wheel, his mind clicking. "There are a dozen abandoned school buildings in KC. Two of them were closed before the late 80's when asbestos was ordered removed."

"Damn, Huck. I knew your trivia bullshit would come in handy someday. You know where they're located?"

"One's on Grover. I'm not far from there. I'll head over. You can check out the one at Fourth and Spires.

Call for back up."

He slipped the phone back into the holder on his belt and pressed down on the accelerator. The spike of adrenaline told him they were onto something. The dread expanding in his chest told him they would be too late.

****

I passed on MPM and stayed at home. The last thing I was in the mood for was a girl's night out. The awkward moment with Lane and Bart and the visit with Katie's parents had my nerves on edge, even if a psycho killer wasn't playing a sick, dangerous game with me.

He hadn't called in days. I should be relieved, but his silence was almost as frightening as his calls. What was he doing? Searching out another victim to present as a gift? Why couldn't I do something to stop him? Get some kind of clue from what he said in his calls?

Maybe I could add something to one of my articles to draw him out. He wasn't stupid, though. The old 'meet me so I can interview you' trick had failed miserably.

I put in an Elvis CD, hoping his music would soothe me as it normally did. Even when one of my favorites, "Walk a Mile in My Shoes" played, my mood remained morose.

I sat at my computer, putting Cameron Cooper's name in the search engine. He'd been in jail for years on rape charges. A few of the murders had taken place during that time. As Lane determined, Johnny Price had also been incarcerated during a few of them. Michael Finlay, the guy who attacked me was dead, and still the killings hadn't stopped. I sat back and clenched my hair in a fist of frustration. If the police couldn't get anything on a suspect, how the hell did I think I could?

The thought I'd tried to keep in the recesses of my

mind once more surfaced. If I'd never written those articles, would he have stayed dormant? Had my writing inflamed him, unleashed a killer back out into the world?

I recalled the look on Katie's mother's face when she'd spoken about the murderer using the pennies. Although she hadn't said so, I knew that one disturbing fact added to her sorrow, her frustration that the person who'd slaughtered her child was enjoying a new reign of terror. With me right in the center of his spotlight.

****

The school was dark and held a musty smell of disuse. Lane could almost hear the sounds of the long ago children who'd stampeded the halls. Somehow, it was interwoven with the heavy silence.

He cautiously made his way down the long corridor, slowing at each classroom, inching the doors open one at a time. Nothing so far, but if the suspect was in the building, the creaking of the hinges might alert him to Lane's presence. Too bad he hadn't brought WD-40.

Lane turned a corner, his glance shooting down the darkened hallway. A faint light shone at a door halfway down. His heart thumped hard in his chest. Silently, he crept toward the door, Beretta drawn.

His blood froze when the murmur of a man's voice reached his ears. This was it. He'd found him. He just hoped he'd found him before the girl had met her end.

The knob turned beneath his hand, and Lane eased the door open, gun pointed.

"That's far enough," a male voice barked. He spoke in a harsh, whispery tone.

Lane halted. A girl sat scrunched against the wall, a blindfold over her eyes. The room was dimly lit, but he could still see her terror. Could almost smell it.

"Come out where I can see you," Lane demanded, taking a step forward.

"If you release the door, she dies. Look above her head."

Lane's gaze traveled upward. His breath seized. Some kind of metal blade contraption was suspended directly above where the girl sat.

What the…?

"The mechanism is connected to the wire on the door. I'm also holding a wire in my hand. Either of us lets go, and she's mincemeat."

The amusement in the bastard's voice was like the sound of nails on the chalkboard hanging on the wall behind the victim. He stood somewhere toward the back of the room, hidden in the shadows, behind the door Lane was now afraid to let go of.

"You can't get away," Lane bit out, but he was very afraid that he could.

"You let go or I let go, she dies. I'll leave out the back door, tie the end of the wire to the knob."

Lane moved the Beretta where it pointed in the general direction of the killer. "I can blow your ass away before you can make it to the door."

"Yeah, and then those big mean blades slice her into little pieces. Toss your weapon aside, and I'll leave, then you can figure out how to save her, hero. But if you let go of the door or don't put your gun down, she dies. Is it worth her losing her life for you to capture me?"

Blood rushed to Lane's head so hard, he thought his brain would explode. *Son of a bitch. Insane, twisted son of a bitch.*

He had no choice. But to let a murderer walk free? They'd never even been close to catching this guy, and now he was within a few feet of Lane's grasp. All he had to do was release the door and...

His gaze went back to the terrified, *innocent* girl.

"Fuck," he growled low in his throat. He gingerly squatted and slid his weapon a few feet away.

A bark of satisfied laughter came from the killer. "I take that as acquiescence. See you on the flip side, Brody."

Lane stood helplessly while the shadowed figure backed toward the door. Lane couldn't make out his features, couldn't see the wire he claimed to have, but he doubted it was a bluff. He wasn't going to risk the girl's life to find out.

Every muscle in his shoulders and neck tightened as he waited. What if the asshole released the wire anyway? What if, in spite of Lane's best efforts, he had to stand here and watch the girl die a horrific death?

His jaw set with determination. If that happened, he had no reason to hold his position. The mother fucker couldn't get far enough fast enough to escape Lane's wrath. And once he got his hands on him...

If he did what he wanted to do, he'd be suspended from the force, maybe brought up on charges.

Knowing the bastard had finally paid for his crimes would make it all worthwhile.

Chapter 18

"It's all right, sweetheart. He's gone." Lane held back the anger, gentling his voice. "Help will be here soon."

Nerves strung tight, he pulled his cell from his pocket and called Tony to put out an APB on the suspect. As he closed his phone, he heard the sound of rushing footsteps. Backup had arrived.

Two patrolmen approached from the hallway. Lane spoke to the younger one. "Hold this door open, and keep it open as if your life depended on it." He didn't bother to tell him that Shayne Burris's life *did* depend on it.

The young officer's brow creased. "Huh?"

"Just do it," Lane gritted.

The guy grabbed the door, and Lane rushed over to the girl and knelt. Gently, he tugged off the blindfold. Terrified eyes blinked like a newborn baby bird's.

"It's all right, Shayne," Lane whispered. "I've got you. Just hold on a few seconds, and I'll have you free."

Her gaze shot upward. "Th-there's a thing... blades," A gasp of terror left her throat. "Above my head. Don't let it fall. Please, please don't let it fall."

"I won't. Don't worry. Help is here now. I won't let anything happen to you." Lane worked her bindings loose as he spoke soft, reassuring words. Once she was free, he hugged her, patting her head while she sobbed against his chest.

Not long after he heard the wail of sirens, two EMT's burst through the door. Lane backed up and let them take over, a small part of him wondering if he'd really done the right thing. How many other girls would die because he'd saved this one?

****

Lane scrubbed a hand over his face. How long had it been since he'd slept? Since he'd slept well, anyway.

"The fucker." Tony rolled a Kush ball between his hands. "That's some diabolical shit, man."

"Yeah." Lane kept envisioning the asshole climbing out the window as he stood there powerlessly watching. Kept hearing the smugness in the whispering voice. Swear to God, if he got ahold of him... *when* he got ahold of him...

They'd been to the hospital to talk to Shayne Burris. She knew nothing. Her little brother was there, and he seemed to be all she could focus on. She hadn't seen the man's face. He'd grabbed her from behind. Nothing identifiable about his voice. Not a goddamned thing they could use. So, what else was new?

Still, he'd asked the girl and her family to come into the station to answer further questions. She'd been released from the hospital within a few hours, no worse off, other than the emotional trauma that would likely stay with her forever.

The desk phone rang, and when he picked it up, the receptionist said, "The Burris's are here."

"Thanks." Lane rose and went into the interview room.

Shayne's father stood and gripped Lane's hand in a firm shake. His eyes clung to Lane's. "I don't know what to—" He shook his head. "You saved our daughter's life."

Maggie Burris looked at Lane as though he were the second coming. She clung to her daughter's hand, tears swimming in her eyes. "Thank you. Thank you so much. You're a bona fide hero."

Lane squirmed at the praise. "Happy I could help, ma'am." He looked at Shayne. "I'm just glad I got there in time."

"Me too." Shayne smiled. She was pretty, with curly dark hair and a figure too developed for a sixteen-year-old. Would the Penny Killer have raped her before he took her life?

Lane shook away the thought. Neither of those things happened, thank God. Now, he had to focus on finding out all he could. Something that would help them nail the bastard.

"I'd like to ask your son a few questions," he said to Shayne's mother. "With your permission, of course."

"Sure." Maggie Burris nodded. "I'm not sure how much help he can be, but ask away."

Lane turned to Jacob. The boy wore a Royals cap tugged down over his blond hair. He pushed his glasses up his nose with a tiny forefinger and stared expectantly at Lane.

"Jake—can I call you Jake, or do you like Jacob better?"

"I like Jake."

"Okay, then, Jake it is. When your sister walked you to daycare, did you see anyone around who might have been watching you two?"

Jacob scrunched his brow and shook his head.

"No one at all that looked a little… scary. Or maybe not even scary. Maybe just kind of like he shouldn't be around your daycare? A stranger who didn't belong."

The boy swung his short legs as he considered the questions. "Didn't see no one. But I was thinking about my Hot Wheel and how my sister wouldn't let me keep it."

"Okay, that's fine. You did great."

Lane smiled at Shayne. "How are you doing?"

She drew in a trembling breath. "I'm okay. Still a little shaken up, but thanks to you, I'm fine."

"Listen, could you do me a favor and take your brother into the lobby so I can talk to your parents? Ask the lady at the desk, Mona, and she'll get you guys a snack and something to drink."

Shayne nodded and stood. Taking Jake's hand, she led him out the door.

Once they were gone, Lane said, "I know this isn't going to set well with the two of you, but I think Shayne could still be in danger. We'd like to put your family up in a safe house for a while."

Hal Burris scowled. "Safe house? You think that's necessary?"

"I think so. This guy's probably madder than a scalded cat that Shayne escaped."

Maggie's hand flew to her mouth. "You think he might come after her?"

"I think it's possible. I think it's a risk you don't want to take."

Hal buried his head in his hands. "What about work?"

"Can you take off for a while?"

He massaged his forehead. "I don't see how. I'd probably lose my job."

"We can't have you driving back and forth to the

227

safe house. Since your daughter's the one in danger, we can put your family up, and you can stay home and keep working."

They looked at one another. Hal slowly nodded. "I guess that would be best. Where will they be?"

"Sorry." Lane grimaced with dread. Hal Burris wasn't going to like what he had to say. "We won't tell you where they'll be."

"What? I can't even know where my own family is?"

"No. It's more secure that way. If the killer decided to get to them through you, he might…" Lane let out a breath between pursed lips. "Might torture you to get the information."

Hal's face blanched. He nodded.

"I'll have some officers escort you home so Maggie and the kids can grab a few things. They'll take them straight to a secure location. Where they'll be until this is over. Until he's caught."

Moisture swam in Hal's eyes. "Isn't this the same guy who's been getting by with murder for twenty-five years?" He barked out a strangled laugh. "Are you telling me I might never see my family again?"

****

"How you doin' darlin'?"

I looked up from the break room table into Asia's worried face and forced a smile. Asia only knew part of what was going on. How concerned would she be if she knew about a demented killer aligning himself with me?

"I'm okay. I'd be better if the Penny Killer were caught. Other than that, I'm fine. I mean, the thing with Lane…" I shrugged, purposely making my voice nonchalant. "It was doomed from the start."

"Sorry."

"No. Don't be. My fault. And you were right. I shouldn't have been holding out for a married man who couldn't break off from his psychotic wife. I'm moving on."

Asia took the chair across from me. "Moving on with a new man? Your hero, Bart?"

I grimaced. "No, 'fraid not. Zero attraction there."

"On your part, I assume? I bet the guy's crazy about you."

Lifting my cup, I took a long drink of coffee. "Not sure how crazy he is about me, but I think he likes me more than I do him. Not going to happen, though."

Asia nodded. "I know I keep pushing you to find another man, but truth is you probably need a break. No sense in rushing into another relationship after getting your heart broken."

I sighed with relief. "My thoughts exactly."

"Better get back to work." She stood and squeezed my hand. "Love ya, girl."

"Love you too." I smiled at her retreating back. No matter how jacked up everything else was in my life, it was nice to know I had her in my corner.

Break over, I returned to my desk and sat, staring at the computer. I was reading over my article about a mugging in Overland Park, Kansas, when my cell rang.

The display read "Burris." Shit. Wasn't that the girl Lane had rescued?

Something frightening unwound in my chest.

"Hello?"

"Monroe." His voice sounded despondent. Was he bummed that he lost out on a kill?

"What do you want?"

Alicia Dean

"It's what I *don't* want. I don't want you to write an article about my failure."

"What?"

"That asshole cop. If I ever run into him again…"

He'll fucking kill you, I finished silently.

"You know the *Chronicle* will have to run the story, right?" I asked, adding a touch of sarcasm to the question.

He didn't seem to notice. "Nothing I can do about that. But I couldn't bear it if you wrote those things about me. I want you to see me as… I don't know… invincible."

Invincible? I'd rather see him dead. Not only was I fed up, crazy pissed over the killings, I was tired of him dictating my career. But what could I do other than go along? "I won't write the article," I promised.

Without waiting for a response, I disconnected the call, then dialed Tony's number to let him know I'd heard from the psycho again.

****

Lane sat in the chair next to Catherine's and listened to her ramble. She'd been extremely communicative the last few times he'd visited. Hadn't uttered more than a few words the past two years, and now she never took a break. She talked about their past, about what they would do when she was released, about all the friends they'd need to catch up with. Like they were a normal couple who'd just had a rough go of it lately. Like she'd ever be normal… or free.

His attention came back when he felt her hand caress his thigh. He hadn't even noticed she'd moved closer, but she was on the edge of her chair, leaning toward him.

His eyes focused on her face. Revulsion washed

230

through him. She had that pouty look, the half-lidded eyes and pursed lips he'd once thought sexy. These days, everything about her made his skin crawl. Cupping a hand on the back of his neck, she pulled him closer, touching her lips to his. He didn't pull back, but also didn't return the kiss. His neck stiffened, and he silently prayed for it to be over, that this would be all she wanted.

Catherine broke the kiss, her eyes roaming curiously over his face. "What is it, Lane? Is something wrong?"

"Nothing," he bit out.

"I want you," she whispered. "Make love to me."

He didn't answer, couldn't bring himself to tell her no, but couldn't stomach her touch a moment longer. Gripping her wrist, he tugged her hand from his neck.

Her face twisted into an ugly mask. "What the hell?" She shot to her feet. "Who is she, Lane?"

He stood, moving a few steps away from her. "What are you talking about?"

"There must be someone else, or you wouldn't deny me."

He turned his back to her, and remained silent.

"Ah, so there is." Her harsh laugh screeched through the room. "That's hilarious. You can't keep one woman satisfied, why would you take on another?"

"I won't discuss this with you, Catherine."

"Oh, but you will, darling." She moved around him until they were once more face to face. "Tell me about her. What's she like? Will she settle for a struggling *cop*? She must be some ghetto piece of trash, if she will."

"Stop it," he bit out.

She's not well. Ignore her.

Tears filled her violet-blue eyes, and her lips drew back in a snarl. "Tell me who she is. Who have you been fucking behind my back?"

He stepped around her and headed to the door. "I'll come back when you're feeling better."

She strode across the room and gripped his arm, yanking hard, her fingers digging into his flesh. He halted, screwing his eyes shut for a few seconds before turning to stare down at her.

"Whoever the bitch is," she spat, her mouth twisted with cruelty. "If I ever run into her, she'll wish she'd never laid eyes on you. Got it?"

The thin piece of thread that had been holding his anger at bay snapped like dry kindling. He'd never despised anyone like he despised his wife at that moment. And he'd seen the worst society had to offer.

"You know what, Catherine?" He shook her grip loose and grabbed her shoulders, squeezing tightly. "Your threats are useless. You'll never lay eyes on her. You know why? Because, you'll be locked up for the rest of your selfish, miserable life."

"What? No." She tugged against his hold. "Let me go."

"Not quite yet." He brought his face close to hers and glared into those beautiful, soulless eyes. "You know why you'll never be free? Because, you murdered Joseph." He ignored her gasp. "Remember him? He's one of the many men you fucked while you were married to *me*."

"No." She let out a strangled cry. "Stop it." She tried to lift her hands to her ears, but he held her arms down to her sides.

"That's right. You murdered your lover because he was dumping your ass. He didn't want you anymore, Catherine, just like I don't. *Fuck* loyalty. Only people who deserve loyalty should have it. I won't be tied down to a commitment I made to someone as heartless and evil as you."

He released her roughly, and she stumbled back, covering her face with her hands. "Joseph. I remember now. I killed him."

"Yeah. Just like you killed our marriage. But that was a mercy killing."

He grabbed the handle of the door, and she rushed to him. Taking hold of his shirt tail, she dropped to her knees. "Please, Lane. Please don't leave me. I'm afraid and alone. Please. I'm sorry for whatever I said. I'm sick. You can't desert me."

He shook loose from her. "You *are* sick, Catherine, and I sincerely hope you get better. That way, justice will finally be served, and you'll pay for your crimes. Other than that, I couldn't give a shit what happens to you."

He stormed down the hallway, stalking past Dr. Posell, who'd just left a patient's room and now stood staring at Lane, wide-eyed.

Lane couldn't breathe until he broke free of the hospital doors and was outside, drinking in the cool, fresh air. Air that tasted like freedom.

Freedom. He'd done it. He'd broken the hold Catherine had on him. He was so fucking *done.*

He wouldn't tell Monroe, he wouldn't continue to jerk her emotions around like that. She deserved a break from him and the pain he'd caused. He needed to go to her a completely free man—once the divorce was granted—see if she'd have him then.

Whether or not things worked out with Monroe, the albatross he'd carried for nearly fifteen years had lifted. Life was good.

Alicia Dean

234

Chapter 19

Lane was getting ready to leave for the day when the front desk called back to tell him a woman was there to see him. For a split second, hope that it was Monroe bloomed in his chest. The next words dashed that hope. "Her name is Sanjai Donagy. Says she has to tell you something about a case. I'll send her back."

Through the door of the detective room, a patrol officer escorted a woman who looked to be in her late twenties. Her hair was cropped close on one side, while the other hung long over her shoulder. A streak of purple ran through the long side.

Lane stood and lifted his brows. "Can I help you?"

"I need to talk to you about Michael Finlay."

Lane's interest perked up. "You knew Michael Finlay?"

"Yes." Black streaks of mascara marred her cheeks, like she'd been crying. "We were... he was my guy."

Lane nodded, trying to feel sympathy, but unable to. That's what you get when your 'guy' was a fucking criminal.

"Do you have some information for us?"

"Alls I know is, he wouldn't do that."

So she was just here to defend his honor. Lane quickly lost interest. "He attacked a woman. He *did* do that."

"No, I mean, he wasn't going to hurt her. He

235

wouldn't have killed the girl. Someone hired him to scare her. He wasn't supposed to die."

"How do you know?"

"He told me. We was going to take a trip with the money he made. He got into a lot of trouble with the law, but he was gentle as a kitten. He wouldn't hurt no one."

"You're just now telling us this?"

She shrugged, her eyes dropping away from his. "I was afraid to come in, but I can't sleep. I had to tell the truth."

Lane offered the girl a seat and turned on his recorder. "Tell me everything you know."

She explained how a man had contacted Finlay and asked him to pretend to mug a woman, but that he wasn't to hurt her. She couldn't give a description of the guy, or any information about where he and Michael Finlay met.

"How much was Finlay paid for the job?"

"Five thousand dollars. I still have most of it if you want it back."

"We'll need to process it for evidence." She nodded, but she didn't seem happy about returning the cash. "Did Finlay tell you this guy's name? Anything at all about him that would help identify him?"

"He never said his actual name. When he talked about him, he just called him Coop."

Coop. Shit. Cameron Cooper had hired Finlay to attack Monroe.

****

Linus hunched over a game of solitaire, his gray brows drawn in a frown as he studied the cards. Even with his concentration on the game, he kept our conversation going.

"I told you, Miss Marilyn. No need to check on me.

I'm right as rain."

A faint bruise on his forehead was the only evidence he'd been attacked.

"Just making sure you're okay."

He lifted his head. "How about you? Since you and that detective parted ways?"

I shifted my eyes away. I didn't want to talk to Linus about my relationship with Lane. Discussing a normal one with him would be awkward enough, but mine and Lane's was definitely uncomfortable.

"I'm good," I said, looking at him again. "This is how things should be."

He peered intently at me with his faded blue eyes. "I know it's hard. It hurts. But it's best. I want you happy, and if I thought he could make you happy, I'd be behind it. But I don't want him toying with your affections. Hurting you. Just like when that son of a bitch attacked you last year. Can't stand to see you hurt, girlie, on the outside or the inside."

I smiled, a wave of affection swelling in my heart. "I know. You're always looking out for me, Linus." I patted his wrinkled hand. "Thank you."

His mouth turned up in a brief grin, then he looked back down at the cards. His voice was suspiciously gruff when he spoke again. "Just bein' neighborly, that's all."

He'd once told me that if he had a daughter, he'd want her to be just like me. That same gruffness had been in his tone then. Try as he might to play the tough guy, he was really just an old softy.

My phone rang, and I looked at the display to see Asia's name.

"What's up?" I stood and moved into the living room so as not to break Linus's concentration.

"Why didn't you tell me?"

There were so many things I hadn't told her—like my visit at the cemetery with the killer—that I couldn't guess what she might be referring to. "Tell you what?"

"That Lane ended things with Catherine."

"He what?" My legs turned rubbery, and I sank onto the edge of a nearby chair.

"Don't tell me you didn't know?"

"I—I had no idea. When? How did you know?"

"It happened yesterday. Darion told me."

Lane had told Darion and not me? Did that mean he'd truly decided he didn't love me and, with or without Catherine, he didn't want a relationship? Not that I'd fall into his arms if he did, but he hadn't even *told* me.

"I'm surprised," I said, bitterness tingeing my voice. "What with her mental instability and the dire need to stick by his commitment. It's baffling how he managed to throw all that away."

"Sorry, girl. I can't believe he didn't go directly to you. Maybe he's busy with the case and waiting for the right time."

"Doesn't matter. We can't just pick up where we left off. Too much hurt. Besides, even though he's decided to leave her, they're still married. No matter what he's *said* to her, what he's decided about their relationship, the almighty commitment hasn't yet been broken."

****

Lane and Tony found Cameron Cooper at Dusty's Lounge after asking around at a couple of his known haunts. Just like Judas had done to Jesus, his pals had sold him out—for twenty bucks rather than thirty pieces of silver.

Cooper's legs were hooked around a barstool, his

hand gripped on a foaming beer mug. "Ah, shit," he muttered when Lane appeared on his right side, Tony on his left. "What the hell do you guys want? I ain't done nothin'."

"One, you threatened Monroe Donovan at the shelter." Tony rested an elbow on the bar and began ticking off on his fingers. "Two, you were getting a little chummy with my daughter at the carnival."

Cooper's mouth set in a pout, and his head swiveled back down to his beer. Lane expected him to cover his ears and start humming so he didn't have to listen to what they had to say.

"Three," Lane said, leaning to where he was only an inch or so from Cooper's face. "We heard a little tale about someone named *Coop* paying this asshole named Finlay to beat up Monroe Donovan."

Cooper's head jerked up, almost colliding with Lane's face. "That's bullshit," he shouted. Spittle and beer flew from his lips.

Lane straightened quickly, just barely avoiding the spray. "We have a witness. We know you're pissed about Monroe Donovan naming you as a suspect in her articles. So why don't you give us one good reason not to haul your ass in and book you right now?"

"Because, man. I didn't do it. Swear to God. Don't even know no one named Finlay. If this dude is giving my name, he's framing me. Covering up for someone else."

"He's not giving your name, since he's dead," Tony said flatly. "Someone else gave your name. Said you paid Finlay five grand to rough up Monroe."

The sour look on Cameron's face fled. He howled with laughter, nearly toppling from the barstool. "You have got to be fucking with me right now." He looked to Tony, then to Lane, and laughed harder, wiping moisture from his eyes. "Where the fuck you think I'm gonna get five grand?"

Lane met Tony's eyes over Cooper's head. They'd already considered that. Neither of them believed that, even if Cooper got his hands on that much money, he'd use it to pay someone to beat up Monroe. He might use if for blow, or possibly a place to live.

Lane didn't let his doubt show. "Don't know. How about you tell us? Dealing, maybe? Prostitution? How does a guy like you get hold of five grand, and what made you want to use it to hurt Monroe?"

Amusement hovered in his eyes, but a grimace replaced his earlier mirth. "I didn't hire no one to beat her up. I just want the bitch to leave me alone."

Tony snatched his collar and yanked him off the barstool.

"Hey, hey," the bartender said. "Take it outside."

Holding up a hand, Tony said, "No worries, dude. Not gonna be any trouble."

Putting his face close to Cooper's, visibly tightening his hold on the man's shirt collar, Tony hissed, "If you know what's good for you, you'll leave young girls the fuck alone."

"I didn't—" Cooper started to squeak, but Tony gave him a final jerk, still holding onto him.

"I catch you anywhere near Monroe or my daughter again, I'll pull your intestines out through your asshole, got it?"

Cooper scowled, but managed a nod. Tony thrust him back toward the barstool.

"Fuck," Tony muttered when they stepped outside

the bar.

"I know. No way he hired Finlay. So who the hell did? Are we looking for another 'Coop,' or did someone use his name?"

Tony stared down the darkening street. "Wish I knew, Huck." He shook his head. "Damn sure wish I knew."

****

The next night, Lane stood on Monroe's porch, waiting for her to answer his knock. His gut knotted with the thrill of seeing her, along with deep searing pain of not having her.

Slowly, the door eased open. The breath left his body at the sight of her. Deep brown eyes latched onto his. Dark silky hair brushed perfect shoulders...

And her full mouth tilted down in confusion... or disappointment... or pain. He'd given her so many of all the negative emotions, he wasn't sure which one she was feeling right now.

"Hi, Lane. Can I help you?"

You can help me heal... help me survive the pain of losing you.

Jesus. He'd almost said it aloud.

"I wondered if I could ask you a few questions."

She hesitated. "About?"

"Cameron Cooper. The case in general, anything you can tell me that you might have left out about the Penny Killer or about when Cooper accosted you in the storage closet."

She stepped back without responding. Lane entered the house, swearing he felt a flash of her warmth as he passed by.

"Would you like a seat?"

He shook his head and remained standing. Struggled to maintain professionalism. "I won't take up much of your time. Did Cooper indicate he knew about someone hiring Finlay to beat you up?"

"No." Furrows appeared in her brow. "Do you think he was behind it?"

"Not really. We're basically starting at square one. Hoping we'll uncover something we missed before. When's the last time the Penny Killer called you?"

"After you rescued Shayne Burris. I've told you about each one of his calls." She crossed her arms, and her lips turned up in a smirk. "*I'm* being totally honest with *you*."

He narrowed his eyes, aware of the load of meaning behind her words, though he didn't have a clue what she was talking about. "Am I missing something here? You don't think I'm being honest with you?"

Dark eyes moistened, and she sucked in a deep breath. "Why didn't you tell me you called it off with Catherine?"

The air deflated from his chest. She knew. Of course she did. He'd told Darion. The rest was easy to figure out. "I wanted to. You were the first person I wanted to tell."

"But?"

"I didn't think it was fair to you. I figured you were tired of the uncertainty. Tired of being jerked around. I wanted to wait until I was actually divorced, until I could come to you as a free man and hope like hell I hadn't lost you."

She inclined her head in a quick, jerky movement. An angry movement.

He stepped closer, hooking a finger under her chin.

He tugged until she was looking up at him. "Would you have wanted me to, Monroe? Do you still feel the same about me?"

Her lips trembled. "I don't know how I feel about you," she whispered. "You hurt me deeply, although I know it was because of your sense of loyalty."

"Misguided loyalty," he muttered.

"Regardless, even though I saw that you could give your loyalty to Catherine, I'm not sure you could give it to me." She pulled away from his touch. "We both need time to see how we feel after your divorce is over."

Lane shrugged. "I get that. But, I already know how I feel, and that's not going to change."

"I'm not sure how I feel anymore."

He tried to pretend the words hadn't landed like a thousand tiny knives in his heart.

"Is it Holland?"

She evaded giving a direct answer. "He's remained devoted to his dead fiancée for twelve years."

"Don't you find that a little disturbing?"

She grinned, releasing some of the pressure in his chest. "A little. But, you have to admit, it's impressive."

He smiled back and settled his hands on her shoulders. "Just know that, whether or not we can ever be together, I'm always here for you. You're the most important person in the world, and there's nothing I wouldn't do for you."

She latched onto her bottom lip with her teeth, her large brown eyes pulling him in, mesmerizing him. Not pausing to consider the consequences of getting so close, he pulled her to him and wrapped his arms around her. The weight of her breasts against his chest heated his blood, sent a bolt of lust straight to his groin. His brain clouded with desire.

What the hell are you doing, Brody? Stop now, or she'll hate you forever.

Mounting her like a dog in heat was not the way to win her back. With super-human effort, he broke his hold and stepped back.

****

I tried not to protest at the chill of being deprived of Lane's embrace. I smiled up at him, putting on a courageous front. Like my heart wasn't cracking… wasn't screaming at me to take whatever I could from this man, married or not.

His eyes roamed my face. He lifted a hand and gently grazed my cheek. "If I've lost you it would be what I deserve. I'm just not sure how I'd survive it." He quirked a grin and placed a lingering kiss on my forehead.

I breathed in deeply, savoring the feel of him, however briefly. All I could manage was a nod when he released me once more.

"I'll get out of your way now. Let me know if anything comes up." He headed to the door. "Or if you need me for any reason. Day or night."

I wasn't sure what insane thrill-seeking peculiarity made me lower my voice and say, "Really? Any reason at all?"

He paused at the door, his brows drawn in confusion. "Of course. You know I'd do anything for you."

I sauntered over and reached past him to push the door closed. Neither of us spoke. I held his gaze, drowning in the blue depths. I willed him to read my mind, to respond to my aching desire.

Lifting a hand, I slowly stroked my fingernails down his cheek and ran my thumb across his lips.

"God, Monroe." His voice was a choked whisper. "What kind of torture is this? Payback for what I did to you?"

"It's not fair," I whispered back. "Why can't he make me feel the way you do? Just one look from you melts my insides. But his touch, his kindness, even his devout praise, leaves me cold."

"Holland?" he barked out.

I nodded. "Uh huh." Moving my lips to within a millimeter of his, I murmured, "This isn't payback. This is me, taking what I want and damn the consequences. Just for tonight, I want to pretend there's no baggage between us." I slid my hand over his chest, inside the 'v' where the top button was unfastened. His skin felt hot beneath my hand. The labored thud of his heart pounded against my palm. "Just for tonight, I want you."

He squeezed his eyes shut, sliding his hands on either side of my hips, tugging our bodies together at hip level. "Are you sure? You'd better tell me now, because in a few seconds, I won't have the presence of mind to ask, let alone back away."

I nodded. "I can't deny myself any longer. I deserve this one night. That's all I'm asking. All I'm taking."

Groaning, he lowered his head. Pressed his mouth to mine. I parted my lips, molding my body to his.

He lifted his head and broke the kiss, looking at me with a hint of uncertainty; as if he were afraid I'd disappear, or change my mind. "Monroe, I…" He shook his head. "God. I've wanted you for so long. So badly."

"Me too," I murmured. I needed to forget about Catherine, about the psycho, about what came next. "All

245

I want is this. You. For this moment."

He kissed me again, his tongue warm and probing. I opened my mouth to him, gasping as he caressed the skin along my sides. My fingers fumbled with the buttons of his shirt, while his worked my tee up over my ribs. We barely broke the kiss long enough for him to tug it over my head and toss it onto the floor.

His hand closed over my breast. His thumb dipped inside my bra and teased my nipple, while the other cupped my bottom, pressing me against his erection.

A low moan broke from my throat. God. His touch, his warm rough whiskers against my flesh felt so good. Better than I'd imagined. More than I'd ever hoped for.

"Condoms," he said harshly.

Dazed, I pulled away. "Huh?"

"Protection. Give me one second." He fumbled his wallet from his back pocket and fished out a condom.

"You carry condoms?" I asked, my passion momentarily abating at the thought of Lane with another woman. "Is there something I should know?"

"I haven't been with anyone since Catherine. I got these when I fell for you."

I arched a brow. "And when was that?"

His eyes turned a darker shade of blue, and his sensuous lips curved into a smile. "Almost the first moment I saw you."

"Oh," I gasped, blinking back tears. Unable to say more with the clog of emotion in my throat. I took the packet from his fingers and clasped his hand. Trapping his gaze with mine, I tugged him toward the bedroom. "Let's go make use of this bad boy."

Chapter 20

Lane awoke the next morning, heart soaring as he looked at Monroe lying next to him. It hadn't been a dream. After all the fantasies, he finally knew what it felt like to make love to Monroe, to be loved by her. To be inside her…

His groin stirred, and he reached a hand out to touch her. He stopped before making contact. What happened between them last night had been a one-time thing. Monroe's own words.

Would trying to initiate another lovemaking session drive her away? His eyes roamed over bare flesh that peeked above the blanket, to the curve where her neck met her shoulder. His lips had nuzzled that hollow, eliciting moans of delight.

Last night had been the best night of his life. Sex with Monroe was like nothing he'd ever experienced. Nothing he'd ever thought existed. He'd slid his fingers over parts of her skin he'd never touched before. Parts that were softer than he'd imagined. But still, his hands had searched for more. His lips, his soul, wanted all of her.

She stirred, blinking her eyes open. His breath caught when she looked up at him. A frown creased her forehead, and she tugged the blanket up to her chin.

"Morning," Lane said.

"Uh… morning. I—" She covered her eyes with her

forearm. "Listen, I have a busy day. Need coffee. Maybe you should…"

An unexpected twinge of pain pierced his heart. He hadn't expected her to declare her undying devotion. Neither had he expected such an abrupt brush-off.

"Yeah," he said casually, as though she hadn't just twisted his gut in knots. "I was just heading out. Didn't want to leave while you were asleep." He climbed from the bed and pulled on his clothes. His instincts of not touching her had proved correct. She regretted what had happened between them. "See ya," he said curtly once he'd dressed. It took all the willpower he could muster to keep his voice neutral.

"Bye," she replied, her eyes still hidden beneath her arm.

He left the bedroom and went into the kitchen. He wasn't sure why he felt the need to make the gesture, but he brewed a pot of coffee, strong, just the way she liked it. The last gurgles of the coffee maker were fading away when she appeared in the kitchen, a pink robe belted over her naked body, hair tousled with sleep—and their lovemaking.

"Coffee's ready," Lane said.

She smiled, causing his heart to expand until he thought it would burst through his chest.

"Thank you." Moving over to him, she placed a quick kiss on his mouth. "That was very sweet."

"You're welcome." He restrained the urge to pull her to him, to deepen the kiss, to slide his hands beneath the robe, over her velvety skin.

Damn. He nearly growled with frustration.

Stepping away, he moved to the kitchen door. When he turned back, she was pouring herself a mug of coffee.

She didn't ask if he wanted some, not even a to-go cup.

So, was that really how it was between them? A soul-rocking interlude that changed nothing?

Disgusted that it mattered so much, he turned and left, childishly slamming the door behind him. He swung by his own place to shower before heading to the station.

A few hours after he arrived, a woman called to say her daughter was missing.

Lane could barely concentrate as he asked questions. He kept running his mind over what had happened with Monroe. The sex had been amazing. She seemed to agree last night. Then, this morning, she'd given him the ice queen treatment.

In all fairness, he couldn't blame her. He'd chosen a vindictive, evil murderess over her. That had to sting.

"Detective?" The voice came over the phone line. Damn. He'd zoned out.

"Yeah. Right here. I'm listening." He forced himself to concentrate on the caller's words.

"My daughter's a troubled girl. She's run off before, but usually not this long."

"Give me her name, her description—the clothing she was wearing when she disappeared. Tell me anything you can think of. We'll check it out."

"Her name is Ranita Jacone. She's five feet tall, weighs about 110. Pretty. Dark hair, dark eyes…"

He jotted notes as she spoke, doubting it would turn into anything. If he had a buck for every call that turned out to be no more than a mix up or a pissed off teen, he could retire today. But, with even a miniscule possibility, they wouldn't ignore the reports. No matter how many futile leads they chased down, they'd keep chasing. Until the mother fucker was caught.

****

I hadn't talked to Lane since he'd left my house Friday morning. I wasn't sure how I felt about our making love, even though I'd initiated it. It had been amazing, but wrong. Having sex hadn't resolved anything, although it gave me a glimpse of paradise, of how in sync we were with one another. As if we were meant to be.

It was nothing more than a fantasy, of course. A mirage. If we were meant to be, we would be. He wouldn't be married to someone else, and I wouldn't feel as though I was the one person in the world who would never earn his loyalty.

My cell rang, causing me to jump, even though it had been days since I'd heard from the Penny Killer. I wasn't sure what that meant. Had he stopped after his failure, or was he gearing up for something really big?

I looked at the display. Tony.

"Hey," I said. "I don't suppose you caught the bastard?" Maybe that was why I hadn't heard from him.

"Wish I could say yes, but 'fraid not. Actually, I need a favor. I hate to ask, but I'm in a bind."

"Sure, what is it?"

"Paxton is helping out at the shelter again. I'm supposed to pick her up in half an hour, but I'm heading to Independence to question a suspect. There's no way I'll make it back in time. Lane's going with me, or I'd ask him to pick her up."

"Not a problem. I'll be glad to do it."

"Thanks, Roe. You know, she thinks a lot of you. I'm glad she has a female figure in her life. She needs someone she can relate to right now."

I laughed. "Somehow, the vibe I get from her isn't

quite so positive. I don't think we're exactly BFF's, but if I can help her out in any way, I'm happy to. She has a lot of issues."

"I know. Me and her mom really did a number on her."

"Teens. They're just… difficult. Even when parents do everything right, doesn't mean the kids turn out to be happy, well-adjusted, upstanding citizens." I really didn't know shit about parenting, but I wanted to make him feel better. I secretly agreed with him. Paxton's parents were a big part of her problem.

"Still, I wish we'd done things differently. Thought about the kids more in the beginning instead of our own bitterness."

"Well, it's not too late. She needs both of her parents to hear her, to understand her. Be there for her."

"Right. When Lisa gets back from her honeymoon, I'm going to talk to her about it. See what we can do to help. Maybe even get Paxton into counseling. Work together for a change."

"That's great, Tony. Good call."

"I hope it helps. Thanks again for getting her at the shelter. She'll be ready at noon. I'll call when I'm done and swing by to pick her up."

I arrived at the shelter a few minutes before noon. When I went inside, I spotted Gable at a table with an older man. One who had the look of someone who'd drank most of his life. His whiskered face was puffy, his eyes red-streaked and watery. Gable's hand was on the man's shoulder, and he was speaking softly. The old man nodded from time to time, a glimmer of hope breaking through the desperation in his expression. I wasn't sure what Gable was saying to him, but whatever it was, it was having a positive effect.

My heart swelled with pride. My brother was an amazing man. No telling how many people he'd helped. He gave and gave of himself, never asking for anything in return. I watched, smiling. Gabe looked up and caught my eye. He winked in greeting, then focused his attention back on the man.

I glanced around, but didn't see Paxton. I searched the storage closet, the kitchen, all the rooms in the shelter. She was in none of them.

When I returned to the main room, Gable rose from the table and shook the man's hand, clasping his shoulder.

The man left, and Gable approached me, brows raised. "What's up, sis? I didn't know you were coming by."

"I didn't either. Tony called and asked me to pick up Paxton."

Gable frowned. "He didn't already pick her up?"

Something fluttery and uncomfortable moved through my lower belly and to my chest. "No. He couldn't make it. He asked me to. Is she gone?"

He shrugged. "I assumed she was. She went outside to wait fifteen minutes ago. She wasn't out front when you came in?"

"No." I tried to draw in air, but my lungs constricted with fear. "She wasn't."

Gable must have seen the fear in my expression. He reached out and squeezed my shoulder. "Don't worry. I'm sure she's fine. She might have just wandered down to the corner market. Maybe she wanted a soda or something."

I nodded, but the movement felt stiff. "I'll go check.

She might be out front by now." I whirled and sped toward the door.

Gable followed. "I'll come with you."

His offer had me more worried than I already was. If he thought she would be out front, why the need to come with me?

I nodded, and the two of us rushed outside. My gaze searched the sidewalk, the streets, but no sign of Paxton.

"I'll head to the market," Gable said. "You go the other direction. Maybe she's just taking a walk around the block."

Worry bloomed to panic. I nodded, but I didn't believe it. The concern in Gable's face told me he didn't either.

We parted ways, and I walked at a fast clip down to the corner, my head swiveling back and forth, searching the streets for Paxton.

Nothing.

Maybe Gable had found her at the market.

Maybe not. You know what you think really happened. Might as well admit it.

No! I wouldn't admit it. He didn't have her. I refused to believe that.

When I found Gable—back in front of the shelter—his pinched expression and the fact that he was alone told me he hadn't found her either.

"I—I need to call..." My voice trailed off.

"The cops. I know."

I shook my head. "No, I mean, yes, the cops. But her father. I-I need to call Tony." I couldn't seem to properly string words together, but I knew what I meant.

I snatched my cell out of my purse and punched in Tony's number.

"Webber's phone," a familiar voice answered.

"Lane?" I hadn't meant for it to, but the word came out in a sob.

"Yes. Monroe? Is something wrong?"

"Where's Tony?"

"He's with a witness right now. What is it?" His voice had an edge of pain to it. We hadn't spoken since the night we spent together, and I knew he didn't like that I'd begun calling Tony with information about the killer's phone calls instead of him. But this time, I had a good reason for calling Tony.

"Do you know if—if Tony's heard from Paxton?"

"No. I don't think he has. I've been right here. I've had his phone for the past several minutes, so he could talk to this guy without interruption. Why? What's going on with Paxton?"

"I don't know," I cried out. "Oh, God. I worried about this, about putting her in danger."

"What are you talking about? What's happened?"

"I can't find her. She's missing, Lane. Paxton is missing." I swayed, and Gable steadied me with a hand on my arm. "I think the killer has her." My voice rose with hysteria.

Lane drew in a sharp breath. "Maybe she's… I don't know, just… out of pocket." In spite of the positive words, his voice was tight with worry. "She's a handful. Maybe she took off on her own."

"Not this time. I have a feeling." My gut seized with the need to vomit… to scream… to dissolve into hysterical sobs. "It's him, Lane. I know it is. Somehow, I know." My knees weakened and the last words were an anguished cry. "Oh, God, Lane. The Penny Killer has Paxton."

Death Offerings

Chapter 21

Cadence had been staying with one of Tony's female friends while Paxton worked at the shelter. I picked him up and took him over to my parents so he wouldn't be around when we were discussing the fact that his sister was missing—that she might be in the hands of a crazed killer. He was quiet on the way over, his small face scrunched in concern, but he didn't ask any questions. Although he knew something was wrong, he was either afraid we wouldn't tell him the truth… or afraid we would.

When I got back to Tony's, he was pacing the floor, scrubbing his hands over his face, cursing. "Son of a bitch," he bit out. "If I get my hands on that mother fucker…"

In spite of the tough words, the catch in his throat and the dampness in his eyes revealed his grief and pain.

I slowly approached him. "We'll find her, Tony. She'll be okay."

"I should be out there looking for her."

"Lane has been looking for hours. The whole police department is out in full force." I soothed a hand over his forearm, gently rubbing. "Everyone is doing all they can. You're better off staying here in case she comes home. Or in case someone calls."

He whirled on me, his face a tortured mask of anguish. "*Someone*? You mean like the Penny Killer?

Like that fucking psycho?"

I purposely made my voice calm, controlled. "We don't know that he has her."

We met gazes, and I saw in his what I was sure he saw in mine. We both knew. He had her.

"Why hasn't he called you?" Tony demanded. It was accusatory, as if my non-ringing cell phone was my fault.

"I don't know." I didn't say that no call was better. When I got a call, it was always too late. "Want me to fix you something to eat? Is there anything at all I can do for you?"

He turned tortured brown eyes—Paxton's eyes—on me. "Can you promise my little girl is alive? That I'll get her back?"

****

Lane quietly opened Tony's front door at five a.m. Monroe was asleep on the couch, her hands folded beneath her cheeks, an afghan covering her lower body.

Tony sat in the recliner adjacent to her, his face pale, haunted. He vaulted to his feet and stalked over to Lane almost before the door shut. "Well? Anything?"

Lane shook his head, wanting to tell him they'd found her—alive and unharmed, found some clue as to what happened to her, but he couldn't. It would be a lie. "I'm sorry."

"Fuck," he roared.

Monroe stirred, blinking her eyes open. She sat up and brushed her hair back from her face.

In spite of the horror of the situation, in spite of his worry and fear, Lane had an overwhelming urge to take her in his arms, to run his fingers through her sleep tousled hair and kiss her slightly parted lips. He shook the feeling away.

"No luck?" Monroe asked, her deep brown eyes looking hopeful, yet worried at the same time.

"No. 'Fraid not."

Tony dug his keys from his pocket and stalked to the door.

"What are you doing?" Lane asked.

"Going out to look for her."

"You know that's not a good idea. The guys are doing all they can. You'd only slow them down. Your emotions would get in the way."

"So, you think I can just fucking *sit* here all day? Like I have been for the past ten hours? While my little girl is out there in danger?"

"Look, you just need to—" Lane reached out to take his arm, but Tony jerked away.

"What? Give up? Hang around here like some kind of useless piece of shit?" He grabbed the door knob, his mouth tight. "I don't want your help, Brody. If it wasn't for you, this wouldn't have happened."

Monroe rose from the couch and came over to them. "Come on, Tony. You don't know what you're saying."

Without acknowledging her, without breaking his gaze from Lane's, he said, "You had him. Had him right there, and you let him go. He wouldn't have Paxton if you'd taken him out at the school."

Lane swallowed the lump that rose in his throat. "Then the girl would have died."

"Yeah? How many more will die because she lived?"

Without waiting for an answer, Tony jerked the door open, then slammed it behind him, leaving Lane on the other side, his friend's words echoing in his head.

****

I looked at Lane, but he was staring at the ground, his fingers pinching the bridge of his nose. I moved over to him and placed my hands on either side of his head, forcing him to look at me. His indigo eyes shimmered with a hint of tears.

"It's not your fault," I whispered. "You couldn't let that girl die."

He nodded, but pulled away and turned his back. "Yeah. I know." He sounded like a condemned man. Tony might be his accuser, but Lane was his own judge and jury.

"No. You don't know. You're blaming yourself." I took his shoulder and made him face me. "Don't do this. You won't be any good to Paxton or Tony if you start to believe that."

His gaze roamed over my face, his eyes bleak with pain. He took a step forward. So did I. He enfolded me in his arms, and I held on tight, burying my face in his shoulder, inhaling his spicy male scent.

"I need you so much," he whispered against my hair.

I nodded. "I'm here for you. Paxton is fine. We'll find her."

I wished I believed my words, but I didn't, any more than Lane did. It made me feel better to say them. Maybe it made him feel better to hear them.

We pulled apart, and my phone rang. Hope bloomed in my heart as I hurried over to the end table where it lay. I scooped it up, hope turning to terrified dread when 'unknown' showed on the display.

"Hello?" I said, my voice shaking.

Lane stalked to my side, watching me intently.

"They fucked up. Big time," the hateful, distorted voice said.

"Do you have Paxton? Is she okay?" He wasn't calling from Paxton's phone. I had her name stored in my cell. It would have shown up on the caller ID.

"You're the only one I can talk to, Monroe. The only one who cares about my thoughts, my feelings. Even though you tried to betray me in the cemetery, I forgive you. I know you were only doing what you felt was right. You didn't betray me in your article, just like I asked. Didn't print that embarrassing incident where fucking Brody screwed up my plan." He continued, his voice rising with anger. "Had to find a new place too. He fucked up a perfect set up, the cocksucker."

"Please," I whispered, holding the phone tilted so Lane could listen too. His cheek was practically pressed against mine, his brow furrowed in concentration. "Please tell me where Paxton is."

"Did I say I had her?"

"No, but—"

"Tell your cop buddies to check under the bridge on 435, just on the Missouri side of the border." He chuckled. "Wish I could see their faces when they do."

The line went dead. I turned to Lane, my heart thudding like a bass drum, my stomach churning with nausea. "No," I choked out. "Not Paxton."

"Shit," he muttered. "Stay here." He grabbed his phone and keys, punching numbers on his cell keypad as he hurried to the door. Someone must have answered, because he said, "Keep it off the radio, but I need a unit at the—"

His words cut off when the door slammed. My legs gave out, and I sank to the edge of the easy chair.

Dear God. Was it Paxton? Would they find her body under the bridge? I covered my face with my hands, sobs tearing at my body. The poor girl. So lost, so confused. *Please, God. Please don't let her be dead.*

Chapter 22

Lane squinted at the sun cresting over the horizon. Dawn was starting to bring in a new day. Another day of Tony not having his daughter. Depending on what Lane found when he arrived at the scene, it could be the first day of forever without his child.

Fuck the speed limit.

He hit the gas and raced down the highway. He'd called a patrol car to the scene, but hadn't told Tony yet. Didn't want to until he knew for sure. He damn sure didn't want Tony finding his daughter in whatever condition the body was in.

You don't know it's her. It might not be Paxton. Might not be anyone. Might just be part of his sick game.

Lane wished he could believe that, but his gut knew they'd find something under the bridge. He just wasn't sure what… or who.

He parked on the shoulder of the highway behind the patrol car. Its lights were off. Good. The less attention brought to the scene, the better.

Lane cautiously made his way down the steep incline. Rocks tumbled under his feet.

Mitchell, one of the patrolmen who'd answered the call, watched Lane come to a halt at the river bed. He pushed his hat back on his head and pursed his lips, his expression grim.

"What you got?" Lane asked, barely able to get the

words out.

"A body. Young girl."

"Shit," he bit out. "Is it Paxton Webber?"

Mitchell shrugged. "I was hoping you could tell us." He turned and headed under the bridge. Lane followed. Each step felt like a slog through wet cement.

He drew closer. The first detail he saw was the dark hair. *Paxton has dark hair.*

The body was facing away, the right arm splayed behind at an awkward angle, the left one underneath her upper torso.

Lane moved around to the other side of the victim and squatted, blood pounding through his head. His vision swam. It took a moment to clear so that he could get a full look at her face.

The face of a stranger.

Not Paxton.

He released a long sigh and rose to his feet, relief making him dizzy.

"It's not her," he said, his voice strangled. His mind went back to the phone call he'd gotten from the concerned mother. Based on the description she'd given, this girl was likely her daughter. What was her name?…Ranita. Ranita Jacone. Son of a bitch. "It's not Tony's daughter."

Mitchell nodded. "That's something, anyway."

"Yeah." Lane tugged his tie loose from his collar. "It's great."

Guilt at his happiness weighed him down. He had no right to be glad the girl wasn't Paxton. His friend might be spared the grief—for now—but some other family was about to have their world destroyed.

Two hours later, the ME arrived. In the victim's

hand, he found a ring with a small emerald setting. This time, though, there were two pennies. One was dated 2010. Lane had learned the fucker well enough by now. Most likely the ring had been a gift from someone—a boyfriend, maybe—two years ago.

The second penny was dated 1997. A quick calculation told him that was the year Paxton was born.

****

Although worry for Paxton kept me from falling into a restful sleep, I was dozing in my recliner when the doorbell rang. I leapt to my feet and rushed to the door, hoping it was Lane with good news. He'd already called to say the victim under the bridge wasn't Paxton. That meant there was hope.

When I flung the door open, mid-morning sun temporarily blinded me before I recognized Bart. I tried to hide my disappointment.

"Hi, Monroe. Are you okay? I called, but you didn't answer."

Which might mean I didn't want to talk to you, I felt like sniping at him, but it wasn't his fault Paxton was missing. I didn't have the energy to entertain, to concentrate on anything other than where she was, and whether she was okay, whether she was alive.

"I'm all right," I said. "Worried, but all right."

He nodded. "I heard about Paxton on the news. I thought you might like some company. I know this must be very difficult for you."

"Yes. It's awful." Tears welled, and I brushed them away. "I'm terrified that she's—" I couldn't finish the words. Wouldn't allow myself to think it, let alone say it.

He stepped inside and closed his arms around me.

"She's going to be okay. Her dad will find her."

I clung to him, even though his arms weren't the ones I wanted comforting me. I thought I didn't want company, but it turned out his presence was better than being alone.

"Thank you for coming by," I said, my voice muffled against his shoulder.

"Of course. Why don't I stay a while? You shouldn't be alone right now."

I nodded and stepped out of his embrace. "I'm afraid I won't be much fun to be around."

"That's not why I'm here. I want to take care of you. How long has it been since you've eaten?"

I frowned, trying to remember. "I'm not sure."

"Then it's damn sure been too long." He took my elbow and steered me into the living room, easing me onto the recliner. "You rest. I'll fix you something to eat."

I nodded, letting him take charge. I didn't feel hungry, but logic told me I needed sustenance.

Bart made some noise in the kitchen for twenty minutes or so while I stared at the television, even though it was off. Turning it on might help take my mind off Paxton, but I'd tried earlier, and all it did was irritate me.

I looked up when Bart entered the living room, carrying two plates. He eased onto the couch, setting the food on the coffee table. He'd heated frozen Swedish meatballs and cooked rice and green beans to go along with it. It looked tasty, but I had no desire to eat. My expression must have conveyed my lack of enthusiasm.

"Here," he coaxed, handing me a fork. "At least try."

I took the fork, speared a meatball, and brought it to my mouth. I chewed slowly, but when I tried to swallow, the food lodged in my throat. I drank from the bottle of Diet Pepsi Bart had brought me.

"I can't," I muttered. "I just can't eat."

Bart's hazel eyes gleamed with sympathy. "I'm sorry. Maybe try just a little more. How about a few green beans? Those have vitamins your body needs."

I smiled with gratitude, and for his sake, forced down a few bites of the vegetable.

"That's a girl."

He spoke to me as if I were a precious gift, someone to be pampered and cared for, cherished. Although too much of that sort of treatment might be smothering, knowing someone cared so much was sort of nice. So why the hell couldn't I feel for him even a tenth of what I felt for Lane? Why did Bart's touch leave me cold?

I only half concentrated on the one-sided conversation from Bart. He was probably trying to occupy my mind, to keep me from worrying too much about Paxton.

"I like the girl," he was saying. "She seems like a sweet kid." Bart shook his head. "What a shame. Even though I don't have children, I can imagine how Detective Webber must feel. Something like this would topple your world."

I was lifting my Diet Pepsi to my mouth when his words registered. I froze in mid motion.

Topple your world.

I'd heard that phrase before. But only once in my lifetime. And recently.

The Penny Killer had used it in the cemetery.

No. You're exhausted, not thinking clearly.

I slowly lowered the bottle and cut my eyes to Bart. Could it be? He'd come on the scene not long after the psycho started calling me. But, still, impossible…

Not entirely, though. Bart was a little unnaturally drawn to me. So was the killer.

As casually as I could, I said, "If you don't mind, I'm going to go take a quick shower. Those few bites of food helped me feel almost human again, but now I need a shower to revive me."

"Sure. I'll be right here. Anything you need me to do?"

Depends. Do you have Paxton? Are you the one who murdered all those girls? If so, I need you to tell me where Paxton is, then fucking die.

"No." I forced a stiff smile. "Thanks, though. Be right back."

I turned on the shower in the bathroom connected to my bedroom, just in case Bart listened for the sound of running water. Quickly booting up my laptop, I typed *Bartholomew Holland* and *Kansas City* in the search engine.

Several unrelated web sites appeared, but one seemed quite related. A high school alumni list. Photos of 1987 graduates of River Park High School in Kansas City. I clicked on the link. A photo appeared of Bart— much younger, but unmistakably him.

He didn't go to school in Denver. He'd been right here in Kansas City all these years. He was here when the other girls were murdered. He was fourteen when Katie died. Born in 1969.

1969. The date of the penny Katie's mother found on her grave.

A shiver raced through my body. Blood went cold inside my veins. Rage and nausea coiled through my soul. Bart was the killer. He'd only been fourteen or fifteen when Katie died, but based on the story he told in the cemetery, he was a sadistic fuck at a very young age.

I clamped my jaws shut to keep from screaming like a crazed lunatic. All this time, I'd been hanging out with him, thinking he was such a great guy. So helpful. So caring.

You son of a bitch.

Tears of guilt and anger rose in my throat, but I swallowed them back. I had to call Tony. Now.

I shot to my feet and looked around. Where was my phone?

Shit. I'd left it in the living room. On the end table just a few feet from where I'd left Bart.

I'd have to go back in there. Play it cool as though I hadn't just found out he was a cold-blooded killer. A killer of innocent young girls. *Of Katie…*

I bit back the sob that wrenched my throat. I had to remain calm. To think.

Go back in there. Act normal. Get your phone. Do it for Paxton.

Wiping sweaty palms on my jeans, I started for the door, then paused as reality rushed in. If I called the police, Bart would clam up. There was no way he'd tell them where he had Paxton. Maybe not ever.

My legs turned to rubber, and I sank to the edge of the computer chair. Panic sped my pulse rate so high, I thought I would pass out. I took a slow, deep breath, drawing in much needed oxygen. Somehow, I had to take care of this on my own. At least until I got Bart to talk.

But how?

A small plan started to come together in my fuddled mind. I wasn't certain it was the best plan, and I wasn't precisely sure exactly how it would play out, but I knew where to start.

I could still be wrong… There could be a perfectly plausible explanation for Bart pretending he'd gone to school in Denver. For him using the same unique phrase as the murderer—to conveniently have come into my life not long after the Penny Killer.

Yes, there was still room for doubt. If it turned out I was wrong, I'd owe him an apology. If it turned out I was right, there would be hell to pay.

I did a quick Google search on Valium. The doctor had prescribed them to me last October after the injuries I sustained during the altercation with the man who'd held me hostage. The pills were to help relax my muscles so they could heal. I'd only taken a few. There were probably twenty-five or twenty-six left in the bottle. How many would it take to knock him out and not kill him?

A scan of a few websites gave me the answer I needed. To the best of my estimation, ten was about right. Problem was, that would likely keep him out twelve to twenty-four hours. I had no other solution, though. I had to get him to tell me where he had Paxton. Even if it took another day.

How would I get him to swallow ten Valiums without noticing the taste? Coke would surely disguise at least part of the bitterness.

No… I had a better idea.

"Monroe, are you okay?"

I jumped when Bart knocked on my door. Hurrying into my bathroom, I turned on the water in the sink and stuck my head beneath the faucet for a few seconds, then towel dried my hair. After changing into jeans and a button up shirt, I pulled on a jacket and slipped the bottle of Valium from the medicine cabinet into one pocket, the .22 into the other. As an added touch of realism—so I'd smell like I just had a shower—I squirted body spray on my skin beneath my clothing.

"I'm fine," I said, opening the door. "The hot water felt so good, I couldn't bring myself to step out of it."

He smiled. "I'm sure you needed to relax. Glad you enjoyed your shower." He frowned as if in concern. "Are you cold? You're wearing a jacket."

"Yeah." I made myself shiver. "I can't seem to get warm. It's like I'm cold on the inside. Fear for Paxton, I suppose."

"I know. I'm sorry." His sigh, his expression, his demeanor was sympathetic. But I knew better.

I searched his face. Where I'd once seen a humble, reserved, giving man, I now recognized evil. Something in the eyes… a light of underlying insanity. His mouth now seemed to tilt at a cruel angle. I knew it could be my imagination, but regardless, there was suddenly something about him that creeped me out.

"I think I'll have some tea, how about you? It's a special blend my grandmother used to make." I hoped I didn't sound phony, overly bright.

"No, thanks. You go ahead. I don't care much for tea."

Damn. You own a fucking coffee shop and you don't like coffee or tea?

I went back into the kitchen, and he followed.

"Please have some with me. It's kind of bitter tasting, but it's also really good for you. Gives you a burst of energy." I forced my lips into a coy smile. "If you stay here a while, you're going to need all the energy you can get."

He blinked rapidly. His voice was breathless when he answered. "Okay, sure, yeah. I'd like some tea."

"Have a seat in the living room, and I'll bring it to you. I need to…" I shrugged. "I don't know. Feel useful."

"Right. I'll be in the living room."

You're so damned easy. I took a deep breath. Better not get cocky this soon. I had a long way to go to see my plan through.

I ground ten of the Valiums into Bart's tea—tea I'd made from Earl Grey bags I had in my pantry for some unknown reason. In reality, I was *not* a tea drinker.

Carrying the steaming cups into the living room, I handed one to Bart, then settled down next to him. I took a cautious sip of the hot brew, wrinkling my nose. "Ugh. It's bitter, just like I remembered. But, worth it if you drink the whole thing."

"Yeah?" Bart took a drink from his cup and frowned. "God. It is bitter."

"Right? It's kind of tough to swallow, but you don't get the full effects of the energizing power unless you finish the whole cup."

"All right, then. Bottoms up."

We toasted, and Bart continued to take sips of his tea each time I took a drink of mine.

Silence settled between us, with Bart casting questioning looks at me from the corner of his eye from time to time. Was he gauging my interest? Trying to figure out if my earlier words had a double meaning? Maybe, but he didn't make a move to find out. He was pretty shy for a fucking serial killer.

After a few moments, I said, "You know how I'm writing articles about the Penny Killer?"

"Yeah. Sure."

"Well, there's something I haven't told you." I took a sip of my tea. Bart took a sip of his. "He's been calling me."

"What? Calling you? Why?"

I rolled my eyes. "Bragging mostly, feeding me inside info about the crimes for me to print in my articles."

"Wow." Another sip of his tea. "Sounds like a real nut case."

"Yeah. He is. He's kind of a dufus too. Thinks everyone is so scared of him, but we're actually not. We mock him behind his back."

He emitted a strained chuckle. Took another drink of tea. "Oh? Seems pretty scary to me."

"Nah. He goes after helpless young girls. Hides behind a phone and disguised voice. He's a wimp."

Bart's brows rose, his mouth tightening. "A wimp, really?"

"I pretend to be afraid when I talk to him, but I actually think he's just pathetic."

"Do you really think it's wise to take him so lightly?" His voice hardened, but the words were starting to slur.

I shrugged. "I'm not worried. He's not very bright."

His hand tightened around the cup, his knuckles white with tension. "Not very bright? He's been get—getting by with murder for... quarter of a century. How—how can you say's not bright?"

"It's just dumb, blind luck. We're closing in on him though."

He frowned, wiped a hand over his mouth, then squinted at me. "We?"

I smiled. "Well, me."

"Huh? You?" He tried to get up, but staggered, then bent over and grabbed the coffee table. His head swayed toward me like a stunned bull's. "What'd you do to me?"

I stood. Leaning close, I whispered, "I'll tell you when you wake up."

Chapter 23

As soon as Bart passed out, I tied his hands and feet with rope, then strung the rope over to the heavy cowboy desk, securing it around the legs. Even when he awoke, the asshole wasn't going anywhere.

I fished his keys from his pocket and headed outside to check his trunk. Any serial killer worth his salt had a murder kit. That would be the final proof. I held my breath as I opened the lid. A duffle bag lay inside. Taking a quick peek around the neighborhood to make sure I wasn't being observed, I pulled back the zipper and released my breath with a whoosh.

Shock rendered me still as I perused the contents. Duct tape, strips of material he no doubt used as blindfolds, a bag of pennies, and small vials. Smelling salts?

I shuddered. Although I'd known on some level he was the Penny Killer, seeing the indisputable evidence weakened my knees.

With shaking fingers, I closed the bag and hefted it on my shoulder. After shutting the trunk, I hurried inside.

I texted Adam that I wouldn't be at work tomorrow, using the excuse of my worry over Paxton, which would have been enough in and of itself. The fact that I had a murderer sedated and tied up in my home was an even better reason, although of course, I couldn't share that detail.

Luckily, no one stopped by while Bart lay unconscious on my couch. Lane had called a few times to update me. The updates were always that there were no updates. With every passing minute, the odds of finding Paxton unhurt and alive diminished.

I suffered a torrent of guilt each time I spoke with Lane and withheld the information about Bart. I so badly wanted him with me… wanted his help. But worry for Paxton kept me silent. My plan was risky—maybe foolish—but with Paxton's life at stake, I was willing to take that risk. Alone.

I spent a good deal of time pacing the floor as I waited for Bart to wake up. Resting proved impossible. Although I needed it for what lay ahead, I was far too wound up to sleep. Adrenaline pumped through my body, suffusing me with the energetic burst I'd falsely attributed to my grandmother's fictional magical tea.

It took nearly eleven hours for Bart to stir even slightly. In thirteen hours, he batted his eyes open and gaped at me. "What—what's happening?" he gasped. He looked around, squinting. Probably because I'd removed his glasses.

"I want some answers. The effects of the Valium haven't quite worn off—at least that's what I assume after my internet search. But, for your sake and Paxton's, I hope they've worn off enough that you can help me."

"Paxton? Help you?" He blinked again. "What are you talking about? Where are my glasses?"

I waved a dismissive hand. "You can do without them for the time being. I understand that when one of our abilities is lessened, the others are more honed. Maybe if you can't see well, you can think better. The amount of Valium you ingested causes slight amnesia, but I bet with a little coaxing, full memories will come flooding back. This might help too." I snapped open a vial and held it under his nose. He sniffed, jerking his head back and coughing.

"What the hell? Monroe, please. I'm at a loss here. What are you talking about?"

Fury washed through my body, preventing me from speech for a few seconds. My words were tight when I finally got them out. "I know who you are. I know you have Paxton. Tell me where she is."

"What? Who I am?" He strained against his bindings. "This isn't funny. Let me loose. You know I don't have Paxton. Why would I do something like that?"

"Because. You're the Penny Killer."

His eyes rolled back in his head, but he managed a burst of laughter. "That's insane. What's gotten into you?"

I drew the .22 from my jacket pocket and leveled it at him. "*You're* insane. I want an answer, and I want it now. Otherwise, I put a bullet through your evil brain."

His gaze went from the gun, up to my eyes, back to the gun, then settled on my face. The innocent mask fell. A touch of smugness came over his features. "I did it for you. For us."

"What do you mean, for us?"

The now unguarded hazel eyes shone with maniacal glint. "Well, partly I took her to punish her dad and that fucking Lane Brody, but I also figured I could use it as leverage."

"Is she alive?" That was the burning question. Once I found out, I could proceed with trying to pick apart his demented mind and get the answers I needed.

"She's fine. I couldn't hurt her. Not knowing what she meant to you. I hoped I could convince you to go away with me if I promised to let the police know where she is. I was going to wait until we were far away from here before I told them. Until it was too late for you to change your mind."

I frowned. "You're crazy. There's no way I'd go anywhere with you. Not in a million years, even if you weren't a murderer, I feel zero attraction toward you. Got it? Zero."

His expression twisted in anger. "You don't mean that. Come away with me, and I'll let her dad know where she is. Otherwise, she dies."

I cocked the hammer and aimed between his eyes. "Or, maybe *you* die."

He shrugged, although it was barely a movement at all, restrained by his bindings as he was. "I'd rather die than be without you. So shoot me. Go ahead. Then you'll never learn where she is."

I let out a long sigh and stepped back. Placing the gun on safety, I slipped it back in my pocket. I tilted my head and grinned, pretending I knew what I was doing. Pretending I wasn't terrified to my very core.

Leaning forward until our noses almost touched, I said softly, "There are other options, you know."

****

Lane's eyes felt like he'd washed them out with gravel. He and Tony had been looking for more than twenty-four hours and not a clue. Not one fucking little clue.

They'd questioned everyone at the shelter multiple times. Everyone who owned a business within ten miles of the shelter. Paxton didn't have many friends in the area, but they questioned every kid they could find that was even close to her age.

"Nothing." Tony's voice was hollow, lifeless. His mouth drooped, and dark bags hung underneath his eyes. If Lane looked in a mirror, he'd probably see the same image.

"We'll find her, bud."

Tony snorted a laugh that sounded like a death rattle. "Right. Even I said that in the beginning. You know as well as I do when someone's been missing this long, the odds are nearly non-existent. Especially when a serial killer is on the loose. One who's been—" He drew in a trembling breath. "Been taking girls just like her."

Lane dropped his head back and blew out a pursed breath. The moon hovered in the black sky as they stood on the deserted sidewalk in front of the shelter.

What now? Where to search next?

His mind went to Monroe. He wanted nothing more than to be with her now, to rest his weary body, his tortured mind, in her sweet presence. But she wouldn't welcome him.

Was Bart with her? Was he the one providing comfort, giving and taking from her what Lane desired?

He squeezed his eyes shut, blocking out an overactive imagination. The pictures forming in his mind were agony. Monroe returning Bart's kisses, her soft lips and supple body locked with another man in a passionate embrace.

He shook his head, trying to dispel the images. Tony's daughter was his priority. If they didn't find her—alive—how would Tony go on?

Tony hadn't said anymore about blaming Lane for not taking the guy out, but the thought probably still festered somewhere deep inside. If Paxton didn't survive, it would likely surface in a big way.

He clasped Tony's shoulder. "What next?"

His partner's large frame shuddered beneath his hand. "You might as well go home. We've done all we can do. Just because I can't sleep, doesn't mean you shouldn't. I bet you're balls-to-the-wall exhausted."

Lane shook his head. "I wouldn't be able to sleep either. I'm not going home until we bring Paxton home."

Tony gave a quick nod. The only sign of emotion was the quaver in his voice. "Then I guess we start all over."

****

I knocked on Don Chathum's door, praying he would be awake at this late hour. A light shone through his front window, but it didn't mean he was up.

He opened the door, wearing blue and white plaid pajamas. The shine from the porch light glinted on his bald spot. "Monroe?" His eyes widened in surprise. "Is everything okay?"

"Yes, fine." I forced a chuckle. "This is going to sound crazy, but I have a friend over, and he's nuts about reptiles. I was telling him about Rambo, and he said he'd love to meet him. Can I borrow him?"

His brows furrowed. "Well, yeah. I suppose so. Want me to bring him over?"

"No, no, that won't be necessary. I'm sure you have other things to do."

"Well, sure. All right." His tone conveyed confusion, the furrow remained. "Come in."

I stepped inside and waited by the door while he disappeared down the hallway. Moments later he returned, carrying a cage with a five feet long corn snake inside. Light orange in color, decorated with black-outlined darker orange circles placed at perfect intervals from the head to the tip of its tail. Although completely docile, they appeared fierce enough to frighten anyone skittish about snakes. I sent up a silent prayer it would have that effect on Bart.

"You sure you don't need me to go with you?" Don asked.

"I'm sure. Thanks, though." I would need Rambo for a while. I didn't want Don popping in to check on his pet unexpectedly. "Look, if you don't mind, I'll just bring him back to you tomorrow. It looks like you're ready for bed, and I don't want to keep you up."

His expression held curiosity, but he nodded. We'd been neighbors for nearly six years. He trusted me. "Sure. Yeah. That will be fine."

I hurried out the door, giving him an over the shoulder wave as I stepped off his porch.

A rush of breath escaped, and I let myself into the house. Bart was right where I'd left him. Not that I'd expected anything different. He was trussed up like a calf at a rodeo event.

The anger in his face was palpable.

"I have a surprise for you," I said.

I pulled the cage from behind my back. His face blanched, and his eyes grew as large as Frisbees. "No!" he screeched out. "God, no."

So he hadn't been faking his fear of snakes. Good. I didn't have a Plan B.

"Oh yes." I set the cage on the floor and opened the door. I reached to take Rambo out. A light shudder ran over me. I wasn't exactly fond of snakes. I knew corn snakes were harmless, and I wasn't freaked out by any snake that wasn't venomous, but it didn't mean I enjoyed getting this close to them. I wouldn't, however, let Bart know that.

"Monroe, please, no." He tried to press into the couch as I approached, holding Rambo aloft. "How can you stand it? Why aren't you afraid?"

I laughed. "I grew up with three brothers. I'm immune to being afraid of almost anything." I hardened my voice. "Tell me where Paxton is, or I swear to God, I'll lay him right on your face."

His chest rose and fell with rapid breaths. "I—I… can't… breathe. No, God. Please, no."

"I bet that's what your victims were thinking when you squeezed the life from them, you sorry piece of shit." I stepped closer to the couch and held Rambo mere inches away from Bart's face. Rambo's tail undulated over his neck and chin.

A sound that was part shriek, part howl left his throat. "Okay. Okay. For God's sake, I'll tell you." A vein bulged in his forehead. The tendons on his neck stood out like blue ropes. His voice strangled, he screamed, "Get that thing off of me, and I'll tell you."

I pulled the snake back, but didn't put him away. "Talk."

He licked his lips and swallowed hard. "I—I have a boat. *Sylvia's Dream.* The girl is on my boat. It's docked at Lake Lotawana by the boat ramp. She's in the cabin. She's fine, I swear."

"She'd better be." I flipped open my phone and dialed Lane's number. When he answered, I said, "Check for Paxton at Lake Lotawana. There's a boat called *Sylvia's Dream* docked by the boat ramp."

"What?" He sounded weary, dejected. And highly

confused. "Why would you think that? What's going on?"

"Please, just go. Call me back as soon as you know something."

Before he could respond, I ended the call. Bart was whimpering now.

"If Paxton isn't where you said, if she's hurt, I'll turn Rambo loose on you and watch you suffer for a while, then I'll put a bullet in your head."

He let out a strangled groan. "She's fine. I promise. Just get the damned thing out of here." He spoke to me, but fear-glazed eyes stayed glued to the snake.

"Not yet. If she's okay, I'll put the snake away, and we'll wait for the police to come."

I took a disturbing pleasure in causing him the same kind of terror he'd unleashed on innocent victims. I'd examine my penchant for sadism later. Right now, I wanted answers.

"I suppose we have a little time," I said, still holding Rambo. "I'm curious about a few things. If you're so terrified of snakes, why take your victims to wooded areas?"

"I—I wanted them—hidden. I didn't go that deep into the woods. It didn't take long to dump them."

Dump them. Like they were nothing more than objects to discard. My revulsion grew. "What really happened to Sylvia? Did you kill her?"

Tears and snot dripped down his face. He shook his head. "No. I loved her. She died in a car accident. That was the truth."

"What about that story you told me at the cemetery? Your father and the babysitter."

"The truth. That was the truth. It made me what I am

today."

The image of the poor, innocent girls he'd savaged rose to my mind. He'd taken their lives like they meant nothing. Rage boiled through my body, but I kept my voice level. "Boo-freaking-hoo. You're such a fucking cliché."

Chapter 24

The mixture of hope and fear on Tony's face was difficult to witness as they drove to Lake Lotawana. If they didn't find Paxton alive, if they didn't find her at all, Lane was afraid Tony's fragile hold on sanity would disintegrate. Lane had no idea how Monroe had gotten the information, but his concern over Paxton battled the fear for Monroe. Had the killer confessed to her? Did he have her now? Had he forced her to lead them on a wild goose chase to get them out of the way, so he could...

He abruptly staunched that line of thinking. Right now, Paxton needed them. Monroe was fine. Her voice had been confident. She hadn't sounded like she was being coerced.

But what the fuck was going on?

The boat came into sight as soon as they pulled into the parking lot. Tony bolted from the car before it came to a complete stop.

Lane slammed the gearshift into park and took off after him.

"Paxton?" Tony shouted as he boarded the boat at a full run.

Soft, muffled whimpers came to Lane as Tony threw the cabin door open. Almost afraid of what they'd find, Lane followed Tony down the step, ducking to look over his partner's shoulder.

Relief pulled the strength from Lane's legs. She was

there. Alive. Sitting on the floor with her hands and feet bound. A blindfold covered her eyes.

Tony rushed to her and dropped to his knees. He made quick work of removing the blindfold and untying her. His daughter flung herself into his arms, sobbing against his chest, clinging tightly. Tony clung to her just as hard, tears making his voice wobble as he murmured, "You're fine, baby. I've got you, and you're going to be fine. Daddy's here."

Lane cleared his throat and thumbed moisture from his eyes. "Paxton, sweetie. Do you know who took you? Do you know the man's name?"

She lifted her head from her dad's shoulder and nodded as she looked at Lane, eyes still expressing the horror she'd experienced.

"It—it was…" She let out a strangled sob. "I went with him. I knew him, so I thought it was okay. I thought you sent him to pick me up." Her confused gaze rested on Tony's face.

"Who was it, baby? Who did this?"

She sucked in a shaky breath. "Bart. Monroe's friend, Bart."

A bomb exploded in Lane's brain. *Bart Holland.* Fucking Bart Holland. He'd been in Monroe's house. Pretended to be her friend. Her rescuer. Her hero.

Tony stood and pulled Paxton to her feet, still keeping an arm around her shoulders. Lane met his partner's gaze.

"The mother fucker," Tony bit out.

Lane jerked his phone from his belt. He didn't know where Monroe was, but before he called her, he'd send a patrol car to her house. They could get to her quicker than he could, just in case she was there. With Holland.

He spoke to dispatch as he headed back up top, Tony and Paxton following. When he ended the call, he dialed Monroe.

Her voice was breathless as she answered. "Did you find her?"

"We found her. She's fine."

"Oh, thank God." Tears choked the words. "It was Bart."

"I know," Lane gritted. "Are you okay? How did you know?"

"He's here."

A fist twisted in Lane's gut. "He's got you? Hang tight. We're heading over. He hasn't hurt you, has he?"

"He doesn't have *me*," she said. "I have him."

"You have him?"

Lane's mind couldn't process the information. What the hell was going on over there?

"I'll explain when you get here. He's not going anywhere. He's not going to hurt anyone else."

"Did you—did you kill him?"

She gave a shaky laugh. "No, as tempting as it was, he's alive. Just hurry."

"I have a patrol car on the way. They'll make it there before I can. You have a lot of explaining to do."

****

Headlights flashed through my living room window. I rushed over and jerked back the curtain. A patrol car pulled into the driveway.

Rambo was back in his cage, and Bart was still bound. Now that the snake was secure, he'd grown more confident, hurling curses one moment, begging my forgiveness the next. I ignored it all. The past few days were taking their toll. My body was drained, my mind and soul exhausted.

I opened the door to Christopher Mitchell, a rookie cop I'd met on a few occasions.

"You have the suspect?" he asked, looking at Bart.

"That's him," I said.

Mitchell went over and drew his gun, pointing it at Bart. "I'm going to cuff you," he said, pulling cuffs from his belt. "You make one wrong move, and I'll shoot."

"No," I said, hurrying over to Mitchell. "Don't untie him. Wait until backup arrives."

Mitchell's smile was condescending. "I think if you handled him, I can too. Just step back, let me deal with this."

"I think you should—"

He paid no attention to my pleas. Holding the gun to Bart's head, he loosened the ropes. My breath caught in my throat as I watched him snap a cuff on one of Bart's wrists. I had a bad feeling about this. I didn't trust that Mitchell could untie him and get him cuffed without help. I snatched the .22 from the side table and leveled it on Bart.

When Mitchell had the ropes removed, he reached for Bart's free hand and started to snap on the cuff. In a move so swift and confident it looked choreographed, Bart rose, snatching Mitchell's gun from his hand and twisting his body around, tugging his arm so far up his shoulder blades, I thought it would snap. Mitchell let out a grunt of surprise and pain. The cuff dangled from Bart's wrist as he buried the gun in Mitchell's neck.

It all happened so quickly, I hadn't made a sound— hadn't given in to the scream building in my throat. *Son of a bitch.* Fear swept through me, even though I had a gun.

Bart's teeth flashed in a satisfied smile as he used Mitchell's body for a shield. "Now who's got the upper hand?"

"Let him go, or I'll shoot." My voice wasn't as commanding as I'd have liked it to be.

"Drop the fucking gun, or I blow his head off."

I hesitated. If I could draw this out long enough, Lane would be here. Then everything would be okay. Lane could take care of Bart—could diffuse the situation. I wasn't sure how, but I knew he could. As well as I knew I couldn't.

Defeated, I lowered the gun and let it fall from my hand.

Bart's smile widened. He slammed the butt of the gun on Mitchell's head. The cop dropped to the floor like a bag of wet noodles.

I backed away, diving for the door, but Bart was too quick.

He grabbed my hair, winding his hand in it so tight, I screamed out in pain. Tears sprang to my eyes.

His face came within centimeters of mine. "This wasn't how I'd planned our escape, but you changed the game. Now, I'll have you, one way or the other."

I didn't remind him that help was on the way, that he wouldn't get by with this. That Lane would be here to save me. I hoped he would be. Hoped it wouldn't be too late.

My hopes dissipated when Bart dragged me out the door. I fought for everything I was worth. Struggled to release his hold. The effects were like a fly against a Tsunami. He clamped his hand over my mouth and his arm around my middle—his hold so tight, I thought my ribs would crack—and pulled me through my yard to the street.

I shot my glance to the other houses in my cul de sac, but they were dark and silent. No one was out. Not in the middle of the night.

My feet tried to gain traction, to stop his momentum, but he was too strong. He tugged me along like a rag doll, the dangling cuff slapping against my neck.

When I realized Bart's destination, my tenuous belief that Lane would rescue me fled. The cemetery. He was taking me to the cemetery where no one would find us. The agony of his grip on my waist was overshadowed by the certainty that I'd die in the very place where I'd taken refuge.

He flung the gate open and jerked me between a row of headstones. The faint glow of streetlights allowed me to see the depravity and fury in his expression when he released me. Before I could run, he threw me onto the ground and fell on top of me. His lower body smashed me into the grass, so heavy, I lost my breath.

His mouth clamped down on mine, his teeth grinding against my lips. I tasted coppery blood. My head swam with fear and dizziness.

The hand with the cuff dug into the tender flesh of my throat while the other gripped the neck of my blouse and yanked, sending buttons flying.

"No!" I screamed against his lips, pushing him with all my strength. My efforts only seemed to excite him. Nausea rose in my throat when I felt his erection press into my hips.

Lifting his head, he laughed, the sound as sadistic as the gleam in his eyes. His hand gripped my nipple, pinching and twisting. Sharp, burning pain ripped through my breast, making me cry out in pain.

He eased his lower body up enough to gain access to the button of my jeans. He tugged until the button loosened. This was it. He was going to rape me. Dear God. He was going to rape me and kill me before Lane could get here.

Sobs tore at my throat. "Please," I gasped. "Please don't. I'll go away with you. I promise. Just please stop."

His hand tightened on my throat. "Too late for that," he gasped. "I tried to be patient with you. Forgave you for betraying me the first time, but you've gone too far. Now, you'll pay."

I stared up into the night sky, at the smattering of stars above my head. Perhaps the last sight I'd ever behold. *No. I wouldn't die this way. The bastard couldn't win.* Drawing in a lungful of air, I let out a scream. It was weak, hindered by his weight crushing the breath from me.

Bart clamped a hand over my mouth, his despicable face twisting with maniacal amusement.

"No one will hear you," he panted. "Might as well lay back and take it."

Get here, Lane, please get here.

But Lake Lotawana was more than forty miles away. No way could he make it here in time. And if he did, he wouldn't think to look for me in the cemetery.

Bart released my throat and slipped his fingers inside my jeans, beneath my panties. Stark terror overtook my body, giving me a strength I didn't know I had. I bucked, hitting and kicking. He didn't pause. His fingers continued to tug and probe. I bit down on his hand as hard as I could.

He yelped, jerking his hand away. I belted out another scream. This one carried more volume.

"Bitch," he grunted. He clasped my throat once more, squeezing my larynx. My chest convulsed with the effort to breathe.

Just when I thought I'd lose consciousness, Bart's weight lifted from me. Dazed, I looked up to see Lane grabbing Bart by the shirt, pulling him to his feet. I'd never seen a more beautiful sight.

Lane's face contorted with rage. His fist slammed into Bart's face. Bart raised an arm, balling his hand, but Lane hit him again. Bart dropped to the ground, and Lane dove on top of him.

I rose to a sitting position, my emotions a whirl of confusion—relief for me, fear for Lane, the desire to see him beat the mother fucker to a pulp.

Straddling Bart, Lane's fists came down, over and over, pummeling Bart's face. Bart screamed, flailing his arms in an attempt to protect himself. But Lane didn't stop. He was like a man possessed, his face red with fury, the muscles in his arms bulging through the fabric of his shirt.

If Lane beat him to death, he'd be in trouble. He'd lose his job, maybe go to jail. I jumped unsteadily to my feet.

"Lane," I choked out. But the sound could barely be heard above the grunts and thumps, above the wounded animal moans coming from Bart.

I stumbled over to them. Bones cracked as I reached them. "Lane, stop," I said more loudly. "You're going to kill him. Stop."

Lane didn't seem to know I was there. A commotion caught my attention. Two patrol cops rushed toward us. Each man grabbed one of Lane's arms and tugged. Lane halted, breathing heavily, looking around like he wasn't sure where he was.

"We've got him, Brody. It's okay."

Lane staggered to his feet. He shook his head, then lifted it to look at me. "Monroe?" He stepped over Bart and rushed to me. His face softened, his eyes a stormy gray-blue in the meager lights of the cemetery. "God, Monroe. Are you okay?"

I nodded as I finally thought to pull my jeans up. I fumbled until I fastened them. Tears prevented me from speech.

Lane lifted a hand, running his fingers gently over my throat. "I thought he—I went nuts. Did he—" His eyes misted, and he sucked in a breath. "Did he rape you?"

I shook my head, drawing the edges of my blouse together. "No," My voice was strained from Bart's chokehold. But I was fine. Lane had saved me. "He didn't—didn't rape me. You got here in time."

Lane dropped his hand from my neck and drew me into his chest. I melted into the warmth, into the safety of his arms. I don't know how long he held me, but I wanted it to last forever.

Chapter 25

One week later

The minor injuries Bart inflicted had healed, but the damage to my soul, to my confidence in my ability to trust my own judgment, was still battered. How could Bart have so thoroughly fooled me? How could I not have seen the monster behind the mask?

I'd barely slept a full night the past week, waking with night terrors that all had the same theme—welcoming hideous-looking monsters into my life, into the lives of those I cared about—endangering them with my gullibility.

I stopped by Tony's to say goodbye to Paxton. Her mother was back from her honeymoon and would arrive soon to take her and her brother home. Paxton hugged me tightly, then pulled away. I studied her face, reassuring myself that she was really okay. That the evil I'd invited hadn't claimed her as one of his victims.

I cupped her cheek. "I'm going to miss you," I said, my voice cracking.

"I'll miss you too." She offered a tremulous smile. "Thanks for what you did. You took a big risk to save me."

"Worth it." I grinned. "I wasn't going to let that asshole get away with hurting you."

She glanced over to where her father stood watching

us. His face was drawn with strain and sadness. The emotional fallout of the past few weeks had taken its toll.

"Dad was worried about me. He didn't sleep the whole time I was—" She paused, swallowed hard. "—was missing. I guess he really does love me. He wouldn't rest until he found me. Until he knew I was okay."

"I know." I smoothed a hand over her silky hair. "Your dad will always be there for you. Always make sure you're okay."

She nodded and wiped tears away with her forefingers.

Tony came over and took me in his arms for a hug. "I owe you, Roe. That was a damned fool thing you did. You almost got yourself killed."

I shrugged. "I seem to make a habit of that."

He grinned and tweaked my chin. "You certainly do."

I said my final goodbyes and headed out to my car. When I slid inside, my phone rang. Even knowing they would no longer come from a psycho killer, each time I got a call, my heart jumped a little. Lane's name showed up on the caller ID, and my heart jumped even more. We'd barely spoken since the night of Bart's arrest. Internal Affairs kept Lane busy with inquiries regarding his attack on Bart. Bart had the nerve to file a complaint.

"Monroe," he said. "I need to ask you something. If the answer's no, I'll understand. In fact, I wouldn't blame you at all."

Ask me something? Surely this wasn't some kind of proposal, an attempt to get back together. If that were to happen—and I was beginning to doubt the likelihood in light of his absence the past week—surely he wouldn't do it over the phone.

"What is it?"

"The lieutenant is the one who insisted I call. For the record, I'm one thousand percent against it."

"Against what?" Disappointment filled me. Obviously this wasn't a declaration of his undying love. That probably wouldn't come via an order from the lieutenant.

"Holland wants to see you."

"What?" I couldn't have heard right. No fucking way would I talk to that piece of shit. No way would Lane ask me to. "You're kidding, right? You want me to see him?"

"*I* don't want you to. But we've been questioning him, and he won't say a word. He hasn't even retained an attorney. Said he wouldn't talk to anyone but you."

"No. No way."

"Good. That's what I hoped you'd say. We'll get the information from him another way."

I frowned. "Wait. What information?"

There was a heavy silence on the other end of the line. "We need to tie him to the murders. To all of them. We need to find out if there are other victims we don't know about. Close the files. Bring closure to the families."

Shit. This put the request in a whole new light. If I could help the authorities—and especially the families of the victims…

"I'll do it. I'll talk to him."

His frustrated sigh sounded over the phone. "You don't have to. I said we'd get the information from him."

"He said he'd talk to me, Lane. I need to do this."

"I don't want you near him."

"I'll be there in fifteen minutes." I hung up the

phone.

My stomach heaved with fear and dread. I thought I'd never have to face the demon again. My nightmares were about to become very real.

****

Bart sat at a table in the holding room, wearing an orange jump suit. Heavy chains shackled him to the chair and to posts in the floor.

I entered, my footsteps slow and reluctant. Two guards stood on either side of him. I knew I was safe enough, that he couldn't hurt me. But being close to him was harder than I thought it would be. My heart crashed against my rib cage like waves on a choppy sea, sending blood rushing into my ears.

I took a seat at the table across from him. He was two to three feet on the other side, bound and helpless, yet I could feel danger emanating from him.

A white bandage over his nose stood out in stark relief against the purple and black bruises on his face. His lips were split and swollen from Lane's blows. I suppressed a smile of satisfaction.

"Hello Monroe. I'm glad you came."

The words were difficult to make out. He barely opened his mouth when he spoke, and I realized his jaw had been wired shut. Damn. Lane really did a number on him.

"I can't say the same. I won't be here long." I released a clenched fist where I held the sheet of paper they'd given me with questions I was to ask. Laying it on the table in front of me, I smoothed it out with shaking fingers. "Give me the names of each of your victims." My voice was surprisingly steady, but my hands trembled violently. I clasped them together on top of the paper for some semblance of control.

I avoided his gaze, waiting for his answer. I didn't have to write down any of the information he gave. Our conversation was being recorded.

"I've missed you. I wanted a chance to apologize. Even though what you did to me was wrong, I shouldn't have reacted the way I did. I never wanted to hurt you."

I swallowed against the bile in my throat. Still refusing to look at him, I said, "Please just answer the question."

He was silent for a few moments, then began reciting names through clenched teeth. Each one was like a blow to my chest. So many girls, so many needless deaths. *Rotten bastard.*

I realized when he was finished, that he hadn't mentioned Katie. Was he still trying to pretend he hadn't killed my friend? Like that would make me think more highly of him?

"Did you hire Michael Finlay to attack me?"

A rueful chuckle left his mouth. "I wanted to meet you. Wanted to make a good first impression. What better way than to save your life? The dumbass was shocked when I grabbed the knife from him. That hadn't been part of our deal. Like I'd let him live so he could finger me. People can be so fucking stupid."

"You tried to frame Cameron Cooper?"

"I knew you'd named him as a suspect in your articles. It only made sense."

He spoke matter of factly, like he was laying out some brilliant business plan. Even with the damaged features and wired jaw, his presence sent a ripple of fright over my flesh.

Only a few more questions to go. You can do this.

"The earlier victims were raped. But not the latest ones. Although you tried to make it appear they had been."

He was silent for a while. I lifted my head to look at him, then immediately regretted it. He stared at me with a twisted, intense worship that was tainted by the evil glint in his eyes.

"I couldn't. Not after I fell for you. Once I started reading your articles, saw that we had a connection that went beyond the physical, I didn't want anyone else. No woman since Sylvia made me feel the way you did."

I shivered at the demented declaration.

Relief swept through me when I realized I'd reached the end of the questions. I stood, pushing from the chair and turned my back to him.

I'd almost made it out of the room before his voice stopped me. "I didn't kill her, Monroe."

I paused, but didn't turn around, didn't speak.

"Your friend, Katie. I swear I didn't kill her. Think about it, and you'll know it's true. I admitted to all the others. If I'd killed her, I'd tell you. There are no more secrets between us."

Taking a deep breath, I rushed from the room, his words echoing in my head.

If I'd killed her, I'd tell you...

He had to have done it. If not, then who? I shook off the question. It was him. To think otherwise would be ludicrous.

****

It was nearly an hour after my talk with Bart before I left the station. The lieutenant—a large, intimidating woman—thanked me for my assistance. The words were grateful enough, but I sensed a lack of sincerity behind her emotionless tone.

I drove home, wanting nothing more than to get inside the security of my own house and fall apart. Seeing Bart was worse than I imagined. It would be a long time before the nightmares left and I'd finally rest.

As I unlocked the front door, a car pulled into the drive. I turned. Breath expelled from my lungs in a fevered rush when I saw Lane's Crown Vic.

He climbed from the car while I froze in place, watching, waiting.

He moved slowly toward me, locked his ocean gaze on me.

"Lane? What is it? What are you doing here?"

He shook his head, his gaze still latched onto my face, mesmerizing in its intensity. I struggled to draw in air through the band clamped around my lungs.

"I can't do this." His husky tone moved through me, shivering over my skin. "I can't take it."

He'd made it onto the porch, but didn't pause, still coming toward me with that languorous but determined stride.

"Can't do what?" I was captured by the emotion on his face.

He didn't speak, didn't pause. He reached out and took my cheeks in his hands. His eyes moved over my features, his expression awash with anguish. "I can't, *won't* be without you another second."

I opened my mouth to reply, but his head lowered, and he took advantage of the position. Locked his mouth over mine. His kiss was hungry, desperate, like a dying man gasping for his last breath.

In spite of my better judgment, I gave into the ardent fierceness. My knees buckled and tingles of fire licked over my skin. I'd craved his touch, needed to know I still mattered to him.

I pressed more tightly into him and wound my arms around his neck. He lifted a hand and cupped the back of my head, his tongue delving deeper, moving against mine. A low, harsh moan vibrated from his chest to my breasts, making my nipples tingle.

This is a mistake… sex won't resolve anything. The thought fought for dominance over my desire-fogged stupor.

Before I could decide which won the battle, Lane decided for me. He broke the kiss and stepped back. He stared down at me, his hooded eyes deepening to cobalt as he drew in ragged breaths.

Groaning, he ran a hand through his hair and shook his head. "I know I shouldn't be here, shouldn't put you through this. I don't deserve you, don't deserve another chance."

I crossed my arms, trying to steady my own breathing. "So, why are you here?"

He grazed my cheek with his fingers, letting them rest on my neck where the bruises had all but faded. "I can't lose you. I've never begged for anything, but I'm begging you now. Please give me another chance. You're the one person in my life worthy of loyalty, and I'll do anything in my power to prove my devotion to you. Even if it takes the rest of my life."

Tears threatened, but I swallowed them back. "I don't trust my instincts anymore. I was so impressed with Bart's loyalty to his dead fiancée that I was blinded to the fact that he was a twisted, evil monster." I gave a short, bitter laugh. "Apparently, my loyalty gauge is a little faulty."

"So where does that leave me? Us? What does that mean?"

I thought about his question. About all we'd been through. All we'd almost lost. Letting out a tremulous sigh, I said, "It means that I love you. You have nothing to prove. You're the best man I know, and I can't stand another second without you either."

The worry in his features disappeared. He drew me into his arms, squeezing me to him, caressing my back with warm, rough hands.

"God, Monroe. You have no idea how happy you've made me. How happy I'll make you."

"You've already made me happy," I whispered. Looking over his shoulder, I saw Linus standing on his porch watching us. I pulled back and smiled up at Lane through my tears. "How would you like to come inside?"

A word about the author…

Alicia Dean began writing stories as a child. At age 10, she wrote her first ever romance (featuring a hero who looked just like Elvis Presley, and who shared the name of Elvis' character in the movie, Tickle Me), and she still has the tattered, pencil-written copy. Alicia is from Moore, Oklahoma and now lives in Edmond. She has three grown children and a huge network of supportive friends and family. She writes mostly contemporary suspense and paranormal, but has also written in other genres, including a few vintage historicals.

Other than reading and writing, her passions are Elvis Presley (she almost always works in a mention of him into her stories) and watching (and rewatching) her favorite televisions shows like Ozark, Dexter, Justified, Breaking Bad, Sons of Anarchy, and Vampire Diaries. Some of her favorite authors are Michael Connelly, Dennis Lehane, Stephen King, Lee Child, Lisa Gardner, Ridley Pearson, Joseph Finder, and Jonathan Kellerman…to name a few.

Email: Alicia@AliciaDean.com
Website: http://aliciadean.com/
Blog: http://aliciadean.com/alicias-blog/
Facebook:
https://www.facebook.com/AuthorAliciaDean/
Twitter: @Alicia_Dean_
Instagram: AliciaDeanAuthor

BookBub: https://www.bookbub.com/profile/alicia-dean

Pinterest: https://pinterest.com/aliciamdean/

Goodreads: http://www.goodreads.com/author/show/468339.Alicia_Dean

www.ingramcontent.com/pod-product-compliance
Lightning Source LLC
Chambersburg PA
CBHW070051030726
47506CB00002B/425